JC's
HOPE

Joyce Byers Hill

Inscript

Bladensburg, MD

Dove Christian Publishers/Inscript Books
PO Box 611
Bladensburg, MD 20710
www.dovechristianpublishers.com

Printed in the United States of America

Books by Joyce Byers Hill

A PLACE CALLED HOPE Series:
Diamond in the Rough
JC's Hope

Dedication

I would like to dedicate this book to my brother and sister-in-law, Gerald and Carri Byers. Together they raised a little boy, Sean Christopher Byers, and helped him become an incredible young man who touched the hearts of everyone he knew. Thank you, Gerald and Carri, for sharing your precious son with the world.

I also dedicate this book to Sean's brother Kevin, and his sisters Naomi and Keli. Being your brother was one of Sean's most cherished roles.

Preface

Our world was shattered on December 17, 2014, when my nephew, Sean Christopher Byers, was tragically killed in a car accident. At the time of his death, I was in the middle of writing my first novel. I stopped writing after Sean died. My heart just wasn't in it anymore. Eventually, I returned to writing and discovered it was cathartic. I had to finish my novel. It was a dream of mine, and I could not give up on my dream. So, I finished writing *Diamond in the Rough*, and got it published.

I never really planned to write a sequel to my first novel. But after Sean's death, I felt compelled to do something special for him. Sean was an extraordinary young man, and twenty-three years with him was not nearly enough. There was a little boy born at the end of *Diamond in the Rough*. Obviously, that little boy was not Sean. He was simply a character in my first novel. But I felt his character would provide a way to honor Sean. So, I wanted to write that boy's story.

JC's Hope was born of my desire to pay tribute to Sean. My desire to write what I think Sean's life might have been like had he not been taken from us in the prime of his young life. It has been a harder story to write because I not only wanted it to be a fictional story that readers would enjoy, but it also had to honor my nephew.

So, I hope you enjoy JC's story. And, my dear Sean, I hope I have done justice to what might have been your story. I'll never forget you, Sean. I love you, my dear nephew, forever and always.

Joyce Byers Hill

Prologue

"Joshua Christopher Harmon!" Meghan yelled across the yard at her rambunctious five-year-old. "How many times have I told you not to climb around on the Bobcat unless your dad or Uncle Todd is with you?"

"But Mommy," he explained with all the logic of a little boy. "I'm wearing my hardhat and I'm being careful."

"Joshua, you need to get down before you get hurt."

"I won't get hurt, Mommy. Jesus will protect me," he replied with a huge smile.

"Josh, you sure do keep Jesus busy!" she said with a laugh. "Your dad will be home from the church in a little while, then you can play on the Bobcat."

Meghan started across the yard toward the shop, shaking her head. Her two-year-old daughter, never far from her big brother, was happily playing with a toy dump truck in a mud puddle next to the Bobcat. Like her brother, she too sported a yellow plastic hardhat and a miniature pair of Levis. Her tiny cowgirl boots, along with her socks, had been discarded in the yard on the way to the mud puddle. Meghan reached for her daughter's hand with a smile and said, "Ryleigh Elizabeth, what am I going to do with you? Good thing you're washable. And at least you took off your boots before you started playing in the mud."

"Look at all the dirt my dump truck hauled, Mommy," Ryleigh beamed proudly as she pointed to a small pile of mud.

"That's quite a pile, Ryleigh! Did Joshie help you with it?"

Ryleigh looked adoringly at her brother, still playing with the controls in the Bobcat, and exclaimed, "Brother showed me how to dump the mud, but I did it all by myself!"

"You two are quite a pair," Meghan said with obvious pride.

"Do you think Daddy will let me play on the backhoe today?" Joshua asked hopefully. "He said when I was bigger. I'm bigger now, Mommy."

"I don't know, Josh. He just told you that a few days ago."

"I'm bigger than I was a few days ago," he rationalized. "So, I think he will let me!"

Meghan reached up and rescued her son from the Bobcat as he held onto his plastic hardhat. Being around construction for his entire short life, he understood the safety rules his dad and mom insisted on obeying, but he didn't always like them.

"Let's go fix you two a sandwich, then you can talk to your dad about the backhoe when he gets home."

"Okay, Mommy," Josh replied as his feet hit the ground running. Suddenly, he came to a screeching halt and started back toward the Bobcat. "Mommy, I left my Bible on the seat of the Bobcat! Jesus doesn't want me to lose it!"

Meghan retrieved the small Bible from the Bobcat and handed it to her son. He clutched it to his chest like a prized possession, then took off running toward the house and the promised lunch. He paused briefly on his way to the house and picked up his little sister's boots and socks. He looked back at her and said, "Come on, Sissy, let's race to the house!"

Ryleigh scrambled out of her mother's arms and took off running across the yard barefoot toward her brother. Josh had slowed to a crawl to give his sister a chance to catch up to him. She was giggling as she ran as fast as her little legs would carry her.

"I'm going to beat you, Brother!" she exclaimed as she zoomed past.

Josh made sure his little sister beat him to the back deck. He came up behind her panting and laughing. "Wow, Sissy, you're really fast! I bet you're even faster than Uncle Todd now! High five!"

Josh gave Ryleigh a 'high five', then took his little sister by the hand and headed into the house.

Meghan followed close behind, hoping her kids remembered to stop in the mud room to get cleaned up before going into the kitchen. But knowing in her heart that it really didn't matter.

Chapter One

As she thought back to that memory from eighteen years ago, Meghan Harmon stared out the window at the traffic below. This small hospital room has been her home for more than a week, at the bedside of her 23-year-old son Joshua. Her husband Travis, pastor of Hope Community Church, sat at the opposite side of the bed, deep in prayer. This has been their life since their son was brought to the trauma center fifty miles from their home. As Meghan held her son's hand, it seemed like an eternity listening to the steady beep of the monitors hooked to his motionless body. But at least there is the constant beep, indicating hope.

Eight days ago, brought the phone call that turned their world upside down. The phone call every parent dreads. The patrol officer on the other end of the line did his best to deliver the news with compassion. "There has been an accident. Is Joshua Christopher Harmon your son? He has been severely injured and is being airlifted to the trauma center. I have a son his age. I will meet you at the front door of the emergency entrance. Please hurry." Those words have been permanently etched into her heart and her memory. "…an accident…severely injured…please hurry."

Still clutching her son's hand, Meghan glanced over at her husband. *Dear God, I don't know how I would ever get through this without Travis. Please give me the strength to be strong for him. I can't imagine what this is doing to him. He has already lost a son once. Please don't take Josh from him too.*

"Travis," Meghan said softly. "Would you like me to go down and get you something to eat?"

When Travis looked up at his wife, she was immediately struck by the fact he looked like he had aged ten years in the past few days.

"No," he replied. "I'm fine. But go get yourself something."

"Honey, you haven't eaten anything in two days. You need to eat. Please?"

Travis looked at his wife with so much love in his tortured heart. She rescued him a quarter of a century ago when he wasn't sure his heart could ever love again. She proved him wrong. He had been struggling with the loss a few years earlier of his wife and unborn son at the hands of a drunk driver. That loss took an enormous toll on him. It made him question his effectiveness as a pastor and made him doubt he could ever love again. Meghan came along and healed his hurting heart. She made him whole again. Meghan and her daughter Kaci became his world. When Josh came along, it was like he had won the lottery. The arrival of their daughter Ryleigh three years later completed his life. He had every-thing his heart had ever dreamed of – a beautiful, loving and supportive wife, two daughters, a son, and grandkids. His ministry was growing, his own spiritual walk was strong, and his kids all had strong Christian lives. A man couldn't ask for anything more.

Meghan broke into his thoughts. "Honey? Food?"

He smiled weakly at his wife. "Sure, babe. You can bring me a sandwich. What time did you say Kaci and the kids would be here?"

"They should be here pretty soon. Jason has to work today so he won't be able to make it until the weekend. Ryleigh will be heading home shortly, as soon as she finishes her last final exam. I'll be right back with some food for you, and I want you to actually eat it."

"Yes, dear."

As Meghan walked away, Travis marveled at the strong woman she was. She was hurting too, but always tried to make sure everyone else's needs were being met. He also knew she was concerned about the girls. Travis had never seen a brother-sister bond like Josh and Kaci shared, with the exception of Meghan and her brother Todd. Even though Kaci was several years older than her brother, no one could love him with more devotion than she did. The news of his accident shook Kaci to the core of her being. She made the fifty-mile trip to the hospital every day with her young twins. If it were possible for her to will her brother out of that hospital bed, she would do it. Then there was Ryleigh. The moment she laid eyes on her older brother she fell in love with him. She had a sort of hero worship relationship with him. She followed him everywhere when they were kids. Josh not only tolerated being shadowed by his little sister, but he also considered it an honor to watch over and protect her.

Travis heard a commotion in the hallway and looked up to see his older daughter and grandkids standing in the doorway. It always warmed his heart to see the five-year-old twins. Aaron, the oldest by four minutes, looked just like his dad Jason, sandy blonde hair, and deep blue eyes. Little Sophie was the spitting image not only of her mom and uncle Josh, but of her grandma as well, sharing their auburn hair and hazel eyes. They both had the soft hearts of their mother, coupled with the adventurous spirit of their dad. It kept life interesting.

"Papa!" Sophie said excitedly, as she ran into Travis's arms. Aaron joined his sister in his grandpa's embrace, then broke free and walked over to the bed. He took his mama's hand and pointed to the monitors. "Mama, the beep means Uncle Joshie will be okay, right?"

Kaci hugged her little boy tightly, her mind instantly going back to when her brother was that age. "The beeping is a good thing, Aaron. But Uncle Joshie needs lots of prayers so he can get better."

"Sissy and I prayed for him last night at bedtime. We will pray now." Aaron took his little sister by the hand, then reached out for his mom's hand and closed his eyes. "Dear Jesus, please make my Uncle Joshie better. Sissy and I want to play with him. He said he will take us to a baseball game. I found my glove so I'm ready. Mama wants to talk to him. She cries at night. I don't like it when Mama cries. Amen. Papa, your turn now."

With tears running down his face, Travis hugged his daughter and grandkids just as he noticed Meghan standing in the doorway. He went to his wife, hugged her tightly, then brought her into the family prayer circle.

Travis struggled to begin. "Dear Merciful God, you know the beginning and the ending. You know what you have planned for your servant Joshua. Only you know when you will call him home. We pray that now is not your time. We ask that you give us the strength to handle this challenge. Our strength will never be enough. We need your strength. If it is your will to leave Josh with us, we will be eternally grateful. We pray you will heal his body and his mind so he can continue his work in your name. We ask these things in the name of our Lord and Savior, Jesus Christ. Amen."

A chorus of quiet amens followed, punctuated by the heartfelt "Amen!" of a little girl.

"Papa," Sophie said as she crawled into her grandpa's lap. "Grandma brought you a sandwich. You have to eat it, 'kay?"

"I will eat it later, honey."

Sophie looked into her papa's eyes with the adoration of a five-year old. "Papa?"

"Yes, sweet pea?"

"Grandma told Mama you're not eating."

"She did, did she?" Travis questioned, looking over at his wife.

"Mama said you're sad. But Papa?"

"Yes?"

"You have to eat. You have to be strong to play baseball with me and Uncle Joshie and Brother. And Aunt Ryleigh told me she's going to play too. But she has to get home from school first."

"Okay, I'll eat the sandwich. Will you and Aaron help me?"

"Sure!"

Little Aaron interjected. "Papa, we will eat one bite. But you have to eat most of it. You're bigger. You need to eat more."

"Is that right?"

"Yes, sir! Uncle Joshie told me big people have to eat more. That's why he always eats the biggest cookie!"

"Well, if that's what your Uncle Joshie told you, it must be right. Okay, let's eat that sandwich."

Meghan stood with her arm around her daughter as they watched the love between the twins and their grandpa. Kaci turned away and looked toward her brother. She reached over and gently stroked his forehead, pushing the hair out of his eyes. "Come on, Joshie," she almost whispered. "You can do this. We aren't ready to live without you. We can't live without you. The kids need you. Dad and Mom need you. Ryleigh needs you. I need you. You're tough and you're strong. You can do this. You have dreams. What about all those kids out there you want to help? They need you."

By now, the tears were flowing freely down Kaci's face. Travis walked over and pulled her into his arms.

"He's going to be okay, isn't he, Dad?"

"I don't know, sweetheart. Only God knows. All we can do is pray. And talk to him. I think he can hear us."

"Dad?"

"Yes, honey?"

"Would it be okay if I stayed here for a little while by myself? Just me and Josh?"

"Sure. I'll take your mom and the kids for a little walk. We can all use some fresh air. We'll be back in a little while. Ryleigh should be here before long. Are you going to be okay?"

"Yeah. I just need some time with Joshie."

"Okay, sweetheart," Travis replied as he gave her a kiss on the forehead. Then he gathered up his wife and grandkids so his daughter could have some time with her brother.

Kaci pulled a chair close to the bed, settled into it, then took her brother's hand in hers. "Oh, Joshie, you have to wake up. I know you're in there. I can feel it. You know, little brother, I remember the day you were born. I remember how excited everyone was when Dad and Mom brought you home from the hospital. You were so cute. You were such a great little brother. You reminded me of myself when I was little. Mom and Grandpa always had a hard time keeping me off the heavy equipment. You were the same way. You thought as long as you had your little yellow hardhat, and your Bible, you were invincible. You could never get hurt. You packed that Bible around with you everywhere. I don't know how many Bibles Dad and Mom gave you over the years. No matter what crazy stunt you pulled, you always said, 'Jesus will protect me.' I hope you were right, Josh, because I sure want Him to protect you now. Are you in there, Joshie? You need to wake up."

Tears cascaded down Kaci's face as she pleaded with both God and her brother. "Please, God, give us something. Some hint. Anything to let us know he can hear us. Come on, Joshie. We all love you."

Kaci was still talking simultaneously with God and her brother when the rest of the family returned a half hour later. Meghan walked up behind her daughter and put her arms around her.

"Are you doing okay, kiddo?"

"Yeah, I'm okay, Mom. I just wish I knew for sure if he could hear us."

Just as Kaci started to pull her hand out of her brother's hand, she felt something. Or did she?

"Oh my God!" she said breathlessly. "Dad, Mom, I think Josh just moved his finger!"

Instantly, Travis and Meghan were at their son's bedside. Everyone started talking at once.

"Son," Travis asked hopefully. "Can you hear us?" He took his son's hand and instructed, "Josh, squeeze my finger. Come on, son, you can do it."

Meghan was holding her son's other hand, begging and pleading for some sign of hope. "Come on, Josh. Let us know you're in there. Please!"

Kaci looked crestfallen. "Maybe I was imagining it. I wanted it so badly."

But then Josh's left index finger moved. Ever so slightly. Then another finger. Little movements, but movements, nonetheless.

"Keep talking to him," Meghan instructed. "I'm going to get the nurse!"

Before long, nurses and doctors were streaming into the room. They ushered everyone back and asked for someone to take the twins out of the room. Kaci gathered up her kids and told her parents they would be in the waiting room down the hall. The room became a flurry of activity, with doctors issuing instructions to the patient while nurses began taking vital signs and checking his pupils for reaction.

Ryleigh arrived just in time to see a doctor rush into her brother's room, and she could hear the commotion on the other side of the door. Her heart jumped in her chest when she walked into the room and took in the scene before her. A half dozen medical personnel were huddled over her brother, working feverishly, while her parents clung to each other in the corner of the room. Without a word, she joined her dad and mom in the corner, never taking her eyes off her beloved brother for a moment. Over the course of a couple hours, things began changing rapidly. There was more voluntary movement in both his hands and feet, and his eyes would open and close occasionally. Everyone became much more hopeful.

Kaci had arranged for her in-laws to come pick up the twins so she could remain at the hospital with her dad, mom, and sister. After being told they were going to try weaning Josh off the respirator to see if he could breathe on his own, Travis gathered his wife and daughters and headed to the hospital's chapel. The four knelt in urgent prayer.

"Dear Loving God," Travis began. "You have brought us this far in Josh's journey. Please don't stop now. You know how much he is loved by his family. You know his heart, and how desperately he wants to help kids who are struggling and need you in their lives. He has so much to offer and has such a Christ-filled heart. He has been a faithful disciple of yours his entire life. Even as a small boy, he packed his Bible around with him as a constant companion. He always knew he would serve you. If it is your will, please restore his health and give him that opportunity. As always, we pray for this miracle in the name of your Beloved Son, our Lord and Savior, Jesus Christ. Amen."

The four stood and embraced in a hope-filled hug before walking back down the hall. By the time they returned to Josh's room, the breathing tube had been removed and Josh appeared to be having no trouble breathing on his own.

After a few cautionary words from the doctor, Travis, Meghan, Kaci and Ryleigh were urged to take Josh by the hand, or touch his arms, and talk to him in an effort to pull him back to the land of the living.

"Josh," Travis began. "Can you hear me, son? Squeeze my finger if you can hear me."

As instructed, Josh squeezed his dad's finger. Smiles erupted on everyone's faces, and the tears began to flow once again. "Praise, God," Meghan said with gratitude.

"Mom?" a quiet, raspy voice asked. Josh opened his eyes more deliberately now.

"Oh, Josh," Meghan replied in a whisper.

"Son," Travis said with tears in his eyes. "You gave us quite a scare, buddy."

His voice still not more than a raspy whisper, Josh replied, "Sorry, Dad. Won't happen again."

"I hope not, son. You have your guardian angels working overtime!"

Without turning his head, Josh moved his eyes from side to side, as if he was searching. "Kaci?"

Kaci moved so she was in her brother's line of vision. "I'm here, Joshie. Where else would I be?"

"Love you, Sis," he rasped.

"I love you, too, Joshie."

"Ry?" Josh asked as his eyes began searching again.

Ryleigh stepped beside her sister and reached out for her brother's hand. With tears flowing down her cheeks, she smiled and said, "I'm right here, JC."

With a sigh of contentment, Josh said quietly, "Love you, Little Sis."

Ryleigh smiled and said, "Of course, you do. And I love you too, Brother."

And just like that, a thousand prayers were answered.

Chapter Two

Travis stepped into the house from the back deck and was greeted by a sound he didn't realize he had been missing. He worked his way through the house he had helped Meghan build before they were married. When he reached the family room, he leaned against the wall and soaked in the beautiful sounds coming from the piano across the room. His son Josh sat at the piano, with his back to the room, oblivious to his surroundings. That's the way it always was when he sat down to play. The music took over his body and soul. Josh had been playing the piano since he was a little boy. It didn't take long before his piano instructor came to Travis and Meghan and informed them she could no longer give him lessons. His talent had surpassed her ability to teach. She had nothing else to teach him. So, Josh began creating music on his own.

A few months ago, Travis wondered if he would ever hear that beautiful sound again. It had not been an easy road for any of them after the accident that nearly claimed Josh's young life. He was in the hospital for almost three weeks, then in a rehab facility near the trauma center for another eleven weeks. Josh was a fighter, and he was young and healthy. The doctors said that was probably what helped him survive the horrific three-car accident. He was luckier than two others involved who died at the scene. They will probably never know exactly what happened. The only thing the state patrol was able to determine with any degree of certainty is that the driver of one of the other vehicles crossed the centerline of the highway and hit another car head-on. Josh's pickup was caught in the crossfire of careening vehicles, one of which flipped over onto his truck before sliding into the ditch along the road. God had definitely been watching out for Josh that day.

But a lot of scars remained from the accident – both physical and emotional. One sizable scar on the side of his head would eventually be hidden by his hair. Travis noticed Josh had begun wearing his wavy auburn hair a bit longer since the accident, maybe in an effort to hide the scar. It now reached to his collar; more than an inch longer than he had ever worn it. The three-inch scar that ran from his chin along his jaw line would hopefully fade with time. Travis had seen his son running his thumb along the scar absentmindedly at times. The emotional scars would take longer to heal. Josh had slipped into a bit of a depression shortly after returning home. He mistakenly felt he should be able to pick up his life right where he had left it. That was proving to be more of a challenge than he expected. However, with the support of his family and the help of a good Christian counselor, he was making remarkable progress.

A couple weeks prior to the accident, Josh had graduated with a master's degree in Psychology. It had always been his dream to find a way to work with young kids. The fact Josh was blessed with a loving and supportive family was not lost on him. He never took for granted what he knew many kids never had. His best friend grew up in an abusive home run by an alcoholic father. Kyle always sought refuge at the Harmon home when things became difficult at his house. Josh was also aware of the fact his older sister spent much of her childhood in the home of an alcoholic father. Josh admired his mom for having the strength to divorce Kaci's dad while Kaci was a teenager. Josh had hopes of opening some kind of center for troubled youth. A place where they could always feel safe. A place where they wouldn't be judged because of circumstances beyond their control, but where they would be held accountable for their own actions. That was his dream, and his hope. Now to turn it into a reality.

The music faded away, then ended, bringing Travis out of his thoughts.

"Is that the first time you've played since you've been home, son?"

Josh turned to look at his dad with a smile on his face. "I didn't know you were standing there. Yeah, that was the first time. I wasn't sure what to expect."

"It was beautiful, as always. You have such a talent for music, Josh. I wish I had half your talent."

"Thanks, Dad," Josh replied sheepishly. "You know, that was one of the things I've been talking to the counselor about. I wasn't sure if I would still be able to play. He told me I wouldn't know unless I tried. I'm glad I can still play. I'm not sure I could live without music."

"I'm glad, too, Josh," Travis replied sincerely. "I love walking into the house and being surrounded by your music. You have a real gift. I hope you realize that."

"I do, Dad. As a very wise pastor once told me, 'God is good.'"

"All the time," Travis finished. That was one of the things Travis used in his sermons a lot. It was a constant reminder for people to remember the blessings God has given them. Josh grew up hearing his dad say 'God is good. All the time.' And he loved finishing the phrase with 'All the time. God is good.'

Seeming to be lost in his thoughts for a moment, Travis waited for Josh to speak.

"Dad," he started hesitantly. "Do you think I have what it takes to be able to run a youth center?"

Travis walked across the room and sat down beside his son on the piano bench. He marveled at how much his son looked like he did when he was younger. The same lean build, hovering just over six feet tall. Putting his arm around Josh's shoulder, he said, "Josh, I do. I really do. I honestly believe you have what it takes to do anything you put your mind to. You have a lot of talent, son. You have a good, compassionate heart. You are great at relating to kids of all ages. You always manage to talk to them at their level, whatever that may be. You have a gift for using not only your love of music, but also your love of baseball to draw the kids in. You also have a fair amount of re-al-life experience because of your friendship with Kyle. And, of course, you have your psychology degree. So, you have the training to back up your gut instincts and your compassion. You'd be a natural, son. I sincerely believe that."

"Thanks, Dad." Josh paused for a moment, but Travis could tell he still had something on his mind. "I was talking to Kaci about it the other day."

"Oh?"

"Yeah. Since she has a business degree, I thought maybe she'd like to help with the business end of the youth center. Business isn't my strong suit, but it's her area of expertise. I know she wants to get back to doing something that uses her degree, and if she helped with the center, she could work from home and still be there with the twins. She really liked the idea. And you know Kaci, give her an idea and she runs with it!"

"That's a fact!" Travis laughed.

"She already has a lot of ideas for grants we could apply for. And Jason knows of a building that would be perfect for a youth center. With his connections, he thinks we could probably get it for very reasonable rent. So, he's going to check into that. It's not far from the schools, so the location would be perfect."

Travis loved how animated Josh became whenever he talked about the center. He definitely had a passion for it, so Travis had no doubt he would be successful. Josh had always had a compassionate heart. After serving on a mission between high school and college, he came into contact with a lot of young kids who needed some direction and a godly influence in their lives. That was part of the reason he decided to major in psychology and minor in theology in college. He returned from his mission with a strong focus on where he was heading.

"Follow your passion, son," Travis advised. "And don't forget to let God lead you. I will support you in whatever way I can."

"Thanks, Dad. I'm going to get together with Jason and Kaci tonight. Jason said he has some news about the building that might work for the center. I'm anxious to hear what he found out."

"Hopefully he has some good news for you. Well, I have to run over to the church for a meeting, so I'll talk to you later. Give Kaci and the kids a hug for me when you see them tonight."

"Will do."

Josh had already started playing the piano again before Travis made it across the room. He paused once again in the doorway to soak in the beautiful music, and to thank God for sparing the life of his son.

God is good. All the time, Travis thought as he headed out to his truck.

* * *

Kaci had invited Josh to join her family for a dinner of homemade spaghetti. Now that dinner was over, and the twins were settled in the playroom with puzzles and coloring books, the adults sat down to discuss JC's ideas for the youth center.

Kaci's husband Jason opened the discussion with a smile on his face.

"Well, JC," he began. "Are you ready for some good news?"

"After the past few months," Josh replied, "I am definitely ready for some good news. Were you able to find out anything about that building you had in mind?"

"Yes, I was," Jason confirmed. "I met with Mike Slater over lunch yesterday. He's the owner of that old warehouse over on Division. It's just a few blocks from both the middle school and the high school. The building has been vacant for a couple years because he really didn't want to have another warehouse operation going in there. With both the schools growing, there are a lot of kids running around the neighborhood. He's been concerned about the safety aspect with a bunch of large trucks going in and out of the parking lot.

"When I approached him with your ideas for a youth center, his eyes lit up instantly, and I could almost see the wheels turning in his mind. We had quite an interesting discussion. He wants to meet with us to flesh out your ideas a bit, and to see exactly how serious you are about this venture."

"That would be great," Josh said enthusiastically. "Would he mind if Kaci joined us in that meeting? If possible, I'd really like her to handle the business end of things. And maybe Dad. He usually has some ideas that I hadn't thought of, so I like getting his input."

"I'm sure that wouldn't be a problem at all. Mike is a great guy. I've worked with him a lot over the years, and he's very easy going and down to earth. You'd never know he was a millionaire!"

"Really?" Josh asked, surprised.

"Yeah. He owns several buildings around town. But he always says, 'I'm just a regular guy. I put my pants on one leg at a time just like everyone else.' He's a very honest and respectable businessman."

"When can we set up a meeting with him?" Josh asked. "I'm really anxious to see if we can get this thing off the ground."

"He said he's available any day this week after four o'clock. Why don't you talk to your dad and see what his schedule is, and Kaci and I can work around that."

"Sounds like a plan. I'll talk to Dad and let you know. And Jason? Thanks. I really appreciate your help on this."

"I will help you in any way I can, JC. You know that."

* * *

With a promise from Uncle Josh to play with them later, the kids had been playing quietly while the adults were talking. Josh stood in the doorway to the playroom, watching Aaron help Sophie fit a puzzle piece into the correct spot. Sophie smiled at her brother when they were able to make the puzzle piece fit perfectly. Still smiling, she looked up and saw her uncle standing in the doorway.

In one swift move, Sophie jumped up and launched herself into Josh's arms.

"Uncle Joshie!" she screamed with delight. "You're going to play with me and Brother now, right?"

In no time at all, Josh had both kids in his arms. And he wouldn't have it any other way. He sat them down, then joined them on the floor in the middle of the room.

"So, munchkins, what are we going to play?"

Always the little diplomat, Aaron asked, "Do you want to color or put together puzzles, Uncle Joshie?"

Josh rubbed his fingers along his jawline, feigning deep thought. "Well, I'm more of a builder than an artist. Why don't we do a puzzle. Would that be okay?"

"You color good, Uncle Joshie." Sophie said as she crawled into his lap. "But if we do a puzzle, we don't have to stay inside the lines."

"Hmm, you don't say." Josh replied with a smile.

Meanwhile, Aaron had been looking through the puzzles on the shelf and had found one of his favorites. It was a puzzle of a bulldozer. He brought it over and sat down beside Josh.

"I think we should do the bulldozer puzzle. Sissy and I like this one."

"That works out great, because that's my favorite puzzle too." Josh gave his nephew a hug, then watched him dump out the puzzle pieces onto the floor.

The twins spent the next half hour in kid heaven as they had their uncle's undivided attention. They successfully put together several puzzles before Sophie finally sweet-talked her uncle into coloring a picture of a baby horse with her. Aaron managed to squeeze into Josh's lap while the other two colored the picture. When they were finished, Sophie joined her brother in the lap while Josh read them a story. By the end of the story, both kids were yawning.

"Okay, kids," Kaci said from the doorway. "It's time for bed."

Aaron yawned as he crawled out of his uncle's lap and reached for his sister's little hand. "Come on, Sissy. Uncle Josh is tired and needs to go to bed."

In a sign of confirmation, Josh yawned and stretched his arms.

"Come here, munchkins," Josh said. "I need hugs before you head off to bed."

Before long, the kids were snuggled in their beds, having received all the necessary hugs and kisses.

Josh gave Kaci a hug and shook Jason's hand. "Thanks for dinner, Sis. As usual, it was excellent."

"You're welcome anytime, Josh. Give Dad and Mom a hug for me, and we'll talk soon. Love you."

"Love you, too."

Josh walked out to his new Jeep with more optimism than he had felt in quite a while. Thank you, God. Maybe things are starting to come together.

Chapter Three

Meghan was happy she would be babysitting the twins this afternoon while the others met with Mike Slater about the warehouse building. She loved being a grandma and treasured her time with the kids. True to form, Aaron and Sophie came running to her as soon as she walked in the door to their home.

"Grandma!" they squealed in unison.

"You came to play with us, huh?" asked Sophie as Meghan bent down to pick up her granddaughter.

"I sure did! We're going to have lots of fun."

Travis had scooped up Aaron and had already planted him firmly upon his shoulders. Aaron was happily bouncing up and down in excitement.

"Papa?" Aaron asked. "Are you going to stay and play too?"

"Not this time, kiddo. I have to go with your mama and daddy and Uncle Josh to talk to a man. But I'll come play with you this weekend. Would that be okay?"

Aaron laughed. "It's always okay for you to play with me, Papa!"

By the time Travis, Josh, Kaci and Jason had gathered everything they needed for their meeting, and had dispensed hugs and kisses all around, the kids were content on their grandma's lap in the rocking chair with their favorite book.

"We'll be back soon, Mom," Josh said.

"Take your time. We'll have fun," Meghan replied.

* * *

On the ride over to Mike's office, Josh eagerly dominated the conversation with talk of his plans for the youth center. It quickly became obvious that he had put a lot of thought into this project. Jason was impressed with how well-thought-out JC's plans were. Kaci and Travis had some ideas and input as well, and within a few moments they were parking in front of Slater Investments.

Jason introduced everyone to Mike Slater, a stocky man in his late sixties, who led them back to a conference room so they could talk without interruption. Once in the conference room, Josh was immediately drawn to a framed baseball jersey on the wall. Upon inspection, he saw it was an autographed jersey belonging to Willie Mays of the San Francisco Giants. Mike chuckled when a barely audible 'Wow' escaped from Josh's lips. He walked up behind Josh, put his hand on his shoulder, and began relating the story of how he obtained the jersey. Mike led the group around the room, pointing out the various baseball memorabilia he had collected over the years.

"You know, Mike," Travis said. "My wife is not going to like that she missed this. She is one of the biggest baseball fans I've ever known. In fact, I proposed to her in center field. And Willie Mays is her all-time favorite ball player. She's going to be incredibly jealous when I happily tell her about this!"

Mike laughed in understanding. "Yeah, Jason has told me how much your entire family loves baseball. You bring your wife by anytime and I'll be happy to show her my collection.

"In the meantime, shall we get down to business?"

Everyone settled in around the conference table, as one of Mike's assistants brought in pitchers of ice water and glasses.

"Josh," Mike began. "By the way, do you prefer to be called Josh or JC?"

"I'm fine with either one," Josh replied.

"I'm going to kind of let you steer the conversation," Mike continued. "I've discussed your idea with Jason a bit, but it's your dream and your vision. Why don't you tell me what you have in mind."

"Okay," Josh began. "I don't know how much Jason has already told you, so if I am repeating things, just let me know.

"I hope to be able to open a youth center for troubled kids, so they have a place to go where it's a safe environment. I know there are a lot of kids out there who need a place where they can feel safe, feel like they are a part of something, and have some good role models. But it's also important to me that it's a place where they can have some godly influence in their lives."

"Why is that important to you, Josh?" Mike asked.

"I was blessed to be raised in a good Christian environment. Dad is a pastor, and he's always been my role model. I know not all kids are as lucky as I was. I know there are a lot of kids out there who come from broken homes, and they are just trying to survive the best they can. I don't want kids to just survive. I want them to be able to thrive. I'm not sure that's possible without God in their lives. I believe a lot of the kids who get involved in gangs or drugs and alcohol know they are missing something in their lives. They just don't realize what they are missing is God. The place he fills in their lives could never be filled by drugs, gangs, or anything else. It can only be filled by God."

"You're pretty wise for someone so young," Mike said with admiration.

"No, I'm not really that wise," Josh chuckled. "I'm just smart enough to realize I have been blessed."

"Tell me, Josh," Mike said. "Have you always wanted to help troubled kids?"

"I can't say always. But at least since high school."

"Any particular reason?" asked Mike.

"Well, my best friend grew up in an alcoholic home. He didn't exactly have the best home life. He used to hang out at our house a lot. I always thought it was just because we were friends. He told me one time that it was because we were friends, but it was also because he felt safe there. He liked the feeling he got when he walked into our house. I've never forgotten that. I think every kid should have a place where they feel good and safe as soon as they walk through the doors."

Mike began playing the devil's advocate because he wanted to draw Josh out even more, so he could see the passion behind his dream.

"Don't you think they could have a place where they feel safe without involving God?"

Travis raised his eyebrow at the question posed to his son and was very curious how he would answer.

"I'm sure it's possible," Josh replied. "And there's no doubt it would be helpful in a lot of situations. But I don't think they would be able to have the all-encompassing feeling of security and safety that only God can provide. I don't know how to describe it. But you can feel physically safe without necessarily feeling a total sense of security. With God, you get the whole package. There's just an extra level of security in knowing that God has a plan for your life."

Travis smiled with satisfaction at his son's response, knowing he felt that to the core of his being.

"You see, Mr. Slater..." Josh began.

"Please," Mike interrupted. "Call me Mike."

"Okay, Mike. As I've mentioned before, I know I have been blessed by growing up in a Christian home. But when I had my car accident..." Josh faltered.

"Go ahead, son," Travis encouraged.

"When I had my car accident, and nearly died, I knew God was there with me. Even though I wasn't conscious, I knew He was there. It gave me a sense of peace and security I wouldn't have had any other way. I knew that no matter how things turned out, I would be okay. If I didn't survive, I would be with God. If I did survive, there was a reason God was giving me another chance. I want those kids to have that sense of security and peace. I want them to know that a youth center can provide them with physical security. But, more importantly, I want them to know that a youth center where God is always welcome can provide them with spiritual security as well."

"Well said, young man," Mike agreed. "Well said."

Everyone around the table nodded their heads in agreement. Mike had additional questions for Josh, and the discussions continued for another half hour. Kaci was able to lay out the basics of how the youth center would be managed from a business standpoint. She had a folder with applications for various grants they could apply for to operate the center and pay salaries. Travis offered his services as a pastor to provide Bible study classes at the center. Travis also mentioned his brother-in-law, Todd, one of the owners of Byers Construction. That was the family business his wife's father had started, and Meghan and Todd now owned the company. Travis was sure Todd would be willing to offer help in any remodeling that might need to be done to make the warehouse functional as a youth center.

After nearly two hours around the conference table, the discussions were winding down.

Mike pushed back his chair and looked at Josh.

"Well, Josh, it's obvious you have put a lot of thought into this project. You have a degree in psychology, so that's definitely a plus. You have Kaci to manage the business end of things, and you appear to have the support of your entire family. However, to me, the most important thing I see is your passion. That passion is what will make the center a success.

"So, young man, it looks like you have a building for a youth center."

Everyone at the table erupted in cheers.

"Wait a minute. Wait a minute, everyone," Mike said as he raised his hand.

"There's one more thing. Do you have a name in mind for the center?"

"I do," Josh replied. "It will be called JC's Hope."

Mike nodded with satisfaction as he stood. "That sounds like the perfect name."

Mike walked around to Josh's side of the table and put his arm around the young man's shoulder as he stood.

"Josh, you're a very impressive young man. You have a dream, and you aren't afraid to go after it. I like that. I want to give your dream every opportunity for success. So...I am going to donate the warehouse to the center."

Everyone in the room looked shocked.

Mike continued. "We can work out all the details later. But I will donate the building, and you and the center will become the legal owners."

Josh stared at Mike in disbelief. "Wow, that's incredibly generous! Thank you so much!"

"It's my pleasure. I'm looking forward to helping you get this project off the ground."

Everyone shook hands with Mike at the end of the meeting, and he assured them he would be in touch in the next few days. The drive back to Kaci's and Jason's home was filled with excited conversation. They were still shocked and astonished at the outcome of the meeting.

Travis glanced over at Josh as he drove and said, "God is good."

Josh flashed a wide grin and replied, "All the time."

Chapter Four

Josh stood in front of the empty warehouse, with his hands in the back pockets of his Levis, and a huge grin on his face. All around him was commotion and lots of conversation. But he was happily at peace. Most of his family was wandering around outside the warehouse. His dad and mom, Kaci and Jason, his sister Ryleigh, his Uncle Todd, and even his little niece and nephew. But Josh simply stood and took it all in. It was still very surreal to him. He had a hard time wrapping his head around the fact that he was now the owner of this property and the large warehouse. Thanks to the incredible generosity of Mike Slater. Now, they were anxiously awaiting Mike's arrival with the keys to the building. Then it would feel real.

Josh watched his dad, mom, and uncle, all very experienced in the construction industry, walk around the perimeter of the building with a notepad. When Travis had mentioned the warehouse to Todd and asked if he might be interested in helping with the remodeling, Todd agreed without hesitation. On behalf of Byers Construction, Todd had offered their services in whatever way was needed to get the youth center functional. Josh still marveled at the support of his family, and at the way God was making all the pieces fall into place for the center.

Travis and Jason met up with Todd and were walking across the parking lot toward Josh just as a pickup pulled onto the lot. Mike Slater climbed out of the truck and walked over to Josh as well. He reached out his hand to Josh as he patted him on the back, then shook hands with the other men.

"Good afternoon, gentlemen," Mike greeted. "Well, Josh, it looks like you have quite a support group here. Who are these two little youngsters?"

Kaci, Ryleigh, and Meghan had joined the group and had the twins in tow.

Jason bent down and picked up Sophie. "These are my twins, Mike. This cutie is Sophie, and that little guy is Aaron."

Mike knelt on one knee to shake Aaron's hand. "I'll just bet a young man like you probably likes baseball, don't you?"

Aaron's eyes lit up. "Yes, sir! I have a glove!"

Not to be outdone, Sophie began wiggling out of her dad's arms and joined her brother on the ground.

"Me too! I have a glove too! And we have a bat!"

Mike laughed in reply. "You don't say."

"And we have baseball names!" Aaron said proudly.

"Is that right?" Mike asked with curiosity.

"Yep. I'm named for Hank Aaron. He hit more home runs than almost everybody! And my middle name is Cooper because Cooperstown is where all the best baseball players go when they're really good! Hank Aaron goes there! I'm going to go there someday too. When I get really good."

"I have a baseball name too," Sophie chimed in.

"Oh? And what is your baseball name?" Mike asked.

"Sophie!" she replied, as if that explained everything.

"So, you're named after a baseball player named Sophie?"

"Yep! She's in the Cooperstown place for girls."

"Mama, what did she do? I can't remember." Sophie said with disappointment.

Kaci smiled as she explained. "She's in the National Women's Baseball Hall of Fame because she stole more bases in a single season than anyone else."

"Yeah, she's the best!" Sophie said proudly. Then she whispered to Mike, "But it's okay to steal bases in baseball because you don't really take them."

"That's good to know," Mike said with a chuckle.

"Why don't you two wait right here. I think I may have something in my truck for you."

Sophie jumped up and down and clapped her hands in anticipation. Then she whispered in her brother's ear, "What do you think it is?"

Aaron whispered back, "Don't know. But I bet it's really good."

Mike returned with two kid-sized batting helmets from the local AAA minor league baseball team, the Hope Angels. He adjusted the sizing straps inside the helmets, then placed one on Aaron's head and the other on Sophie's head.

"Perfect fit," Mike said. "It looks like they were made for you."

Aaron and Sophie both patted the helmets down on their heads and grinned as they hugged each other.

"What do you say, kids?" Kaci reminded.

"Thank you!" they yelled in unison.

"Papa?" said Aaron. "Can we play baseball now?"

Mike chuckled as Travis replied. "We'll be sure to play this weekend, okay?"

"Yay!" the twins squealed.

"Josh," Mike began as he reached out his hand. "Here are the keys to your building. Why don't we go take a look around."

Josh grinned nearly as wide as his niece and nephew did when they received their baseball helmets. Travis put his arm around his son's shoulder, then they started walking toward the building, with their entourage close behind.

Everyone gathered at the main door and waited for Josh to unlock the building. Once inside, Travis, Meghan and Josh headed in one direction, while Todd and Mike went the opposite way. It was a very large warehouse, so everyone went exploring. The twins happily ran circles around each other in the middle of the large empty space, while their parents kept an eye on them.

Travis watched his son as they wandered around the building and could almost see the wheels spinning in his head. Josh had stopped in one large area and began looking around.

"What are you thinking, son?" Travis asked.

"Wouldn't it be great, Dad, if we could make a gym in here? You know, maybe a basketball court, a weight room, a rock-climbing wall over there," Josh said pointing.

"That would be a good idea," Travis agreed. "It will be interesting to see how this all comes together."

Out of the corner of his eye, Travis noticed Mike and Todd in deep conversation, both pointing at various things around the building.

"Josh," Travis said. "Go ahead and look around. I'm going to go over and talk to Todd for a few minutes."

Josh was already deep in thought and simply nodded in acknowledgement.

As Travis walked up behind Todd and Mike, he heard them discussing various aspects of the remodeling that would need to be done.

Todd turned to Travis and said, "This will be a great building for the center, Travis. It has a ton of potential."

"I agree. It's large enough for some classrooms where kids can study and do homework without interruptions. A couple of those offices could be easily remodeled to be used for administration and things. There's already a kitchen here and it could be updated without a ton of work. And Josh is already dreaming of maybe a gym with a basketball court, weight room and a rock-climbing wall," Travis added with a chuckle. "He has some pretty ambitious dreams!"

Mike laughed with admiration. "I can see that. Todd and I were just talking about some of the work that needs to be done to convert this to a fully functional center. The building is structurally sound. I updated all the electrical, HVAC and plumbing after the last tenant vacated, so those things would be minimal. Just whatever needs to be done for the various rooms that are added, and that kind of thing.

"Todd tells me his construction company will donate their time and labor to do the work," Mike continued.

Travis reached out and shook Todd's hand. "Thanks, Todd. That will help a lot. And I'll help with the labor whenever I'm not tied up at the church."

Mike had been watching the family explore the building and could see how the entire family shared in Josh's excitement. Josh himself had been walking around with a notepad, and Mike could see him feverishly jotting things down as he explored.

"You have quite a boy there, Travis," Mike commented.

"Thanks. He's been through a lot in the past few months since the accident. But he has never lost sight of who he is and why he's here. I have a lot of respect for him."

"I want to help him out," Mike said with determination.

"You have!" Travis replied. "Donating this building and land was an amazing contribution! We were just hoping you would be willing to rent it to him for a reasonable amount so he could move ahead with things. Your generosity is unbelievable."

"If Byers Construction is willing to donate time and labor to do the work, I will donate whatever supplies are needed," Mike said with affirmation.

Todd and Travis simply stared at each other.

Mike caught Josh's attention and waved him over. "Josh, come on over here and join us for a minute."

As Josh approached the group, he was already talking excitedly. "This is going to be great! I have so many ideas. Mike, I can't thank you enough for your generosity."

"Hold that thought, son," Travis said with a smile.

"Josh," Mike began. "I've been talking to your dad and uncle. There is no doubt your entire family is supporting your project. It's refreshing to see families who really help each other out. You have your own built-in cheerleading team. It's important to have that kind of support, and I know you don't take it for granted."

"No, sir," Josh replied. "I certainly don't."

"Your uncle tells me his construction company will donate their time and labor for all the remodeling that needs to be done. So, I will donate the material. Whatever is needed to get the center up and running."

Josh couldn't believe what he was hearing. He looked at his dad, and Travis simply nodded and smiled.

"Wow," Josh said in amazement. "But, Mike, you've already done so much. You gave me this land and the building!"

"I want to help, Josh, and I have the means to do so. I love your concept and your passion. And I know there is a need for a youth center here in town. I don't want its opening to be slowed down because of a lack of funds."

"You won't regret it, Mike," promised Josh, as he shook the hand of his benefactor.

Then Josh walked over and gave his uncle a big hug. "You won't either, Uncle Todd. Thank you so much! I don't know how I can ever repay everyone."

"You can put a piano in this place," Todd replied, only half joking. "That way I can stop by occasionally and listen to you play."

Mike pointed to Josh's notepad and said, "Add a piano to your list, young man. We need to keep these construction workers happy!"

Josh laughed in amazement as he happily added a piano to his growing list, and silently thanked God for His behind-the-scenes orchestration.

* * *

Over the next several weeks, the center was a hub of activity. Trucks from the local lumber and hardware supply store were frequently showing up to unload supplies, trucks and crews from Byers Construction were a daily sight, and there was a near-constant parade of family members stopping by to offer support or assistance. Mike Slater stopped by on a regular basis to make sure Josh was getting anything he needed for the center, in hopes it would be able to open in a couple months.

Word had gotten out around town about the new youth center, so Travis was fielding a fair amount of phone calls from local pastors offering their support and expressing their gratitude for the much-needed center. Even a local Boy Scout troop had stepped up to offer help. Several scouts had already cleared a small area in the center of the parking lot and had hauled in dirt and planted sod for an outdoor picnic area.

That was the scene before Josh as he pulled his Jeep into the parking lot. He simply sat there for a few minutes, shaking his head in amazement, and offering up another prayer of thanks. Just as he was getting out of his Jeep, he was approached by a man he knew to be a Scoutmaster working with the young men on the picnic area.

"Hi, Alan," Josh said as he shook hands with the man. "I can't thank you enough for all the hard work you and your scouts have been doing. The picnic area is looking great!"

"It's my pleasure, Josh," the man replied as he patted Josh on the back. "Actually, I can't take credit for anything other than coordination and heavy labor," he added with a chuckle. "The boys came up with the idea on their own. When they heard about the center, they thought it would be a great community service project for the entire troop. When I agreed with them, they took the idea and ran with it."

"Well," Josh replied, "they have sure been working hard. They are a great bunch of boys. I have fond memories of my time in the Scouts. It always feels good to be helping out in the community."

"Logan," Alan called as he raised his hand to wave over one of the boys. "Would you come over here for a minute, please."

A tall young man, appearing to be about fifteen years old, dropped a shovel and jogged over to Alan and Josh. "Hey, Mr. Walker. Did you need something?"

By way of introduction, Alan said, "Logan, this is Josh Harmon. He is the owner of the youth center."

"Hi, Mr. Harmon. I'm happy to meet you. This is a great place you have here."

Josh shook the young man's hand and replied, "Thanks, Logan, but please just call me Josh."

"Sure thing, Mr. -, I mean, Josh," he replied with a grin.

Alan chuckled at the exchange, knowing it would be hard for the young man to call Josh by his first name. "Josh, Logan was chatting with me the other day, brainstorming, and trying to come up with an idea for his Eagle Scout project. He had an idea that I think has merit, but I wanted him to run it by you to see what you think.

"Logan, why don't you tell Josh about your idea."

The young man's face lit up as he began explaining his idea. "As Mr. Walker said, I need to do a special project as part of achieving the Eagle Scout rank. When we started working on this picnic area, I thought that might be a great area to erect a sign identifying the center. You know, a nice wooden sign. Maybe something with the name carved into it and painted so it would stand out. We could maybe even put a light on it somehow so people could see it in the dark."

"You know, Logan," Josh said enthusiastically. "I think that's a great idea! I was already planning to paint the name of the center on the building somewhere, and I will still do that, but I really like your idea of a separate sign that stands out. And erecting it in the new picnic area would be the perfect place for it."

Alan smiled at Logan's huge grin, knowing how excited he was about the idea. "So, Josh, what's the next step for the sign?"

"I think I will let the two of you work up your ideas, and the design, then you can show me what you have in mind, and we can take it from there. How does that sound, Logan?"

"That sounds great. I already have a few ideas, so it won't take me long to come up with something to show you. Thanks for the opportunity, Mr. Har-, I mean, Josh. I better get back over and help the guys finish up. Don't want them to think I'm slacking!" With that, Logan shook Josh's hand and jogged back over to the picnic area, immediately picking up a shovel and getting back to work.

Alan chuckled as he said, "Logan's a good kid. And a hard worker. Just so you know, he's also a very gifted artist. He would never have mentioned that, but he already has several potential designs drawn up. I have confidence you will be able to find one you like."

"I can't wait to see them! Stop by anytime, I'm usually here."

"Thanks, Josh. I'll let Logan know." Then he chucked as he added, "Don't be surprised if you don't see us in a day or two. As I said, I know he already has some designs drawn up. If you're like me, your biggest challenge will be narrowing it down to the one you want! Now I had better get back over there before those boys think I'm the slacker!"

Josh watched Alan join back in, working side by side with the boys, then he walked toward the door of the warehouse, still marveling at how quickly everything was coming together.

* * *

As Josh walked into the building, he quickly spotted his uncle Todd talking to a tall young man who had his back to Josh. Todd was pointing up toward the rafters and along the wall, obviously discussing some part of the remodel being done. Josh called out to his uncle as he approached, triggering the young man to turn around.

Josh suddenly stopped in his tracks, let out a yell, then jogged over to the young man, embracing him in a big bear hug.

"Aiden! Man, it's been a long time!" The cousins embraced like long-lost best friends.

"Hey, JC!" Aiden exclaimed. "It's great to see you, buddy! Dad was just showing me around the center. This is going to be amazing!"

"Thanks! I sure hope so! I can't believe everyone who has jumped in to help make it possible. Hey, when did you get home? I knew you would be getting out of the Army soon, but didn't realize you were already out."

"I got home yesterday," Aiden replied. He looked at his dad and chuckled. "I barely dropped my duffel bag when Dad started telling me about the center you were going to be opening. I knew I would be going into the family construction business when I got out, but didn't know I would be put to work quite so quickly!"

JC playfully punched his uncle's arm and laughed. "You could have at least let the poor guy unpack first!"

Todd smiled and said, "I figured all that time in the Army Corps of Engineers would come in handy with this project. I didn't want to take a chance that his skills would get rusty!"

Todd reached over and put his arm around Aiden's shoulder in a fatherly hug. "Besides, with so much going on over here, I really needed a take-charge guy to be the crew foreman on this project. I was just telling Aiden about the rock-climbing wall you want to put in. He said this wall would be perfect. He knows exactly what needs to be done to be able to anchor the safety ropes for the climbers. See, I knew all that engineering work would come in handy."

The three men laughed as they continued discussing some of the work that still needed to be done.

Josh slapped his cousin on the back playfully and said, "Man, what have they been feeding you in the Army? You must have grown two inches! You've got to be at least six four now. Finally taller than your dad!"

Aiden chuckled as he replied, "I have no doubt Army grub is a lot better now than it was when Grandpa served during the war."

"Speaking of grub," Josh said suddenly. "Why don't we order some pizza so we can all eat lunch and visit for a bit. I'm sure those scouts working outside would be willing to help eat pizza."

Aiden rubbed his stomach in agreement and said, "Sounds like a great idea. It seems like I haven't eaten in forever!"

Todd laughed and said, "Well, not since the two donuts you ate on the way over here. Not to worry, we've got it covered. Meghan already ordered pizza from Luigi's, and she and your dad will be here shortly with it. We've got to keep you guys fed so we can get some work out of you!"

As if on cue, the main warehouse door opened, and Travis and Meghan walked in carrying several large pizza boxes and a cooler of soft drinks. They were being trailed closely by a hungry-looking group of Boy Scouts.

Meghan sat the pizza boxes on the kitchen counter and hurried over to give her nephew a big hug. "Oh, Aiden, it's so good to see you! Welcome home!"

Travis gave Aiden a good-natured slap on the back as he shook his hand. "Welcome home, son. It's great to see you! I see it didn't take your dad long to recruit you for our latest project."

"It's great to see you too, Uncle Travis. Yeah, you know Dad," Aiden chuckled. "If there's a construction project going on, the whole family gets to be involved."

Todd threw up his hands in mock surrender. "Hey, you can blame your grandfather for that. He's the one who started it." Everyone chuckled at the family joke.

"Oh, before I forget," Travis said, "Kaci wants us all to go over for spaghetti tomorrow night. She's going to make a big batch so we can sit around and discuss the progress we've been making, and see if we can get a timeline for finishing the remodeling."

"That's a great idea," Josh agreed. "Leave it to Kaci to keep us on track!"

Meghan spoke up in agreement. "Your sister is definitely a planner. And it will give us all a chance to visit with Aiden."

"Yeah," Aiden quickly agreed. "I haven't seen those little munchkins of hers in nearly a year. They're probably half grown by now!"

"It sure seems like it," Josh agreed. "They need another uncle around to take some of the pressure to entertain them off me!"

"They probably won't even remember me," Aiden said.

"You'll do just fine," JC assured him. "As long as you can talk construction equipment or baseball, they will know you belong to the family."

Everyone laughed in agreement, as they dug into the pizza.

"Come on, boys," Meghan called to the scouts. "Dig in. We're going to need your help to eat all this pizza!"

Enthusiastic expressions of thanks were heard as the scouts quickly descended on the hot pizza, filling their plates.

Chapter Five

Jason met the family at the door and ushered them into the living room. "Come on in, guys. Kaci is in the kitchen, but you can wander on in to say hi."

"Yep, it definitely smells like spaghetti at the Hayes house," said Travis with a smile. "That daughter of mine sure knows how to cook."

Todd and Aiden followed Travis, Meghan, and Josh into the house, with Meghan heading straight to the kitchen to see if Kaci needed any help.

Jason reached out to shake Aiden's hand. "Aiden, welcome home! You look great! Army life must have agreed with you."

"Hey, Jason. The Army certainly has its good points, but it's great to be back home around family. I have to admit, though, I wouldn't trade my time with the Corps of Engineers for anything. It was a great learning experience."

At the sound of voices, the twins erupted from the playroom and ran toward their family.

"Papa!" squealed Sophie, as she launched herself into Travis's outstretched arms. "Where's grandma?"

"She went into the kitchen to see if your mama needs any help."

Sophie slipped out of her grandpa's arms and made a beeline toward the kitchen. "I'm going to go find grandma." On the way to the kitchen, she slowed down long enough to give Aiden a quick glance before saying, "I don't know you." Then she hurried off on her mission to find grandma.

Aiden chuckled, then noticed Aaron eying him while standing beside his Uncle Josh. Aiden knelt in front of Aaron with a smile and said, "Hey, buddy, do you remember me?"

Aaron studied him carefully for a moment before saying, "Maybe. I think you're Uncle Josh's friend. But I haven't seen you for a long time."

Aiden nodded with satisfaction as Josh smiled. "Well, buddy, that's pretty close. Your Uncle Josh is my cousin. And your mom is my cousin. So that makes you and your sister my cousins too."

"Are you sure?" Aaron asked skeptically. "That's a lot of cousins."

Josh laughed as he knelt beside little Aaron. "You're right, buddy, that's a lot of cousins! But he's right. This is our cousin Aiden. Uncle Todd is his dad."

"Oh!" Aaron replied in delight. "I know you! You're the Army man! Uncle Todd told me you were coming home from the Army. Hey, do you have a gun?"

"Not anymore," Aiden replied. "Most of what I did in the Army was build things. You know, like bridges, roads, and stuff."

Aaron's eyes grew large like saucers as he asked in admiration, "Did you get to drive a backhoe?"

"I sure did! Lots of great big backhoes! And huge trucks and road graders. Some of the equipment was almost as big as a house!"

"Wow!" Aaron marveled in amazement. "My papa is going to let me drive a backhoe when I'm bigger. Maybe next week. I have my own hardhat!" With that, Aaron took Aiden by the hand and led him off to his bedroom to show him his hardhat and construction toys.

Todd looked over at Josh and said, "Well, Josh, it looks like you've been replaced!"

Josh just laughed and said, "Well, it's hard to compete with a construction man. Especially an Army construction man!"

The men were still chuckling when Meghan and Kaci emerged from the kitchen.

"Dinner's ready everyone," Kaci announced. She walked over and gave her Uncle Todd a peck on the cheek. "I'm sorry Aunt Nicole couldn't make it. Working again, huh?"

"I'm afraid so. Being an ER nurse has its drawbacks, but she sure loves what she does. And it keeps her off the heavy equipment!"

* * *

After filling up on a satisfying dinner of spaghetti, salad and garlic bread, the kids headed off to their room to play while the adults sat down to discuss the progress of the youth center. Over the next couple hours, the adults hashed over the status on the various phases of the remodel project, satisfied with the progress.

"Well, Josh," Todd began. "It looks like everything is getting close to wrapping up. The classrooms are finished, except for the painting. The kitchen just has a few final touches, and it will be done. I think the last big project is the gym. Aiden is going to coordinate getting the rock wall put in and the floor laid. Once the basketball hoops are installed, it won't take long to finish the gym after that."

"How long do you think the gym will take, Todd?" asked Travis.

"I would think two or three weeks, tops," Todd replied. "That would allow time for finishing the gym floor because there can't be much else going on in there while the finish is being put on the floor."

"The last of the carpeting will be finished in the next couple days," Josh added. "I think the speakers and piano are scheduled to be delivered to the music room on Friday."

"It's beginning to sound like we can probably plan the open house sometime around the first of the month," Kaci suggested. "How does that sound, Josh?"

Josh sat back as a big grin slowly enveloped his face. "I still can't believe all this is happening. The support from all you guys has been beyond incredible. Even though it seems like a lifetime ago, just a few months ago I felt like I was floundering and wasn't sure where my life was going. Then suddenly things just started falling into place."

Travis smiled at his son. "Prayer is a powerful tool, Josh. You wouldn't believe all the people who have held you in their prayers."

"Your dad's right, JC," Aiden added. "Our engineering unit had Bible studies in the barracks every Friday night. You were always on our prayer list."

Josh shook his head in amazement. "I have definitely been blessed."

Josh turned to his sister, "Well, Kaci, if you think we could shoot for the first of the month, I guess you can start making plans for the open house. Try to keep the plans flexible, though, in case we run into a snag with something.

"Oh, and I almost forgot something. I was talking to Kyle the other day, and we definitely want to let him know when the open house will be. He wants to be sure the boys on the baseball team know about the center. A few of them have really been struggling at home."

"Baseball team?" Aiden asked. "I'm a bit out of the loop. What's Kyle up to these days?"

Travis jumped in to field the question. "Aiden, you would be really proud of Kyle. You know what his home life was like, especially as a teenager. Thanks in large part to Josh, Kyle finished high school and graduated from the university with a teaching degree. He is in his first year as one of the math teachers at the high school, and he is the assistant coach for the baseball team."

"Wow!" Aiden said enthusiastically. "That's great! I'm not surprised, though. He was a good kid, and was smart enough to steer clear of the problems his parents got sucked into. He made some good choices for friends as well. That can make a big difference, especially for a teenager."

Josh nodded as he added, "That's one of the main purposes for the center. If kids know they have a safe place to hang out, and can make friends so they develop their own support system, it can go a long way in keeping them grounded and out of trouble."

After a bit more discussion, the group decided to call it a night. Everyone felt they had a good handle on what still needed to be done, and an idea on the timeline to get things finished. Josh promised to keep Kaci informed if they ran into any delays, and Kaci would go ahead with making plans for the open house. Kaci and Meghan had offered to design some flyers that would eventually be passed out to scout troops, neighborhood churches, and the schools. It appeared that Josh's dream was quickly becoming a reality. And JC's Hope would provide hope and support to the youth of the neighborhood.

* * *

Josh pulled his Jeep into the high school parking lot alongside the baseball fields. He sat in the Jeep, watching Kyle work with the teenagers. He was a natural, and it appeared the boys all liked and respected him. It helped that Kyle worked right alongside the boys, which helped him maintain his athletic build. As he looked around the field, Josh noticed a young lady sitting alone in the bleachers. She appeared to be about Ryleigh's age. She was reading a book, occasionally glancing up to watch the boys on the field. She looked a bit out of place, and Josh wondered about her story. He made a mental note to ask Kyle once practice was over.

As baseball practice was winding down, Josh got out of his Jeep and started walking toward the ball field. Kyle saw him and waved him over. Josh jogged over to where the boys were gathering around the pitcher's mound. He reached out to shake hands with Kyle, and said hi to the group of boys.

"Guys," Kyle addressed the group. "This is Josh Harmon. A lot of people, me included, call him JC. I asked him to stop by this afternoon to talk to you guys for a few minutes about a project he's working on."

"Hey, guys," Josh began. "Thanks for letting me steal a few minutes of your time. Are you guys familiar with that big vacant warehouse over on Division? It's just a few blocks west of here."

Several of the boys nodded their heads. Hope wasn't a very large town, so most people were familiar with things happening in town.

"I walk right by there going home every day," offered one of the younger boys. "I think I've seen your Jeep there a few times."

Josh chuckled. "You're right. I seem to be spending a lot of my time there these days. That's what I wanted to talk to you guys about. I own that building and property now, and have been converting it into a youth center. Our little town has been growing, and there really isn't a place where kids can hang out. I want to provide a place where kids your age can go after school and on weekends if you're looking for a place to play basketball, study, play music, or just hang out with friends."

Several of the kids began nodding their heads, smiling, and whispering to each other.

Josh continued. "There are going to be classrooms where you can find a quiet place to study or work on homework. The largest classroom is going to be a music room. We'll have a piano, and maybe eventually some other equipment. Like guitars and amps, possibly. So, if you have an interest in music, it might be a good place to work on that. The center will have a kitchen, and I'll try to keep it reasonably stocked with some basic snacks, water, juice, sodas, and things like that. It will also have a gym, with a full-size basketball court, a weight room, and a rock-climbing wall. And we will be offering Bible study classes and counseling for whoever may be interested.

"I wanted to be sure you guys know about it in advance. I'll also let Kyle know when we schedule the open house, hopefully in a couple weeks or so, so you can stop by to check it out. Does that sound like something you might be interested in?"

One of the older boys spoke up. "I think it's a great idea, Mr. Harmon."

"Please," replied Josh with a smile. "You can call me Josh or JC."

"Right, sorry," the boy said before continuing. "I think it would be great to have a place like that. Somewhere to go after school, to hang out with friends. Is there going to be an age limit? I kind of watch my younger brother after school, and it would be nice to have a place to shoot hoops and stuff with him."

"That's a good point," Josh agreed. "We probably won't be geared for kids who are very young. We are kind of targeting kids who are pre-teens and teens. So, most likely kids who are maybe ten or so, on up. How old is your younger brother?"

"He's thirteen, so it sounds like he would fit okay."

"Absolutely," Josh replied.

"Well, I don't want to take up too much of your time this afternoon. If you have questions, or want more information before the open house, Coach Kyle knows how to get in touch with me. I hope to see some of you at the open house."

Kyle shook Josh's hand in thanks. "Thanks for stopping by JC. I'll look forward to hearing when the open house is scheduled.

"Okay, guys, since we used a little extra time at the end of practice, we'll skip the laps today."

A chorus of cheers erupted from the group.

"Yeah," Kyle laughed. "I thought you might like that. See you guys tomorrow. And those of you who are in my Algebra class, don't forget we're having a quiz tomorrow."

A few mumbled groans were heard as the group of boys dispersed. One of the boys started toward the bleachers where the young woman sat.

Josh, still standing beside Kyle, nodded in the direction of the bleachers. "Do you know who that young lady is, Kyle?"

Kyle looked toward the bleachers before replying. "I don't know her name, but I think it's Matthew's sister. She shows up most days when we're out here having practice. She's always by herself. When she's here, Matthew always leaves with her. I've never really asked him about her. If she is Matthew's sister, it might not be a bad idea for us to get to know her. He's one of the kids I hope will make use of your center. I've always gotten the impression that his home life isn't that great."

Josh rubbed his thumb along his jawline, a common practice when he was thinking about something. "When is your next practice?"

"Tomorrow, right after school," Kyle replied.

"Maybe I'll stop by tomorrow," JC said. "Hopefully, she will be here, and I can talk to her about Matthew. If, like you suspect, his home life isn't great, he's exactly the kind of kid I'd like to see at the center."

"Agreed," said Kyle. "Well, buddy, I'd better get back into the school. I seem to remember promising the kids an Algebra quiz tomorrow, so I'd best get it ready."

The two friends chuckled as they parted ways.

* * *

The next afternoon, Josh was parked next to the ball field when the boys came out for practice. He kept one eye on the boys and the other on the bleachers in hopes of seeing the young lady. About twenty minutes into the practice, the slim ginger-haired lady walked up and sat down on the bleachers, then pulled a book out of her bag and began reading.

Josh got out of his Jeep and walked toward the bleachers. As he approached, he said hi to the lady and asked if she minded if he sat down.

By way of introduction, he pointed toward the boys and said, "Some of those kids are pretty good. I'm Josh Harmon. Is one of those boys your brother, or do you just like baseball?"

The young lady eyed him hesitantly before replying. "Yes, my younger brother is on the team. I like watching them practice. Do you have a brother on the team?"

Still watching the boys, Josh replied. "No. The assistant coach is a good friend of mine. We grew up together. I'm trying to get to know some of the kids a bit because I will be opening a youth center a few blocks from here. I'm hoping some of them will see it as a good place to hang out."

The young lady seemed to perk up at that news, and tentatively offered her hand. "I'm Amelia. Amelia Phoenix."

"Ah," Josh said curiously. "Phoenix. Like rising from the ashes?"

"Yeah," she chuckled softly. "Something like that. My brother is Matthew. He plays shortstop."

"He must be pretty good, then," Josh commented. "That's a tough position."

Amelia smiled and said, "Yes, he's pretty good. When he doesn't get too cocky. He's a good kid, though. So, you're opening a youth center, huh? Is it just like a gym or something, where kids can go after school to play basketball and stuff?"

"Well, that's part of it," Josh explained. "There will be places where they can study and do homework, play games and music, or just hang out. I want it to be a place where the kids can feel safe, and it gives an alternative to roaming the streets where they may get into trouble, or fall in with the wrong crowds. A lot of kids don't have a great life at home."

"Yeah, tell me about it," Amelia said so quietly Josh almost missed it.

Josh and Amelia continued talking for the duration of the baseball practice. Before long, Amelia looked up and saw her brother coming across the field toward her. Seeing his light brown hair looking scruffy under his baseball cap reminded her that she needed to give him another haircut.

As he approached, he looked at Josh and said, "Hi, JC. What are you doing here? Do you know my sister?"

Looking a bit confused, Amelia asked her brother, "JC? Do you know Josh?"

"Not really," Matthew replied. "He's a friend of the coach. He came by practice yesterday to tell us about a youth center he's opening. It sounds pretty cool."

Josh reached out his hand, "I remember seeing you at practice yesterday, but we weren't introduced. Aren't you the shortstop?"

Matthew smiled proudly. "Yeah, I'm the shortstop. I'm Matt."

"You're pretty good. I've been watching you out there," Josh said. "So, you think the center sounds like a good idea? Does that mean you'll come to the open house in a couple weeks and check it out?"

"Sure. Maybe. I'll have to see. Could my sister come with me to check it out?"

"Absolutely," Josh replied. "Your sister, your parents. The more the merrier."

"Not my parents. Just my sister and me. If that's okay," Matthew replied shyly.

"That would be great, Matt." Josh looked around for a car and, not seeing one, asked, "Do you two need a ride home or somewhere? I can give you a ride if you'd like."

Matthew looked at his sister hopefully. She replied, "No. That's okay. We'll just walk. It's not far."

Josh sensed there was more to their story than he knew, but didn't want to pry. Instead, he reached into his pocket for a pen, and pulled a slip of paper from his wallet.

"Here," Josh said as he wrote on the small slip of paper. "Here's my name and phone number. I'll let Kyle know when the open house will be. In the meantime, if you have any questions…" Josh looked directly into Amelia's eyes. "Any questions at all, please don't hesitate to contact me."

Amelia tucked the slip of paper into her bag, put her arm around her brother's shoulder, and said, "Thanks, I will. See you around." And they walked away.

Chapter Six

Josh pulled his Jeep into the parking lot at the center and noticed Amelia sitting at one of the picnic tables out front. Dressed in faded jeans and an over-sized t-shirt, she could have easily passed as another teenager at the center. He gathered a few things he needed from the Jeep, then walked over to the picnic area.

Amelia glanced up as he approached. "Hi, Josh," she said shyly. "I hope you don't mind that I stopped by."

"Not at all," Josh replied. "I'm happy to see you."

"Did you mean it the other day when you said I could contact you if I had questions?" Amelia asked hesitantly.

"Of course," Josh replied, sensing her insecurity. "What can I help you with? Would you like to come into the office so we can talk?"

"No. If you don't mind, would it be okay if we talk out here?"

"Sure," Josh replied. "Let me just take these things in and put them on my desk and I'll be right back out. Would you like me to bring you some water or juice or something?"

"No thanks, I'm fine," she replied.

"Okay. Give me two minutes and I'll be right back."

Josh hurried into the center to drop things on his desk. On the way, he sent up a quick prayer to God, thanking Him for sending Amelia to the center, and asking for guidance in their discussions.

Back at the picnic table, Josh sat down across from Amelia, then smiled. "It's probably a good thing you wanted to talk out here. It's a bit noisy inside. There's still a fair amount of work being done to finish things up before the open house. It will probably be easier to talk and hear each other out here."

Amelia just nodded and smiled.

Not quite sure what was on her mind, Josh didn't want to scare her off, so he decided to tread lightly. "Kyle tells me Matthew is doing great at shortstop. He appears to have some natural talent and good instincts. And he apparently did well on his Algebra quiz the other day."

Amelia looked at Josh with interest. "You seem to know a lot about the kids. Are you a teacher too?"

Josh chuckled. "No. I'm not sure I would make a very good teacher. But I like kids and have a soft spot for them. I studied child psychology in college."

"So that's why you want to open a youth center?"

"That's part of the reason," Josh explained. "As a teenager, one of my best friends really struggled at home. So, he spent a lot of time at my house. My dad is the pastor over at Hope Community Church, and he's come across a lot of kids who needed a positive influence in their lives that they just weren't getting at home. There is a big need for a youth center in town. Especially now that Hope seems to be growing. I also saw a lot of that while I was on my mission trip after high school. It always amazes me how many kids live in a negative environment at home. People don't always realize how big a problem it is. I just think every kid deserves a chance to have a good life. If there's something I can do to help make that possible – even for just one kid – then I think it's my job to do so.

"Does that make sense?"

"Yes, it does," Amelia replied, nodding. She stared off into space for a moment before continuing. "Matt's a good kid."

Josh waited for her to continue, not wanting to push.

"I try to protect him as much as I can," she finally continued. "It's not easy. I don't want him to fall into the wrong crowd. He's such a good kid." Amelia's eyes misted over a bit. She seemed to need to regroup before continuing. "I'm really all he's got. It's really always been just the two of us."

Amelia sat quietly for a few moments, just staring off into space. Josh didn't want to rush her, but hoped she would continue talking.

When she remained quiet, he spoke up. "I noticed the other day when we were talking about the open house, Matt mentioned maybe just you and he would stop by. Not your parents. I don't want to pry, but are your parents not in the picture? And you don't have to tell me if you don't want to."

Amelia looked at Josh. Her eyes were filled with sadness. She let out a heavy sigh before asking, "Are you sure you want to hear this?"

Josh reached over and touched her softly on the arm. "Yes, I do," he said compassionately. "I really do. You obviously came here because you needed to talk. I'm here to listen." He smiled and said, "Really. I'm a good listener."

Amelia smiled and replied, "Well, don't say I didn't warn you.

"Our home life isn't great. Dad and Mom are both hopeless alcoholics. They have been my entire life. Many years ago, they would try rehab off and on, but never stuck with it. Whenever it got difficult, it was just easier to hit the bottle again. Mom would sometimes disappear for days at a time. I don't remember either of them ever having a job when I was growing up.

"So, I pretty much took care of everything at home from the time I was little. I did all the cooking and cleaning. They usually managed to do the shopping for groceries, but that was about it. They fought all the time. I don't ever remember a time when my parents weren't fighting. I thought it would be different when Matthew came along. But it wasn't. The only difference was that I now had someone else to take care of. I never minded taking care of Matthew. He was such a sweet, happy baby. I did a pretty good job taking care of him. Even though I wasn't much more than a kid myself."

"That's a big burden, and a huge responsibility for a kid," Josh said quietly.

"You're right, it is," Amelia agreed. "But I never really had a choice. We don't have any other family. So, it was up to me to make sure Matthew was taken care of and safe. But it's harder now that he's a teenager.

I worry about him all the time. There are so many bad influences out there in the world, not to mention what he sees at home every single day. He's a good kid. I just can't bear to see him fall in with the wrong crowd…and end up like our parents. He doesn't deserve that."

Amelia was openly sobbing now, so Josh moved to the other side of the picnic table and sat beside her. He put his arm around her shoulder and gently pulled her close. He was relieved when she seemed to just sink into his shoulder. He held her close for several minutes while she sobbed, then tried to regain her composure.

When she finally pulled away, Josh began speaking again. "Amelia…"

"My friends call me Amy," she said as she wiped the tears from her eyes.

Josh smiled and began again. "Amy, I would really like you to meet my dad and mom. As I mentioned earlier, Dad is the pastor over at Hope Community Church, so he has seen a lot of things and is also a good listener. And he gives great advice. Mom was married to an alcoholic before she divorced him and eventually met and married my dad. She raised my older sister in the home of an alcoholic before she figured out how to get out of the marriage. She had so much courage to divorce her husband and raise a kid by herself. But she knew it was best for her and my sister. So, Mom would understand what you're going through.

"If you'd like, I could set up a time for them to meet you here at the center so you can talk. You could even bring Matt if you'd like."

Josh and Amelia talked for another half hour or so before she stood up to go. "I've taken up enough of your time, Josh. Thanks for listening. But I should let you get back to what you need to do."

"Anytime, Amy. Anytime," Josh replied. "You can let me know if you would like to talk with my parents. I can set that up. In the meantime, please don't hesitate to stop by, or call me, whenever you need to. I'd like to help you if I can. And I would really like to see you and Matt come to the open house. I'd like you to look around to see what we have to offer here at the center. I think it would be good, not only for Matt, but for you too."

"Thanks, Josh. Please let me know when the open house will be."

"I will, Amy. In fact, I'll give you a call, in case you don't hear about it through the flyers we'll be sending out. And Amy, please take care of yourself. You won't be any good to Matt if you don't take care of you."

She simply nodded, then walked away.

* * *

The center was gearing up for the open house. Flyers had been delivered to both the junior high and high schools, the local Boy Scout troops, and local churches. The community support had been overwhelming. The finishing touches were being put on things both inside and outside the center. Josh and his entire family had just arrived at the picnic area to check out the new sign that had been erected.

Josh stood back, with his hands in the back pockets of his Levis, and admired the new sign. "What do you guys think?"

Meghan spoke first. "Son, I think it looks great! Logan did a fantastic job on it! I'm glad they were able to figure out a way to shine a light on the sign. That will make it easier to see at night."

Everyone echoed Meghan's thoughts, clearly pleased with the outcome of the sign.

Travis walked over and put his arm around Josh's shoulder as they looked at the front of the center. The building no longer looked like every other drab concrete warehouse in town. The fresh pale yellow paint, highlighted with black silhouettes showing some of the center's activities, was the perfect backdrop for the graphics Ryleigh designed identifying the building as JC's Hope.

"Well," said Travis. "Should we look around and make sure we didn't miss anything? Todd why don't you and Aiden check out the exterior and make sure nothing got missed and there isn't any paint touchup that needs to be done. Then you can join the rest of us inside to give one last double check on all the interior rooms. But I think we're probably ready for tomorrow's open house."

Everyone split up to check out all areas of the center. It took about an hour before they met in the middle of the gym, satisfied that everything was ready to go.

"Before it gets away from me," Josh began. "I just want to thank all of you again for not only your constant and unwavering love, but for the incredible support you have shown for the center. This dream never would have been possible without each one of you. I am so blessed to have such an amazing family. I love you all."

"You've worked hard for this dream, Josh," Kaci said. "Not a one of us has worked harder than you have. You deserve this."

"Thanks, sis," Josh replied. "That means a lot to me."

About that time, Aiden walked out of the kitchen with a chocolate chip cookie in one hand and a soda in the other. "Hey, did you guys know there are cookies in there?"

Everyone laughed. "Son, I swear you are a bottomless pit!" Todd said with a laugh. "Leave it to you to find the food."

"It's a good thing we brought extra cookies," Meghan laughed. "There are enough for everyone to have a snack now, and still have plenty for the open house tomorrow. So, enjoy!"

* * *

Cars continued to stream into the large parking lot prior to the official start of the open house. There was already a huge crowd of people milling around outside the center. There appeared to be a good turnout from the junior high and high schools, both in students and teachers. The principals of both schools were in attendance, as well as some members of the school board. Two of the local Boy Scout troops were there, as well as most of the varsity and junior varsity baseball teams from the high school. Several local pastors were also in attendance.

Although Josh had not had a chance to talk to him yet, he spotted Mike Slater talking to his dad and uncle Todd near the front entrance. Josh turned to his cousin in amazement. "Aiden, I can't believe the turnout! This is fantastic!"

Aiden nodded in agreement. "You're right. You couldn't have hoped for a better turnout. But, when you think about it, it's not really that surprising. The center is a great thing for Hope. Something like this has been needed for several years, even while we were in high school. It's nice to see it happening."

Josh patted his cousin on the back and said, "I'll be back in a couple minutes. I see someone over there I need to talk to."

Spying Amelia and Matthew standing in the shade of one of the trees, Josh hurried over to them.

"Hey, Matt!" Josh greeted, as he reached out to shake Matt's hand. "I'm glad to see you were able to make it. We're going to be getting started here in a few minutes, then you'll be able to go inside and check things out."

"Thanks, JC," Matt replied. "It really looks cool. I like the big black graphics of kids playing basketball. The piano and music notes are pretty cool too."

"Thanks, Matt," Josh replied. "I like those a lot too."

Josh smiled, then touched Amelia on her arm as he whispered. "I'm really glad to see you. Thanks for coming."

She simply smiled in return.

About that time, Travis tapped the microphone set up on a podium in front of the main entrance to the center.

"Can I have everyone's attention, please? Let's get started, so everyone can get inside to check things out."

People started moving in a bit closer as Josh and several others stepped up behind the podium.

"First of all, I want to thank all of you for coming. Many of you already know me, but for those who don't, I'm Pastor Travis Harmon from Hope Community Church. This is an exciting day, not only for our community, but for our family as well. This center is the brainchild of my son, Josh.

"Step over here, son."

Josh stood beside his dad and raised his hand to the crowd.

"This center is truly a group effort. When Josh had the idea for a youth center, my son-in-law Jason mentioned knowing someone who might have a building he could rent for the center. This former warehouse belonged to this man right here, Mike Slater." Travis put his arm around Mike's shoulder, then continued. "Without the incredible generosity of this man, the center might not have become a reality."

Mike interrupted Travis. "Enough about me. This is Josh's day. As Pastor Harmon mentioned, it was Josh's brainchild. I was simply one of many players involved who helped make it happen. The credit goes to Josh.

"Josh," Mike continued. "Why don't you step up here and say a few words?"

Josh smiled as he stepped to the microphone. "As Dad said, thank you all for coming. I'm not much of one for public speaking, so I'll try to keep it brief." Josh chuckled as several people in the crowd laughed.

Josh continued. "This truly has been a group effort. My entire family jumped in to do the physical work involved in the remodel, as well as tons of behind-the-scenes work that was necessary. Because of everyone's support, we're here today ready to open the center. So, let me tell you a little bit about the purpose of the center and how it will work.

"JC's Hope is designed to be a community youth center. The plan is for it to provide a safe place for young kids, primarily pre-teens and teens, to hang out. A place where they can go after school or on weekends, as an alternative to aimlessly wandering around town. The center has several classrooms where kids can study or do homework in a quiet environment. There is a kitchen that we'll try to keep stocked with an assortment of basic snacks, as well as water, juice, and soda. The largest classroom is set up as a music room. We have a piano in there, and hope to add maybe guitars and amps later. And the kids will be welcome to bring their own instruments to the center as well. That room will also serve as a worship room. We will have periodic group or individual Bible studies and counseling for whoever may want to participate. We also have a gym with a full-size basketball court, a weight room, and a rock-climbing wall.

"The center will also have a Code of Conduct, which is posted in several places throughout the facility. The Code of Conduct is pretty basic. This is to be a place where everyone can feel safe. A place where each person is expected to treat others with dignity and respect. A place where everyone is held accountable for their own actions, and a place where each person can feel comfortable knowing there is an adult they can talk to when they need someone.

"JC's Hope is here to serve the youth of the community. We want you to feel happy and safe when you enter the doors. So, without further ado, let's open those doors so you can check it out! Feel free to look around, and don't hesitate to ask questions. All of us associated with the center are wearing bright yellow name tags, so you should be able to locate one of us when you have a question."

Travis opened the doors and the crowd descended on the center. Groups split off and headed in different directions once inside. Josh and his family split up to make themselves easily available in different parts of the building. A large group of teens congregated in the middle of the gym, then began checking out the rock-climbing wall and the weight room. Several teachers and pastors made their way to the classrooms, while some parents of the teens wandered into the music room. Before long, a popular worship song was heard coming from the music room.

Meghan searched the crowd for her son, assuming he was the one who had sat down at the piano. Spotting him across the room, she smiled at him, and they both headed toward the music room. They stepped just inside the door and found a teenaged boy playing the piano while several people sang along. The young dark-haired boy was clearly in his element. Josh walked over and sat down beside the boy, smiled as the boy slid over slightly, then began harmonizing on the upper end of the keyboard. The teenager was grinning from ear to ear as they finished the song. He quickly launched into another popular worship song and smiled as Josh seamlessly joined right in. Before long, a good-sized crowd had gathered inside the music room, as well as outside in the hallway.

After finishing the second song, Josh put his arm around the boy's shoulder and said, "That was fantastic!"

The teen smiled shyly, then looked at Josh and replied, "You're pretty good. That was a lot of fun. I hope you don't mind that I sat down to play. We don't have a piano anymore, so I don't get to play very often. By the way, I'm Brandon."

"Nice to meet you, Brandon," Josh replied. "We certainly don't want all that talent going to waste, so you feel free to stop by anytime to play. I hope I'll be seeing a lot of you here at the center. It would be nice having someone to jam with occasionally. Do you know other types of music besides worship songs?"

"Oh, yeah!" Brandon replied enthusiastically. "I also play contemporary songs and classical music. But my favorite is playing rock and roll!"

Josh patted Brandon on the back as he stood up and said, "Oh, yeah, you and I are going to get along just fine!"

* * *

After the last of the crowds had thinned out, and the parking lot was nearly empty, a tired group sat down at the picnic tables outside.

Mike Slater walked up behind Josh, patted him on the back, and said, "Well, son, I'd say your open house was a rousing success. I heard nothing but positive comments and feedback. You and the center are going to be a hit!"

"Thanks, Mike!" Josh replied. "None of this would have been possible without your generosity. I can't begin to thank you for everything."

"You helping out the neighborhood kids is thanks enough," Mike replied sincerely.

Everyone sat around for another hour and talked about the overwhelming success of the open house. All the adults who attended were thrilled at everything being offered at the center, and the kids couldn't stop talking about it. They loved the gym and the rock-climbing wall, and were even impressed with the classrooms where they could study and work on homework.

"Well, son," Travis said. "We'd better head home and get some rest. It looks to me like you're going to have a busy first day tomorrow. I'm proud of you, son. This is going to be great for our town."

"Thanks, Dad," Josh replied. "Thanks for everything. We're going to be busy, and we'll finetune and adjust things as we go. I'm going to be very tired for a while, but I think it's going to be a good kind of tired."

"God is good," Travis said.

"All the time," Josh replied with a smile.

Chapter Seven

Time had flown by quickly once the center was open. True to their expectations, the place was a hit and they adjusted things as the need arose. Every afternoon, shortly after school released, there was a large crowd of teenagers who showed up at JC's Hope. Initially, most of the kids hung out in the gym, shooting hoops, playing a pickup game of basketball, or climbing the rock wall. Once they began feeling a little more comfortable, some of them ventured into the classrooms with their backpacks and were found studying or doing homework at the tables.

One afternoon, a teenaged girl and boy stopped by and asked if it was okay if they played their guitars in the music room. After being assured it was perfectly okay, they began showing up every afternoon and spent a couple hours playing their guitars. They soon had a group of kids who looked forward to them every afternoon and hung out in the music room with them. There was even one young pre-teen boy who asked if they could teach him how to play the guitar, and they eagerly agreed.

Josh walked into the music room to see how things were going. He found two kids playing guitars over near the piano, while an older teenaged boy was patiently teaching another how to play chords on the guitar.

"Hey, Justin," Josh said as he approached the beginner. "You seem to be picking up those chords fairly quickly. You're going to be playing before you know it."

"Thanks, JC," Justin said with a smile. "Zach is a good teacher."

"He sure is," Josh agreed as he patted Zach on the back. "You should consider giving guitar lessons as a regular gig."

Zach smiled as he replied. "I wouldn't mind doing that. My uncle taught me to play, and I remember how great it felt when I was able to play songs. I've always thought it would be cool to be able to do that for someone."

"You know," Josh suggested. "Why don't we post your name on the bulletin board saying you would be willing to teach guitar. See what kind of response we get. If there is some interest, maybe you could set aside an hour or two a couple times a week dedicated to guitar lessons. If necessary, I'm sure I could probably scrounge up another guitar or two you could use."

"Really?" Zach asked in amazement. "That would be great!"

"Well," Josh said. "I'll let you get back to your music. You two are making great progress."

Josh stopped by the gym to check on a group of boys in the weight room, reminding them to be sure to have spotters when they were lifting. Two young boys were working their way up the rock wall, and Josh was pleased to see they were also adhering by the rules to have a spotter.

Josh seemed to always have a smile on his face these days as he worked his way through the center, checking on all the kids. He stopped by one of the offices and poked his head in the door when he saw his dad poring over his Bible.

"How's it going, Dad?"

Travis looked up from his work and replied, "Not bad, son. There seems to be a good response to the Bible studies I started the other day. The first little group only had three kids, but yesterday seven kids showed up. Matthew joined the class yesterday. He sat at the back of the group and didn't say anything. But at the end of class, he asked if it would be okay if he brought his sister to one of the classes."

"Really?" Josh said. "That's a positive sign. I'm glad Matt has been coming on a regular basis. He really needs this place. I hope you told him it was okay to bring his sister. Have you met Amelia yet?"

"No, I haven't. I assume that's his sister?"

"Yeah," Josh replied. "I've talked to her a few times. She's not a teenager. She's about Ryleigh's age, I think. But they have had an awful time at home. Their parents are alcoholics. Amelia has always taken care of Matt. They would both benefit from being here."

"I told him to bring his sister by anytime. Hopefully, he will."

"Dad," Josh started. "Tell me if Amelia stops by with Matt. I'd really like to find a way to make sure she feels welcome here. Even if she's not a teenager. I keep hoping she will take me up on my offer to have you and Mom talk to her. I think you'd be a big help."

"Matt's sister is the one you were telling me about?"

"Yeah. She's been carrying a huge load her entire life. Little kids shouldn't have to be parents to their younger siblings."

"I'll let you know if Matt brings her with him next time. I'm sure we'll be able to find a way to make her feel welcome. We're certainly not going to turn her away because she falls outside our target group."

"Thanks, Dad. I'll let you get back to what you were doing. I'm going to take some snacks into the classroom. Kyle is in there tutoring a couple kids from his algebra class, so I'm sure they need some nourishment."

Travis laughed as he replied. "Algebra always requires extra nourishment! You better take extra chocolate chip cookies in there."

"I think you're right," Josh agreed, laughing as he walked away.

* * *

Travis watched the kids enter the classroom for Bible studies after school. He smiled, thinking how great it was that God was growing this little group of beginners. From what he had been able to figure out, it didn't appear that any of the teenagers had been exposed to much of the Bible. In their world, surviving from one day to the next in a challenging home was about all their young hearts could manage. His Bible studies began with three hesitant kids. Now, more than a dozen showed up on a regular basis. Even though many of them never took part in the discussions, it was encouraging to see them show up with a willingness to learn. That gave Travis a lot of hope that he would be able to break through some barriers and show the students how much they needed God in their lives.

"For God so loved the world that He gave His one and only Son, that whoever believes in Him shall not perish but have everlasting life. John 3:16.

"Have any of you heard that quote before?" Travis asked the small group of teens.

Several of the teenagers raised their hands. More than half those gathered. Travis was encouraged.

"Have you ever thought about what that means? Or, more specifically, what it means to you?"

A young boy in the back of the classroom timidly raised his hand. "It tells me that God thinks I'm important."

"Good, Mike," Travis said, nodding his head. "That's making it very personal, isn't it? That kind of gets right to the meat of things." Turning to the entire group, Travis asked, "How important do you guys think you are to God? How important do you think I am to God?"

"You're a pastor," replied one of the girls. "My guess is God thinks you're pretty important."

Travis chuckled. "Well, believe it or not, He doesn't think I'm any more important than you are. Each one of us is a child of God. You are every bit as important to Him as I am, or Mike, or Matt, or anyone else in this room. God loves each one of us so much that he sacrificed His only Son for us. That's pretty powerful stuff! Every single one of you is important to God. Don't ever forget that. And nothing you do can separate you from God's love."

A couple of the boys began whispering back and forth, each wanting to have a question asked, but neither wanting to ask it.

"Did you guys have a question?" Travis asked. "Don't hesitate. This is an informal discussion. We're just here to learn and discuss things."

One of the boys squirmed in his seat before asking, "Does it really say that in the Bible? Does it really say that God will love us no matter what?"

Travis looked at the boy before responding. "You're Rick, right?"

"Yeah," the teen replied.

Travis walked toward him, flipping the pages in his Bible, and laid the Bible on the desk. Pointing to a spot on the page, he said, "Why don't you read what that says to the class. Right there. Romans Chapter 8, verses 38 and 39."

"I don't have to stand up or anything, do I?" Rick asked.

"No. Not unless you want to," Travis replied.

"Okay," Rick began. "It says 'For I am convinced that neither death nor life, neither angels nor demons, neither the present nor the future, nor any powers, neither height nor depth, nor anything else in all creation, will be able to separate us from the love of God that is in Christ Jesus our Lord.'"

"Thanks, Rick," Travis said as he placed a hand on the boy's shoulder. "Did you guys get that? Nothing in all creation can separate you from the love of God. That's pretty incredible."

"So, if someone, say a kid, did something that wasn't so great, are you saying that God won't stop loving that kid?" Rick asked skeptically.

"Absolutely," Travis assured him. "If someone makes a mistake, or even if they do something they know is wrong, God won't stop loving them. That person needs to tell God he's sorry, won't do it again, and ask God to forgive him, but the love doesn't stop."

"And just like that, God forgives the person?" Rick still sounded skeptical.

"If someone is truly sincere, and asks God to forgive them, God will," Travis replied. "First John, Chapter 1, Verse 9 says 'If we confess our sins, He is faithful and just and will forgive us our sins and purify us from all unrighteousness.'

"What you need to understand is that when you put your faith in Jesus, nothing will stop God from loving you. You are His child, and He will never stop loving you. He always wants what's best for you. He's got your back."

Even though Matthew had been attending the Bible study classes regularly, he never spoke up. Now he did. "If the Bible says that we are God's kids and He always loves us and wants what's best for us, why doesn't that apply to parents and their kids?"

"Well, Matt," Travis began. "That's a tough one. People aren't perfect. Far from it. Every one of us is a sinner and falls short of the glory of God.

People disappoint us. Because they are human. There are a lot of parents out there who put their needs and wants before the needs of their kids. That's a real shame. But it's a fact of life. It's risky business to love and trust someone. It opens us up to hurt, and no one wants that. Sure, it would be great if all parents, and all kids, were perfect. It would certainly make life easier, wouldn't it? But no matter what, even if someone's parents aren't perfect and don't seem to love their kids, our Heavenly Father always loves us. And even if we feel like we've been let down by our parents, our friends, or someone else, we can rest assured that God will never let us down. Ever. And He has big plans for you, Matt. He has big plans for each one of you. It says in Jeremiah Chapter 29, verse 11, 'For I know the plans I have for you, declares the Lord, plans to prosper you and not to harm you, plans to give you hope and a future.'"

"Hey," said one of the girls. "That's what it says on the plaque in the entryway."

Travis smiled, "That's right, Heather."

Travis walked to a table in the corner of the room and reached into a box, pulling out a handful of small pocket Bibles.

"Before you all leave, I just want to let you know that I have some pocket Bibles up here. Please feel free to take one, if you'd like. It would be yours to keep. You can bring it to class with you, if you want, so you can look up things we're talking about. No pressure. Just take one, if you'd like. Let me say a brief word of prayer before we leave.

"Dear loving God, please watch over these precious children of yours. Keep them safe in Your arms. Remind them every day how important they are to You, and how much You love them. Amen."

Several of the teenagers stopped at the table to pick up one of the pocket Bibles. As he was leaving the room, one of the older boys chuckled. "Do you suppose God will watch over me when I'm taking my algebra test tomorrow?"

Travis smiled as he patted the boy on the shoulder and said, "God may not like algebra any more than you do, but before you go into class, make sure to ask Him to help you do your best. And don't forget to study tonight as well."

The boy chuckled, "Yeah, probably not a bad idea. Thanks, Pastor Harmon."

All the kids had left the classroom, except Matt. He was loitering by the box of Bibles, gently running his fingers along the cover of one of the small books. When Travis walked over to him, he asked, "Would it be okay if I took two of these little Bibles? I want one for me. But I also would like to give one to my sister too, if that's okay. If not, maybe I could just share mine with her."

Travis put his arm around Matt's shoulder as he handed him two small Bibles. "It's not a problem, Matt. You be sure to give one to your sister. And please tell her she is always welcome to come to our Bible studies. I would be happy to have her in class."

Matt smiled shyly before putting both Bibles in his backpack. "Thanks, Pastor Harmon. I'll probably see you tomorrow after school."

Travis patted him on the back as he said, "I'm counting on it, Matt. I'm counting on it."

* * *

Brandon was walking up the hallway to the music room when he heard an amazing sound coming from the room. He quietly sat his backpack on the floor, then leaned against the wall with his arms folded across his chest. Within a couple minutes, three other teenagers came down the hall approaching the music room, two of them carrying guitars. Brandon put his index finger to his lips in a motion to silence the kids. The four teenagers were silently listening to the sounds coming from the music room when Travis approached from the opposite direction.

"Hey, guys," Travis greeted, wondering why the boys were simply standing in the hall instead of going into the room. "How are you doing?"

By now the music had stopped. Brandon replied to Travis, "Did you hear that music? It's the most incredible thing I've ever heard."

"I just caught the end of it. Who's in there?" Travis asked.

"I don't know," Brandon said, shaking his head. "I was just going to see if the piano was available so I could play for a bit. It's obviously in use."

Travis opened the door to the music room and walked in, followed by the teenagers. Sitting at the piano, staring off into space, was Josh.

Brandon walked up beside him and said, "Wow, JC, that was the most incredible thing I've ever heard! What song was that? I've never heard it before."

Josh smiled shyly, "It's nothing special. It's just a song I wrote a couple years ago."

"Nothing special?" Brandon asked incredulously. "You *wrote* that? That's the most peaceful song I've ever heard. If someone was trying to describe pure tranquility, they would play that song. Man, I knew you were awesome playing the piano, but I had no idea you composed your own music."

"Used to," Josh clarified. "I haven't written anything since before my accident." Most of the teenagers who came to the center on a regular basis knew about Josh's accident.

"He began writing his own music when he was a teenager, about your age," Travis told the boys. "He has written some really great stuff! Every time I hear him play one of his original compositions, I am in awe of his talent. He sure didn't get his musical ability from me."

"But you play the guitar," one of the boys commented.

"Well, I can get by in a pinch with the guitar," Travis said with a chuckle. "But my very limited musical abilities aren't even in the same category with Josh."

Travis patted one of the boys on the back and said, "I'll leave you guys to discuss your music. I'll be down in the office if anyone needs me."

The three boys with the guitars went over to another corner of the room to work on their music. Brandon pulled a chair up to the piano bench and sat next to Josh. "Do you have that song written down somewhere, or is it just in your head?" Brandon asked Josh.

"It's just in my head," Josh replied with a smile.

"Would you teach it to me sometime?" Brandon asked hopefully.

"Sure," Josh replied. "I should probably write it down one of these days."

"Yeah, you should!" Brandon said, laughing. "That's too good to forget it and not have anyone be able to hear it. In fact, you should record it!"

"I don't know about that," Josh laughed.

"Have you written down any of your original compositions, or do you just keep them all in your head?"

"I wrote my earlier ones down," Josh replied. "That was the last one I wrote, and I just never got around to writing it down."

Brandon moved from his chair and sat down on the piano bench beside Josh. "You know what I think, JC? I think, first of all, you need to write down that amazing song. Then I think you need to gather up all your other original compositions and record them. If they are anything like the one I just heard, you need to get them out there for people to hear. And, of course, you need to teach them to me so I can play them!"

Josh laughed. "Maybe you're onto something there, Brandon. It's certainly something to think about.

"And another thing, JC," Brandon continued as he jokingly crowded Josh off the piano bench. "You need to stop hogging the piano, so I have a chance to play. Then you need to go write some more music."

Josh stood up, "Well, I can definitely turn the piano over to you. But writing more music, I'm not sure I can do that anymore."

Brandon pinned Josh with a stare. "Are you telling me, JC, that you don't believe what you tell us all the time? You tell us to believe in ourselves, to reach for our dreams, and to never quit trying to better ourselves. Is that just good advice for us, or does it apply to you too?"

Josh laughed as he put his arm around the insightful teenager's shoulder. "You got me there, Brandon. You're right. I should practice what I preach. I'll tell you what, why don't we set aside some time and work on writing some stuff together?"

"Really?" Brandon asked excitedly.

"Sure, why not. You have a lot of talent, Brandon. I'll just bet between the two of us we could compose some good stuff. What do you say?"

"Well, if that's what it's going to take to get you writing music again, then count me in!"

Josh patted Brandon on the back. "Okay, my friend, you've got a deal! Now I'll get out of here and let you take over the piano. Keep those ivories warm for me. I may be back."

"I plan to hold you to that, JC," Brandon said with a smile as he turned his attention to the piano.

Chapter Eight

Travis had spent the morning at the center before heading outside to go over to the church to work on his sermon for the weekend. As he started across the parking lot, he noticed a young woman sitting at the picnic table reading a book. He was certain he had seen her around before, but didn't know who she was. He decided to walk over and introduce himself.

The young woman glanced up as he approached.

"Hi," Travis began. "I'm Pastor Harmon. Can I help you with something?"

"Oh, uh, no," she replied, unsure of herself. "I'm just waiting for my brother so we can walk home together. I hope that's not a problem."

Travis smiled. "It's no problem at all. Your brother is in the center, I take it?"

"Yes," she replied. "He usually comes by for a while most days after school. Sometimes right after school. But if he has baseball practice, he comes by after practice."

"What's your brother's name? Maybe I know who he is."

"Matthew," she replied. "He's a sophomore at the high school."

"Oh, I know Matt," Travis replied in recognition. "He's a great kid. He's been coming to the Bible studies I've been giving. So, you're his sister. Did you get the little pocket Bible he got for you the other day?"

"Yes, I did," she replied with a nod. "Thanks for letting him take one for me too."

Travis looked at the young woman who was so unsure of herself, and his heart went out to her. "I don't remember Matt mentioning your name."

"Oh, sorry. I'm Amelia."

"That's right," Travis nodded as he began mentally putting the pieces of the puzzle together. "My son, Josh, has mentioned you. You know, you don't have to wait outside for Matt. You could wait inside. Maybe in one of the classrooms or the music room, or just hang out. It's not a problem." Travis was thinking back to his conversation with Josh about wanting to make Amelia feel comfortable and welcome at the center.

"I don't mind waiting for him outside. I don't want to intrude on the kids."

Travis sat down at the picnic table, across from Amelia. "I hope you don't mind, Amelia, but Josh has told me a little bit about your situation. You are welcome at the center any time. In fact, I would love it if you could sit in on the Bible studies. I think you might enjoy them."

Amelia's eyes were filled with uncertainty. "No, that's okay. I don't want to intrude on the kids. The center is for teenagers. I don't exactly belong here."

They both looked up when they heard a vehicle pull into the parking lot. Josh's Jeep. Travis might have misread things, but it looked like Amelia's eyes lit up when she saw Josh get out of his Jeep.

Josh waved, then started walking toward the picnic table. "Hey, Amy, it's great to see you here. Hi, Dad."

"I hope it's okay. I was just waiting for Matt," she replied with a smile.

"Of course, it's okay," Josh replied as he sat down next to his dad. "You don't have to wait outside. You know, you could go inside to hang out."

"We were just discussing that when you pulled up," Travis explained. "She feels like she would be intruding on the kids, and she doesn't want to do that."

Josh looked at his dad, then decided to mention something they had discussed several days ago.

"Amy," Josh began. "I want you to know that you are always welcome here at the center. Seriously. You can come by anytime. You can take advantage of anything we offer here at the center. I mean that."

"But I wouldn't fit in here," she protested. "They are all teenagers."

"What if you had something to do here?" Josh suggested hopefully. "Maybe you could help out around the center. There are a few of the girls who would probably love to have a big sister. Maybe you could help some of the kids with their homework. There are lots of things we could use some help with here."

Amelia looked down at her hands, resting on the closed book on the table, before raising her head shyly and meeting Josh's eyes. "Maybe I could help clean the center? Maybe keep the kitchen clean and tidy? And maybe I could help some of the kids with homework if they wanted me to. I'm really good at math and history."

"I think that would be great, Amy," Josh nodded enthusiastically. "In fact, Dad and I were just talking the other day about hiring someone to help part-time around here. The center is growing quickly, and we could really use some help."

"Oh," Amelia began to protest, nervously tucking a loose strand of her red hair behind her ear. "You don't need to pay me. I just thought I could help out in exchange for being able to come to the center and hang out while I'm waiting for Matt."

Josh reached over and gently covered Amelia's hand with his own. "Amy, you can come to the center whenever you want to, whether Matt is here or not. You are always welcome. And I honestly think you could be a big help with some of the kids, especially some of the girls. We really could use some part-time help, especially once school lets out for the summer. It wouldn't have to be any set hours. Just whenever you are available."

Amelia looked at Josh, then over at Travis as she appeared to be considering their offer. "I have another part-time job in the mornings. I've been trying to find a good full-time job so I could get my own apartment. And maybe Matt could come live with me. But it's hard to find full-time jobs in town. No one seems to be hiring. Are you really serious? I wouldn't be able to work mornings, because of my other job, but I would be available in the afternoons."

"That would be perfect!" Josh replied. "Obviously we are busiest in the afternoons after school. And you could still take advantage of the things we offer here at the center. You could sit in on the Bible study classes if you'd like, or use the music room or gym."

Travis stood up and put his hand on Josh's shoulder. "I will leave you two to work out the details. I need to get over to the church or I'll never get my sermon ready for this weekend."

"Amelia," Travis said, as he reached out to shake her hand. "It was a pleasure meeting you. I hope we'll be seeing a lot more of you around here."

"It was nice meeting you too," she replied.

As Travis headed to the parking lot, Josh smiled at Amelia then reached for her hand. "Well, why don't you come on in and we can get some of the details worked out. It will be nice having you around the center."

* * *

JC's Hope was booming. Word had spread quickly about the positive impact the center was having on the local youth. Pastors from all the local churches stopped by the center on a regular basis to meet with Travis and Josh, and to offer their services in whatever way was needed. Occasionally one of the pastors would show up with a teenager or two who wanted to check out the center, but didn't feel comfortable doing so on their own. The community support had been overwhelming, although not surprising since Hope was such a close-knit little town.

About once a week Mike Slater stopped by to see if the center had any immediate needs that weren't being met. He had enjoyed getting to know Kyle as they bonded over a mutual love of baseball. Having also been a baseball coach many years earlier, Mike loved comparing coaching techniques and getting to know the young players on the high school team.

Even Josh's family were regulars at the center. Since Kaci managed the business end of the operation, she frequently worked in one of the offices, with the twins close by. Aiden stopped in to help Josh when he could, and had talked to a couple of the teenagers about the benefits of joining the Army after graduation. Todd had worked with the shop teacher at the high school, and together they had come up with a program to offer apprenticeships for some of the boys to work at Byers Construction. And Amelia seemed to have found her place to fit in at the center. She helped with a lot of the chores around the center, but had found her calling when she discovered how much she enjoyed tutoring the kids.

Josh and Travis were walking down the hallway toward the gym when Mike Slater walked in the front door.

"Just the men I wanted to see," Mike said in greeting. "I need a couple extra sets of hands to unload a few things from my pickup."

Travis looked at Josh, who simply shrugged his shoulders.

Mike slapped Josh on the back as he laughed. "I just brought over a few things I thought you might be able to use. Come on, and I'll show you what I have."

Travis and Josh followed Mike out to his pickup, which was parked just outside the front door. "It's always an adventure when you stop by, Mike," Travis said with a chuckle. "We never quite know what you're up to."

Mike just laughed. "I like to keep people guessing. It's more fun that way."

Josh looked in the back of the truck, then looked at Mike. "I don't believe it. All this stuff is for the center?"

"Oh, it's just a few little things, son. Why don't you grab that hand truck there and unload the water and soda. Your dad and I can grab the food, then the three of us can unload those two little games."

"Little games?" Josh asked with a smile. "You mean those two arcade machines? That one looks like a flight simulator!"

"Yep," Mike replied. "And the guy told me that other one is a great baseball game. He showed me how it worked. I may have to fight off some of those young kids so I can have a shot at it!"

Josh just shook his head as he started unloading cases of water and soda. He still couldn't believe everything Mike had done for the center. Gifting him the land and building, paying for remodeling supplies, keeping the kitchen stocked with snacks and drinks. The man was amazing. A gift from God, to be sure.

While inside the building, Josh recruited a couple of the teenaged boys to help unload Mike's truck. They had a hard time taking their eyes off the arcade games. They were sure to be a hit.

Once the back of the truck was unloaded, Mike gestured to Josh and said, "There are a couple more things in the front passenger seat and in the extended cab seat. You and the boys can grab them as well."

Josh opened the passenger door, shook his head, and simply smiled. He grabbed a guitar, then handed a second guitar to Matt.

"Brandon," Josh said. "You're not going to believe what Mike has in the other seat."

Brandon opened the door to the extended cab, then looked at Josh with wide eyes. "A Yamaha keyboard! That's going to be awesome! Can you imagine the fun we'll have with a piano and a keyboard!"

"I can only imagine," Josh quickly agreed.

"And it'll sure make composing music together a lot easier," Brandon added. "We're still going to do that, right, JC?"

"If you're still interested in doing it, sure," Josh replied.

Travis and Josh got busy getting the arcade games into place and plugged in. Before long, there was a crowd around the new games, anxiously waiting for a turn to play.

"Josh," Travis began. "I think we'll probably need to establish some guidelines for using the arcade games. We're going to want to make sure no one spends too much time at the machines, so everyone has a chance to play."

"Not a bad idea," Josh agreed. He turned to the group of boys crowded around the two machines. "Hey, guys, since these are new, I know everyone wants to take a crack at them. Please be considerate of each other and make sure you don't hog the machines. We want everyone to have a chance to play. We'll work up some guidelines in the next few days. But in the meantime, I'm going to rely on you to be considerate and take turns. Thanks, guys." Josh looked at Mike Slater and added with a chuckle, "Oh, and don't forget to give this guy a turn too. After all, he did supply the games."

Mike laughed along with Josh and Travis. Several of the boys went right over to Mike and thanked him for the games.

"These are awesome!" said Rick. "I can't wait to get a chance on the flight simulator. Thanks."

Mike shook hands with each of the boys. "You boys enjoy the games. Just don't be surprised if I show up occasionally and want to take a crack at them. Especially that baseball game."

Mike was still chuckling as he walked toward the door. He raised his hand toward Travis and Josh as he said, "See you guys later."

Before he escaped out the door, Josh ran to catch him. He reached out to shake Mike's hand and said, "Thanks for everything, Mike. Every time I convince myself that you have outdone yourself with your generosity, you come up with something else. The kids are going to love the arcade games and the extra instruments. Brandon is already in the music room setting up the keyboard."

"I'm always happy to help, Josh," Mike replied. "You just be sure to let me know if you need anything."

"Thanks again, Mike. I better get back in there. I suspect I'll probably have to do crowd control around those games."

Mike laughed as he walked back to his truck. He raised his hand once more and said, "Catch you later, JC."

* * *

When Travis entered the room where he held Bible studies, he was surprised to find Rick already sitting at one of the tables.

"Hey, Rick," he greeted as he sat his Bible down on the desk. "You're here early. I didn't expect to find anyone in here."

Rick lowered his head before replying. "Sorry. I hope it's okay that I came in here before class."

Travis walked over and pulled up a chair to sit across the table from the teenager. "Of course, it's okay, Rick. Is something on your mind, or were you just hanging out until class?"

Rick glanced up shyly, his hands folded on the table. "I kind of wanted to talk to you, if you have a few minutes."

"Sure," Travis replied. "Class doesn't start for another twenty minutes. What's on your mind?"

"Remember the other day in class when you told us that God will never stop loving us, no matter what we've done?"

Travis nodded, remembering that Rick was the boy who asked that question in class.

Rick hesitated before explaining. "I did something a few months ago that was wrong. I'm not proud of it. A bunch of other kids were doing it and I guess I kind of got caught up in it."

"Do you want to tell me what you did?" Travis asked.

"Yeah," Rick replied. "It's been bothering me ever since you talked about that in class." He began fidgeting, before continuing. "I shoplifted something from the computer store. It was just a little jump drive. One of the guys swiped a tablet. I was surprised he got away with it. At the time, I figured it was no big deal. It was just a little jump drive, and I just slipped it into my pocket. I don't know why I did it. I didn't even need it. But I know it was wrong. I knew it was wrong when I did it. It was a stupid thing to do."

Travis's heart went out to the kid. He understood how hard it was to resist peer pressure, especially when things were rough at home.

"So, Rick," Travis began. "What do you think you should do about it?"

Rick sat quietly for a few moments before reaching into the pocket of his jeans and pulling out a jump drive, still in the original packaging. He laid it on the table in front of Travis.

"I want to give it back. It's not mine. I never should have taken it. It was stupid." Rick looked up at Travis and hesitated before continuing. "And I want to apologize to God. I don't want him to stop loving me." He chuckled nervously. "I need all the help I can get. But I don't know what I'm supposed to do."

Travis reached out and put his hand on the boy's hand. "That took a lot of courage, Rick. You're a good kid. You're right about needing to return it. If you'd like, I can go with you."

"Really?" Rick asked with relief.

"Sure. I can take you over to the store after class. Since you already have it here, it's best to make things right as soon as you can." Travis slid the jump drive back across the table to Rick. "Put it back in your pocket and we'll return it this afternoon."

"Okay, thanks. What do I do about God?"

Travis smiled. "Why don't we take care of that right now. God already knows what you did, but you can tell him you're sorry and you won't do anything like that again."

Rick looked uncertain. "I don't know what to say. I've never talked to God before."

"How about if I get you started. Then you can just tell Him what's on your mind. Just talk to Him like you're talking to me. Remember, He loves you and wants what's best for you. Are you ready?"

Rick nodded before bowing his head.

"Dear Loving God," Travis began. "Rick has done something wrong, and he wants to make it right. He doesn't want to be separated from your love. He knows that when he confesses his sins and asks for Your forgiveness, that You will forgive him. Go ahead, Rick."

"Okay," he began hesitantly. "Uh, God, I've never talked to you before, so I don't really know what I'm doing. Pastor Harmon said to just talk to you. Uh, anyway, I guess you know what I did. I stole that little jump drive from the store. It was wrong. I'm going to take it back. Pastor Harmon said he'd go with me this afternoon. I'm sorry I took it. It was a dumb thing to do. I promise I won't do anything like that again. So, uh, I guess that's all. I just want you to know I'm sorry."

"Amen," Travis added. Then Rick quickly followed with his own "Amen."

Travis reached over and patted the teen on his shoulder, then stood. He smiled as he said, "Good job, Rick. We'll meet up right after class and get that taken care of."

"Thanks, Pastor Harmon. I really appreciate it. And I promise, I won't do anything like that again."

About that time, kids began entering the classroom for Bible studies. Travis greeted them at the door with a smile as he realized the group was growing every week. Just as he was about to close the door and begin class, he saw Matt hurrying toward the classroom. Following close behind was his older sister, Amelia.

Chapter Nine

Amelia had been helping out at the center for a couple months, and was fitting in well with everyone. True to her word, she showed up nearly every afternoon and had become quite popular with the teenaged girls. Josh discovered she was an amazing tutor. She had a gift for explaining all levels of math to the teens. Kyle had expressed his thanks to her for helping the kids with algebra. She also had a love of history and a talent for helping the students remember dates and details. She had become quite an asset to the center, and Josh was thrilled to see her opening up more and allowing herself to show her true personality. He also was surprised to find himself wanting to know all about her.

Travis and Josh were both thrilled that Amelia had begun attending the Bible study classes. She attended sporadically at first, but had recently begun attending more regularly. Josh had also made a habit of attending the classes occasionally when he wasn't tied up with monitoring other activities. It always warmed his heart when he could see Amelia grasp something said in class.

Josh sat down beside Amelia at a table in the back of the classroom. She turned and smiled at him.

"I'm glad you were able to come to class today," she whispered.

"Me too," Josh replied quietly. "I won't be able to stay for the whole class because I need to spot some kids at the rock-climbing wall in about twenty minutes. But I like to sit in when I can."

On this day, Travis's lesson was centered on the Gospels of John, some of Josh's favorite teachings. The kids had been very attentive and were feeling more comfortable engaging in the discussions. Josh noticed that Amelia seemed to be concentrating heavily on what Travis was saying.

"As we have been learning over the past few days," Travis said. "The Bible teaches us the importance of love because it's at the core of God's being. It says in First John, Chapter 4, Verses 7 and 8, 'Dear Friends, let us love one another, for love comes from God. Everyone who loves has been born of God and knows God. Whoever does not love does not know God, because God is love.' Did you guys get that? God is love. Since we were all created in His image, we are supposed to behave in a Christ-like manner and love one another."

Suddenly Josh heard Amelia quietly whisper, "I found it. I finally found it."

Josh leaned toward her and asked quietly, "What? What did you find?"

She looked at him, her hazel eyes filled with wonder. "I finally found what's been missing my entire life."

* * *

The sporadic music coming from the music room, interspersed with animated voices, drew Amelia's attention as she walked toward the gym, hoping to find Josh. She stood in the hallway for a few minutes, simply listening, before quietly opening the door and stepping inside the room. She spied an empty chair toward the back of the room and sat down quietly. At the front of the room, Josh was seated at the piano, while a teenaged boy sat at the keyboard next to the piano. The two were oblivious to anyone else in the room, as they sat huddled over the keyboards, talking excitedly. The boy would play something on the keyboard, then Josh played something similar on the piano, while they chatted, and Josh scribbled notes on what appeared to be blank music sheets.

Even though Amelia wasn't certain what the two musicians were doing, she enjoyed watching and listening to them. Periodically, Josh would scribble notes on the sheet of paper, they would play something, he would shake his head, erase what he had written and write something else. Whatever they were working on was intriguing. The music seemed to speak to Amelia's heart, and she found herself not wanting it to stop.

After about a half hour of what Amelia finally realized was a new song being composed, she watched Josh scribble down a few more notes, then lay the pencil on top of the piano. He and the teenager talked a bit more as the boy pointed to a couple places on the sheet of music. Josh put his hands behind his neck, lacing his fingers together, then stretched his back. He looked over at the boy with a smile on his face.

"Well, Brandon," Josh said. "Are you ready? Shall we take it from the top?"

Brandon looked at Josh with a grin that lit up his entire face. "Let's do it!"

With a subtle nod from Josh, Brandon began playing an introduction on the keyboard. Josh soon joined in on the piano, blending their talents perfectly. Before long, music filled the room and wafted out into the hallway. Only Amelia noticed the door open, and several curious heads peaked around the door, into the room. The music continued for a few minutes before reaching an amazing crescendo. The two musicians dropped their hands from the keyboards, turned toward each other, and gave a very animated "high five" as they slapped each other's palms.

The room erupted in cheers and applause.

Startled, Josh and Brandon turned to see quite an audience behind them. They had been so engrossed in their music that they hadn't realized a crowd of about a dozen teenagers had slipped into the room. Josh looked over to Brandon, nodded, and the two stood and took an overly theatrical bow, to more applause and some laughter.

Brandon laughed as he nudged Josh in the ribs. "It looks like the song's a hit, JC."

"That appears to be the case," Josh agreed. "Now we'll just have to come up with a title for it."

Josh looked over their small group of fans and spotted Amelia at the back of the room, sporting the most genuine smile he had ever seen on her face. As Brandon began talking to some of the other teenagers, Josh walked toward Amelia.

"Wow," Amelia began in amazement. "Josh, that was fantastic!"

"Thanks, Amy," he replied. "We didn't know anyone else was in here."

"I was looking for you and heard the music and talking from the hallway. I came in and sat at the back of the room so I wouldn't disturb you guys. Before your song finished, several others apparently heard the music and slipped into the room as well. I'm not surprised you guys didn't notice. You were pretty wrapped up in the music. Did you and Brandon write that song?"

"Yes, we did," Josh confirmed. "It's something we've been working on for about a week. Brandon has a lot of talent."

Amelia looked into Josh's eyes as she reached out to touch his arm. "He's not the only one, Josh. I'm no music expert, but I know good music when I hear it. And I know what I like. I definitely like what I heard a few minutes ago. It was almost as if it reached inside me and touched my soul."

Josh chuckled softly as he said, "You should be a music critic. I could get used to hearing reviews like that."

Josh pointed to a chair, inviting Amelia to sit. He took the chair beside her. "You mentioned you had been looking for me. Is there something I can help you with?"

Amelia folded her hands in her lap and tipped her head down, suddenly unsure of herself.

"Amy," Josh said as he reached over and put his hand on her forearm. "Is everything okay?"

She looked up to see compassion filled his eyes. "I think I'm ready to talk to your dad and mom. Do you still think they would be willing to talk to me?"

Josh nodded as he replied, "Absolutely. Amy, I really think they would be able to help you. And they're both good listeners. Is there any time that would be best for you?"

"I don't want to infringe on their schedules," she replied. "So whenever works for them, I'll just make it work."

Josh stood and reached out for Amy's hand. "I need to go check on the kids in the gym, but I'll talk to Dad and Mom before the end of the day. I'll let you know when you can meet. Did you want Matt to be there too, or just you?"

"No," she replied. "I think I'd better do this on my own. Depending on how things go, maybe Matt and I can talk to your parents together a bit later."

"Okay, however you want to handle it. And Amy, don't worry. They are both very easy to talk to."

Josh started toward the door, and Amy fell in step beside him. "Thanks, Josh. And I'll be your music critic anytime. Your music is beautiful. You can tell it comes straight from your heart."

"Hmm, from my heart to your soul. I like that." Josh began whistling the freshly-created song as he walked down the hall, becoming more and more intrigued by this beautiful ginger-haired lady from the bleachers.

* * *

Meghan had suggested they meet with Amelia at the center where she would probably feel more comfortable. Travis and Meghan were already sitting at a table in the office when Josh walked in with Amelia. There was a large pitcher of water, along with several glasses, in the middle of the table. Off to the side was a small box of tissues.

Travis stood as Amelia approached the table. He reached out to shake her hand as he said, "Hi, Amelia. I'm really glad you came. You remember my wife, Meghan, don't you?"

Amelia smiled at Meghan and said, "Yes, I do. I've seen you around the center before. It's nice to see you again. Thanks for agreeing to meet with me."

Josh reached out for Amelia's hand. "Do you want me to stick around with you, Amy?"

"No. Thanks anyway, Josh," she replied. "I'll be fine."

Josh gently squeezed Amy's hand and said, "Okay, I'll see you guys later. I'll be down in one of the classrooms helping some of the kids if you need me for anything."

Josh closed the door on his way out, and the others sat back down at the table.

Meghan was the first to speak. "Josh has told us a little bit about your situation, Amelia."

"Please," Amelia interrupted. "Call me Amy."

Meghan smiled as she replied, "Okay, Amy. Would you like to fill us in a little more? Travis and I both have some experience with what you're dealing with, and I think we can probably help you out. Maybe give you some pointers on how to deal with things."

Amy shifted uncomfortably in her seat. "I'm not quite sure where to start."

"Start wherever you'd like, Amy," Travis replied. "We can ask questions as we go if we need some clarification. And, Amy, there is absolutely no pressure. You can tell us as much or as little as you're comfortable with."

"Okay," Amy said as she settled in. "I think Josh told you that both my parents are alcoholics. Have been my entire life. I don't know what they did before I was born, but I don't remember either of them ever having jobs. So, I didn't get a lot of attention as a kid. When I was big enough to do chores, I began taking care of everything around the house. I started cooking about the time I was old enough to begin school."

Amy stopped to gather her thoughts before continuing. "I thought it would get better after Matthew was born, but it didn't. If anything, it got worse. I have always done everything I could to protect and shield Matthew from as much as I could. But it was hard to do. As he got older, it was even harder because he started voicing his opinion more to our parents. They didn't like that. They didn't want anyone to question them. And they certainly didn't want their kids telling them what to do. It's been hard. That's why I always encouraged Matthew to play baseball. He's good. Really good. And it kept him away from home longer. When we heard that Josh was opening this center, I thought it might be a dream come true. A way for Matthew to have a safe place to hang out."

Meghan handed the box of tissues to Amy as she noticed tears gathering in the corners of her eyes.

"I think Josh told you that I had been married to an alcoholic before divorcing him and eventually marrying Travis," Meghan began. She reached over and covered Travis's hand with her own.

"I'm not going to pretend it was easy," Meghan continued. "But you already know that. Danny, that's my ex-husband, was an abusive alcoholic. So, that always made life turbulent. There was nothing normal about our homelife. Like you, I thought it would get better after our daughter Kaci was born. Also like you, I quickly discovered that wasn't going to happen. He prevented us from going to church, and that had always been an important part of my life. Eventually, I figured out that if I wanted our daughter to have any kind of normal life, I was going to have to get out of that marriage. I got out with my daughter, a few meager possessions, and not much else. He very nearly destroyed both me and my daughter."

Meghan reached across the table and put her hand on Amy's hand. "I don't want to see that happen to you, Amy. Or to Matthew. I can tell you both are good people and deserve a better life than you've been dealt."

Amy reached for a tissue and gently wiped away her tears.

"I've been encouraged to see you attending the Bible studies, Amy," Travis said. "I think that's a very good start. I know it sounds like a cliché, but God is always there to help you. He's never going to leave you, Amy. And nothing is too big for God to handle. You just need to reach out to Him."

Their discussion continued for almost an hour, and Amy was beginning to feel better about her situation. She felt a certain sense of hope for the first time in her young life.

"Amy," Meghan said. "I want you to know you can contact us whenever you need to. We're going to be here for you and Matthew. We want to help, and we want you to be safe."

Travis asked, "Are there any immediate needs the two of you have? Do you have enough food at home?"

Amelia hesitated before replying. "There is one thing I could use some help with, if you can."

"What is it? We will try to help in any way we can," Travis said.

"I've been trying to save money from my part-time job," Amy began. "And what I've been making at the center has helped too. I think I'm close to being able to afford an apartment for me and Matthew. Do you know of any small, affordable apartments that might be available?"

"I have a lot of contacts here in town," Travis replied. "Let me do some checking around and see what I can find out."

"Thanks," Amy said in appreciation. "That would be great."

Meghan slid a small piece of paper across the table to Amy. "Here are our cell phone numbers. I included Josh on there too. Don't hesitate to call us if you need something."

Meghan looked directly into Amy's eyes. "And Amy, if you ever feel unsafe, if you ever feel that you or Matthew are in danger, please call one of us. Day or night. Please."

"Thank you," Amy replied with tears in her eyes. "I will. Thank you both for everything."

The three stood, and Meghan walked around the table and pulled Amy into her arms. "I mean it, Amy. Day or night."

Travis gave Amy a brief hug, as he smiled. "She means it, Amy. She's like a mama bear when it comes to protecting kids. It doesn't matter how old they are, and they don't even have to be her kids. Call us."

Amy simply nodded, then turned to walk out the door.

Travis put his arm around his wife's waist and pulled her close, thanking God for her compassionate heart. "She'll be fine, honey. They both will. We'll make sure of that."

"I hope you're right," Meghan replied as she rested her head on her husband's chest. "She is so young to have that much responsibility. She needs to be able to enjoy life. I plan to stop in here at the center more frequently to check up on her and see how she's doing."

"I never had a doubt, dear," Travis said with a knowing smile. "I recognize the mama bear look in your eyes."

Chapter Ten

Jordan Stevens, the head coach of the Hope High School varsity baseball team, stood along the third base line watching practice. Today's practice was important. The next two games would determine if the team advanced to the State playoffs. Hope's baseball team had never made it to State, but their odds looked favorable this year. The team was having their best season in more than five years, due in large part to the addition of Kyle to the coaching staff. He seemed to have an instant connection with most of the boys on the team, and had even been able to recruit some to try out for the team who had talent but didn't feel like they belonged. Jordan knew Kyle understood that feeling.

Jordan had seen the raw talent of some of the local teenagers who used to hang out at the park, but he had never been able to convince them to try out for the team. When Kyle joined the staff, he made it his mission to seek out those boys in hopes of being able to add them to the team. If he was successful, he knew it would give the boys a purpose and a sense of belonging. He was able to relate to the boys on their level, and the difference it made to the team had been nothing short of phenomenal. Yes, Jordan could feel it in his bones that the team was heading to State this year. It brought a smile to his face, which only grew wider as he watched one of the boys send yet another hit over the center field fence.

Mike Slater sat beside Josh on the bleachers along the first base line, watching this crucial practice. Mike had become a regular out on the ballfield since getting to know some of the kids from the center. He had made it to every game this season, even the out-of-town games. He also secretly subsidized the out-of-town travel so all the boys would be able to go, even if their families were less than supportive.

Turning to Josh, Mike asked, "Well, JC, what do you think? Do you think they will make it to State this year? They have to win these next two games."

"I know Kyle thinks they have a great chance," JC replied. "Like you, I've been watching a lot of their practices, and all their games. They're very good. They have even surprised some of the coaches of the best teams in their division. I think they'll make it. I know they sure want it bad enough."

Mike rubbed the afternoon stubble on his chin as practice was winding down. He stood, with a gleam in his eye, and said, "Well, let's just give those boys a little more incentive."

Josh stood beside his benefactor with a smile on his face, shaking his head. He never knew what Mike would come up with next, but it was always fun to watch and see.

Mike climbed out of the bleachers and strode toward the baseball field like a man on a mission. He caught Jordan's attention as he continued walking toward the head coach. Josh watched the two men talk for a few minutes before Jordan turned and walked onto the field toward Kyle. The two coaches had an impromptu meeting near the pitcher's mound as the players began gathering in the infield.

Once the players were gathered in the infield, Jordan turned to Kyle and said, "Coach, why don't you tell the guys what we were just discussing."

"Before I get into that," Kyle began. "I just want to tell you guys what a great practice this was today. You guys are pulling out all the stops. It's almost as if you know a trip to State is riding on these next two games."

The boys were still pumped up from the practice and gave an enthusiastic reply, punctuated by several loud whoops. One of the seniors on the team yelled, "We got it, Coach! I plan on ending my high school career with a trip to State. Those Bulldogs don't stand a chance!"

Kyle listened patiently as the boys expressed their enthusiasm and determination about winning the next two games. The players were slapping each other on the back, while giving lots of words of encouragement, and their confidence soared.

Kyle raised his hand to gain their attention. "That's the kind of confidence and enthusiasm we're going to need for these next two games. As you know, the Bulldogs have been in first place in our division most of the season. But, we have beat them once this season, so there's no reason we can't beat them again. And Mr. Slater has just graciously added a little extra incentive to the pot."

The boys looked around at each other, wondering what Mike was up to now. Most of the team had gotten to know him quite well since he delivered arcade games to the center and became a frequent visitor. Several of them had begun looking up to Mike as a surrogate father figure, and some suspected he was the reason they were all able to go to the out-of-town games.

"As most of you undoubtedly know by now," Kyle began. "Mike is quite a baseball fan."

"Baseball fanatic, you should say!" one of the boys interjected. "We almost have to beg the man to let us have a chance at the baseball game at the center." The boys laughed in agreement.

Kyle laughed as he continued. "I've heard he's becoming quite the legend down there."

Mike chuckled as he held out his hands and shrugged.

"Well," Kyle began again. "Our resident baseball fanatic has presented a challenge, tied to a reward, for the team. If we win these next two games and earn a trip to the State finals, Mr. Slater is going to take the team to Cooperstown, New York this summer to visit the Major League Baseball Hall of Fame!"

The team erupted in applause and cheers. Several of the boys immediately went over and shook Mike's hand and slapped him on the back.

Jordan looked over at Mike, now surrounded by the entire team, and said, "I think the guys may like your idea!"

The grin covering Mike's face was every bit as big as the grins on the faces of the teenagers. After letting them voice some of their excitement, he raised his hand to get their attention.

"So," Mike said, laughing. "Do I take all this noise to mean you might be interested in my idea?"

Their excitement exploded again, much to Mike's delight.

"We can work out all the details later," Mike said. "But I want you to know that the trip is not contingent on winning at State. Although that would be fantastic! The trip is a reward for you boys earning the right to play in the State playoffs. If we come home with a trophy, that's a bonus. And the trip is for the entire team. No one will be left behind. You have all worked hard this spring, and you deserve a reward for that hard work."

"Okay, guys," Jordan said, addressing the team. "That's it for today. Great practice, everyone. Remember, Saturday's game is out of town. The final game, against the Bulldogs, will be here so we'll have the home field advantage. Make sure you're getting plenty of rest, and don't live on French fries. Throw an apple into your diet occasionally."

Josh, Mike and the two coaches watched as the boys ran across the field, whooping and hollering the entire way.

* * *

The two school buses pulled into the parking lot at the high school, where they were swarmed by what looked like half the town. The coaches pulled the buses to a stop, and the exiting players were nearly mobbed by the enthusiastic crowd. Someone in the back of the crowd began a chant that quickly took off and the roar filled the neighborhood. "One more game! One more game!"

The team had won their out-of-town game in a near rout. It didn't take long for word to get back to town ahead of the returning school buses. The high school principal was seen making his way through the crowd to one of the buses. He stopped to talk to the coaches, then stepped onto the bottom step of the bus and raised his hand.

"Before any of you guys start wandering off," the principal began.

"A lot of people apparently anticipated a victory today and planned an impromptu barbeque for dinner. If you head on over to the gym, they have everything set up. They have been barbecuing hamburgers and hot dogs, and there are tables full of all kinds of side dishes and desserts. It's all set up buffet style, so you can just grab a plate and work your way through the line. I heard it was a great game today. You made short work of the Titans, so you can take on the Bulldogs in a few days! Everyone is welcome at the buffet, so eat up!"

The hungry teenagers didn't need to be told twice. The entire crowd took off at a near run in the direction of the gymnasium.

Mike put his arm around Josh and said, "We'd better hurry or those boys won't leave us with anything but empty dishes to wash!"

They laughed as they joined the rest of the crowd in a mad dash to gym.

* * *

Standing next to Josh and Mike in front of the home team dugout, Kyle could feel the electricity in the air as the bleachers were rapidly filling up prior to the last regular game of the season. Emotions were high in the boys' locker room as well, as the excited teenagers were suiting up for the game.

Josh looked over to the bleachers along the third base line where his family filled a large portion of the seating. "Well, Mike," he said. "It looks like we'd better go grab our spot in the bleachers before we miss our chance. We'll catch you after the game, Kyle. Good luck!" He pointed toward the bleachers, then added with a chuckle, "There's Kaci, Jason, and the kids. I know those little rug rats are going to want to sit next to you."

Mike laughed just as the twins saw him approaching.

"Mr. Mike! Mr. Mike!" Aaron and Sophie yelled in unison as they ran over, and each grabbed onto one of his hands. Aaron patted the plastic baseball helmet on his head and said with a grin, "Look, Mr. Mike. We remembered to wear our baseball helmets!"

Mike pulled his hand from Sophie's little hand and patted the helmet on her head. "I see that. That's very good planning. You never know when a foul ball may head your way."

Smiling up at him, Sophie latched onto his hand once again, then added, "Mama and Daddy brought our gloves too. Maybe we can catch one of the balls."

The twins tugged Mike toward the bleachers. "Come on, Mr. Mike," Aaron said. "Let's sit with Grandma and Papa."

Travis and Meghan laughed as the twins approached, with Mike in tow. They scrambled up onto the bleachers beside their grandparents, then Aaron began assigning seats.

"Mr. Mike," Aaron began, as he took charge. "You can sit next to Papa."

Sophie quickly voiced her objections. "But, Aaron, I want to sit by Mr. Mike."

"Well, I want to sit by Mr. Mike too," Aaron replied. He climbed over the bottom bleacher to get to the ground, then stood back to look at the situation as he rubbed his thumb along his jawline like he had seen his Uncle Josh do.

The adults smiled as they watched Aaron work through the problem.

Aaron pulled his sister over beside him and pointed at his family in the bleachers. "Okay, Sophie, we can figure this out. Cousin Aiden, Uncle Todd, and Aunt Nicole are already sitting behind Grandma and Papa. Miss Amy is sitting by them, and you know Uncle Josh will sit next to Miss Amy. He always does."

The adults were having a very hard time keeping a straight face as Josh climbed up the bleachers and took his assigned seat next to Amy.

Aaron continued, "Mama and Daddy can sit over there, next to Papa and Grandma. They will like that because Mama is Grandma's little girl."

Meghan tried unsuccessfully to stifle a laugh.

Sophie grabbed Mike by the hand and led him over, so they were standing directly in front of Travis and Meghan. "Aaron, I can sit by Papa and Mr. Mike, and you can sit on the other side of Mr. Mike."

The twins clapped their hands in satisfaction, then hugged each other and climbed back onto the bleacher and took their spots beside Mike.

The adults were settling in and visiting while waiting for the players to come out of the locker rooms. Amy was talking with Nicole when Josh's cell phone dinged with a notification of a text message from Kyle. He glanced down at the message which read, "Have you seen Matt? He's not here for the game yet."

Josh quickly looked around just as he caught a glimpse of someone ducking and running behind the outfield bleachers. But was it Matt? He couldn't be sure. He sent a reply text to Kyle. "Haven't seen him, but a kid is running behind the outfield bleachers, heading toward the gym. Can't tell if it's him. Want me to check?"

Kyle replied with a follow-up text. "No. I'll let you know in a few minutes if he shows up." A couple minutes later, Josh received another text from Kyle. "He's here now. Gotta go."

* * *

Matthew ran into the locker room and headed straight to his locker to change into his uniform. Jordan began gathering the players in the middle of the locker room for the pre-game pep talk, while Kyle headed toward Matthew.

"Is everything okay, Matt?" Kyle asked.

"Yeah," Matt replied, still trying to catch his breath. "Sorry, Coach. I forgot my glove and had to run back home to get it."

As Matt hurried to get into his jersey, Kyle thought he noticed a large red mark along Matt's ribcage. "Are you sure everything is okay, Matt? It's not like you to forget your glove."

Matt bent over to tie the laces on his cleats as he replied, "Yeah, Coach, can't believe I forgot it. Let's go beat the Bulldogs."

Matt joined the rest of the screaming players as they rushed out of the locker room toward the field. Kyle had a sinking feeling there was more to the story than a forgotten glove, so he planned to keep an eye on Matt.

* * *

Four innings into the game and the crowd had been on their feet more than they had been in their seats. Every time the home team scored a run, the Bulldogs answered back with a run of their own. Both dugouts struggled to contain the players not on the field, with shouts of encouragement filling the air. All the players were giving the best they had, and not a one was willing to give up. Both teams realized a trip to the State playoffs was on the line, and each team hoped to be the one to fill that final slot.

The Hope Huskies were in the field, with one out, and the Bulldogs had a runner on first base. The batter hit a sharp line drive between the shortstop and second base. Matt dove for the ball, captured it in his glove and tossed it to the second baseman. After a quick throw to first, the double play ended the top half of the inning.

From his spot in front of the dugout, Kyle watched as Matt seemed to take a little longer than usual to get up and head off the field. He cornered Matt just before he stepped into the dugout.

"Are you okay, Matt?" Kyle asked with concern.

"Sure, Coach," Matt replied as he turned away. "Just hit the ground a little hard on that snag."

The score went back and forth as the game neared the final inning, with neither team ever having more than a two-run lead. The crowd didn't bother sitting in their seats any longer, with everyone standing and shouting encouragement to the players. After no score from either team in the sixth inning, the Bulldogs had scored two additional runs in the top of the seventh, and had a runner standing on second base with two outs. The Bulldogs were ahead ten to eight, and were trying to scratch out a couple more insurance runs. The Huskies, knowing they only had one more chance at bat, were doing everything they could to prevent another run.

The Bulldog batter at the plate had watched three pitches cross the plate without swinging the bat. Two strikes and one ball. He connected with the next pitch and sent it deep into left field. Both the left and center fielders started running toward the outfield fence. The left fielder jumped for the ball about three feet shy of the fence. It slapped into his glove, and he quickly closed his glove around the ball. The two outfielders bumped their gloves together in a high five as they took off running for the dugout. The crowd roared their approval, with the blast from an air horn piercing through the noise.

Jordan and Kyle quickly gathered the team around for a last-minute pep talk.

"Okay, guys," Jordan said as the first three scheduled batters crowded to the front of the group. "This is our last chance. You guys have had a great game and a fantastic season. It would sure be nice to put the Bulldogs away and head to State. But whatever happens, you can hold your heads high, knowing you gave it your best. So, what do you say? Shall we go out there and win this ballgame?"

The team and coaches put their hands together in a final rousing cheer, much to the crowd's delight, as the first batter approached the plate. He took his first pitch and hit it down the third-base line for a single. The next batter didn't fare as well as he popped up short behind first base. The third batter dropped a single in short left field that the fielder bobbled, so the base runner made it safely to second. After fouling off several pitches, the next batter went down swinging for the second out.

Matt slowly walked toward the plate. Bottom of the final inning, two outs, and runners on first and second. He knew he needed to advance the runners. They were down by two runs. Before stepping into the batter's box, above the roar of the crowd, Matt heard his sister scream, "Come on, Matthew! You can do it!"

He shot her a quick smile, then stepped into the batter's box. He watched the first two pitches cross the plate. Both out of the strike zone. He fouled off the next three pitches, refusing to quit. Suddenly, Matt raised his hand in a time-out fashion and stepped out of the batter's box. Kyle hurried to the plate, calling "time out!" to the umpire.

Matt was holding his side and stretching.

Kyle ran up to him and put his hand on his shoulder. "Are you okay, Matt? Does your side hurt?"

"It's nothing, Coach," Matt replied, with a hand still on his side. "My ribs just hurt a little. Probably from landing hard earlier. It's okay, Coach. I got this."

"Are you sure?"

Matt just nodded.

"Okay, Matt," Kyle said. "Take a deep breath, and wait for the ball. Don't get ahead of it. And remember, it's just a game."

Matt smiled back at the coach as he stepped toward the batter's box. "Yeah. Right, Coach."

Matt stepped into the batter's box while holding his left hand up toward the pitcher as he settled into his stance. The first pitch was high and outside for ball three. The next pitch, he slammed high and deep into right field. Just as he rounded first base, he watched the ball land behind the outfield bleachers. He started toward second base with both arms raised in the air in victory. The crowd went wild! As he rounded third base, Matt watched his teammates rush toward home plate, with the two base runners waiting on the other side of the plate to greet him. The team swarmed home plate as he triumphantly jumped onto the plate with the winning run.

After a brief celebration at home plate, the coaches from both teams began lining the players up to greet the opposing team. The players filed through the line, congratulating each other on a well-fought game, and a great season. The coaches were at the end of the line. The head coach for the Bulldogs shook Jordan's and Kyle's hands as he simultaneously shook his head.

"You know, Jordan," the coach began. "Two years ago, I never would have thought you guys would ever make it to State. You have a great bunch of kids this year. Any chance they're all seniors and won't be back next year?"

Both Jordan and Kyle laughed as Kyle replied, "Sorry, Coach, only two seniors on the team this year. Most of them will be back next year."

"I figured," the Bulldogs coach replied with a laugh. "Any chance your shortstop is one of those seniors?"

Kyle chuckled. "Nope. We hope to get two more years out of Matt."

The coach slapped Kyle on the back as he walked off the field, shaking his head.

All the players and coaches for the Hope Huskies were gathered in the infield, as the crowd spilled out of the bleachers, breaking off into smaller groups. Mike Slater and his self-appointed entourage made a beeline for the team, hugging and congratulating all the boys.

Kyle put two fingers to his mouth and let out a shrill whistle to gain everyone's attention.

"Okay, guys," Kyle said. "Mike has something he wants to say to you."

"Thanks, Kyle," Mike started. "Well, you boys sure know how to keep the game interesting! Great season! And it looks like we're heading to State! As promised, you have all earned a trip to Cooperstown this summer! We'll keep you posted on all the details as we make the arrangements."

The boys erupted in another blast of excitement.

Mike raised his hand to regain their attention. "But I'm pretty sure the first order of business is food. Am I right?"

More shouting and fist pumping in agreement.

"After you boys get cleaned up and changed, pizza is on me over at Luigi's. It's all set up to start in about an hour or so. You can head on over anytime. Be sure to let me or the coaches know if any of you need a ride."

One of the younger players on the team said, "What do you mean, it's all set up? What if we would have lost?"

Mike put his arm on the boy's shoulder as he replied with a smile. "I had faith, my boy. And either way, you boys need to eat." Then he leaned over and whispered into the boy's ear. "I knew you could beat those Bulldogs. That's why there's also a victory cake waiting over at Luigi's."

Mike turned and walked toward the parking lot, leaving the young boy standing near the pitcher's mound smiling.

As the crowd began to disperse, and the boys hurried to the locker room, Josh noticed that Kyle had singled Matt out off to the side of the group. The fact that he showed up to the game later than he should, gave Josh the feeling something was not quite right. He watched as Kyle walked Matt back into the building with his arm around his shoulder. He was going to have to catch up to Kyle later to find out what happened. Although he already knew in his heart there was more to the story than appeared on the surface.

Chapter Eleven

It was a gorgeous spring day outside, yet the mood was somber as Josh, Travis, and Kyle were seated at a table in one of the classrooms, with the door closed. The center was quiet, awaiting the afternoon rush of kids after school let out for the day. In about an hour, the building would be filled with kids releasing pent-up energy as the school year was winding down. Some of those teenagers would seek out one of the quiet classrooms to study for final exams, so they didn't want to tie up the classroom longer than necessary.

"Well, Kyle," Josh began. "Did you have any luck getting anything out of Matt?"

Kyle shook his head in frustration. "No. He's sticking to his story that nothing is wrong. He still says his sore ribs are from snagging that ball during the game the other day."

"And you don't quite believe that?" Travis asked.

"No, I don't," Kyle replied, shaking his head. "Sure, he hit the ground when he grabbed that ball. But that wouldn't have caused the bruise I've seen. And it certainly wouldn't explain the large red mark I saw along his ribs when he was changing into his jersey before the game."

Travis looked at Josh before asking, "Have you mentioned any of this to Amy? Do you know if she knows anything about it?"

"No, I haven't talked to her about it. I didn't want to upset her if it turns out to be nothing."

"Kyle, is there anything you want me to do?" Travis asked.

Kyle thought for a moment as he looked down at his hands. "Since

I have personal experience in this area, I think we need to tread lightly. The last thing I want to do is scare Matt off, so he stops coming to the center. And stops talking to us. We need to make sure we're his safe space. It's important that he doesn't lose that."

"I agree completely," Josh added, as he reached over and put his hand on his friend's shoulder.

"The team will be heading to the State playoffs in a couple days," Kyle added. "That will keep him away from home for the weekend. It might give him a little more freedom to talk about it. In the meantime, I plan to keep an eye on him as much as I can. Coach Stevens is aware of my suspicions, so he said he'll watch for anything out of the ordinary as well. I'm not sure there's much else we can do right now."

Knowing that Josh and Matt's sister had become good friends, Kyle turned to Josh. "Do you think we should bring Amy into the loop? Or should we wait a bit? You know her better than any of the rest of us."

Josh hesitated before answering. "No, let's wait. There is still the possibility that he simply got the bruise by doing something stupid, and he's embarrassed about it. I don't believe that any more than you do, but I think we should wait a bit before involving Amy.

"What do you think, Dad?"

"It's a tough call, son. But Kyle is right. You know her better than we do, so I think we need to go with your instincts."

As the three men stood and started for the door, Travis reached out and put his arm around Kyle's shoulder. "You have been like a son to me for years, Kyle, and I know your suspicions about Matt must be causing some emotional turmoil for you. You be sure to give me a call if there is anything you need. Whether it's for Matt or for you. Understand?"

"Thanks, Travis," he replied. "I will."

* * *

Amy was just finishing wiping down the kitchen counters when Josh walked in. Seeing him always brought a smile to her face, and today was no different.

"Hey, Josh. I thought you were out in the gym playing basketball."

Josh returned her smile, as he reached into the refrigerator for a bottle of water. "I was, but they have enough guys now, so I thought I would check in on Brandon."

Amy looked around the kitchen, empty except for the two of them. She smiled as she said, "As you can see, Brandon isn't in here."

Josh leaned against the kitchen counter as he opened the bottle of water and took a long drink. He looked around the empty room with a mischievous grin on his face. "Hmm, it appears you are correct, Miss Phoenix. My mistake. But, as long as I'm here, maybe you'll share a couple of those chocolate chip cookies with me," he said, pointing to the plate of cookies on the counter.

"Well, I suppose," she said with a grin. "I mean, as long as you're already here." She reached into the cupboard to get some paper napkins, put two cookies on a napkin and placed it in front of him. She then took one cookie for herself, leaned against the counter opposite him, and took a small bite from the cookie.

After polishing off one of the cookies in just a few bites, Josh reached for his second cookie. Before taking a bite, he reached over with a napkin and gently wiped a few crumbs off Amy's mouth. He stared into her hazel eyes and said quietly, "Uh, you had cookie crumbs."

Amy's cheeks blushed slightly as she raised her hand to her face. "Oh," she said in almost a whisper. "Thanks."

Neither of them spoke for a moment before Josh broke the silence. "I was wondering if you wanted to ride to the playoffs with me this weekend. My whole family is going."

Amy hesitated before replying. "I hadn't really planned on going. It involves an overnight stay, and I really don't have the extra money for that."

"It wouldn't cost you anything. Dad and Mom have already re-served hotel rooms. They got a room for me and my cousin Aiden, and also reserved a room for my sister Ryleigh. There are two beds in her room, and I know she'd love a roomie for the weekend. It was actually her idea. I think you are about Ryleigh's age. She would love it. Come on, Amy, what do you say? It would be fun."

"Well, I don't know. It would be kind of nice to be able to watch the games. And Matt will be there. Would we be riding with your parents?"

"Yeah. Dad and Mom, you and me, and Ryleigh. The family will have a caravan. Uncle Todd, Aunt Nicole, and Aiden will go together. And my sister Kaci, her husband Jason, and the kids will be following us in their car."

"Okay," Amy said with a nod. "It sounds like fun. And it will give me a chance to get to know Ryleigh. I'm sure she has lots of stories to tell about her big brother."

"Oh, great," Josh groaned, through a smile. "Maybe this wasn't such a good idea after all."

"Too late," Amy replied with a laugh. "I already agreed to go. I have a feeling Ryleigh and I will find lots of things to talk about." Amy turned around to cover up the plate of cookies before adding, "Oh, yeah. I'm sure Ryleigh and I will be best friends by the end of the weekend."

Josh walked toward the door of the kitchen, shaking his head. As he walked down the hallway to the music room, he began whistling the tune to a new song he had been working on. A song about a ginger-haired beauty who seemed to fill his thoughts.

* * *

Ryleigh really liked Amy. They spent the entire drive talking and getting to know each other. She could tell from the look on her brother's smitten face that he was more than a little fond of Amy as well. She tried not to tell too many stories about her big brother's childhood antics. Well, okay, maybe she didn't try too hard. After all, the best stories could wait until they were alone in the hotel room.

Between the team and coaches, families of the players, and a fair amount of baseball fans from home, the crowd split up and went in several different directions to find dinner. The coaches wanted the players to get a good night's rest, so they were not going to be out late. Josh's family, along with Mike Slater and a few others, found a family-style restaurant, while most of the team hit a pizza place next to the hotel.

After dinner, everyone found their hotel rooms and settled in for the evening. Ryleigh plopped down on one of the beds in her room, getting comfortable, while Amy sat on the edge of the other bed.

Ryleigh had been playing the little sister role for more than an hour, filling Amy in on all kinds of fun stories about Josh.

"You've told me a lot of great stories about Josh," Amy said, as she watched Ryleigh kick off her shoes. "He sounds like he was a typical little boy. What was he like as a brother?"

Ryleigh leaned back on her pillow, stretched out her long legs, and smiled. "He was the best brother a little girl could ever have. I used to follow him around everywhere, and he didn't mind it a bit. We grew up in a construction family. Mom and Uncle Todd own the family construction business. So, we grew up climbing around on backhoes and bulldozers. It was great. Josh loved playing on the Bobcat, and he never told me I was too little to climb up on it. He always helped me, and never treated me like a little kid." Ryleigh sighed as the memories washed over her.

"Was it the same way as you guys got older?" Amy asked.

"Yeah, it was. He always included me in everything. He's pretty special. I've always known he was destined to do good things. The center is great for him. I can't think of anything he would rather be doing."

"I've heard a little bit about his accident. It sounded pretty traumatic," Amy said. "Did it change him at all?"

Ryleigh sat up on the edge of the bed, her long dark hair pulled into a messy ponytail, and looked at Amy. "Yes, it did. I don't really know how to explain it, but it changed him in a good way. We were all so scared after his accident. We were afraid we would lose him, and I couldn't bear thinking about that possibility. JC always knew he wanted to work with kids, and he kept that focus when he was on his mission, and while he was in college. But it was almost like he was the one driving the train. After he almost died, a sort of peace settled over him. It was like he stopped driving the train, and turned control over to God. He now treats his dream of the center like he has always treated his music. He lets God do the steering. I can't wait until he starts writing music again. It will be incredible."

"He is writing again," Amy said. "He and Brandon wrote a song not long ago. It was the most amazing thing I've ever heard."

Ryleigh nodded in understanding. "He lets God control the music. That's his secret. I'm glad he's composing again. I know it took him awhile after the accident before he was brave enough to sit back down at the piano."

Ryleigh looked over at Amy, who seemed deep in thought. "Can I ask you something, Amy?"

Amy looked up and replied, "Sure."

"You really like Josh, don't you?"

The light blush that crept up her cheeks gave away her answer.

"I thought so," Ryleigh replied. "You know he likes you too, don't you?"

"Do you think so?" Amy asked with uncertainty.

"Yes, I do. I've seen the way he looks at you. It's pretty obvious."

Ryleigh crawled under the covers of her bed before saying, "Well, goodnight, Amy. And by the way, I'm really glad you decided to come. I think we're going to be great friends."

* * *

The Hope Huskies were battling their way through the State tournament, making their coaches and fans proud of their grit and determination. The team was resting in the shade at the ballpark, waiting for their final game. The boys were more pumped up than the coaches had ever seen them. It was hard for them to wind down enough to get some rest before they hit the field again.

The boys were sitting at picnic tables, or sprawled out on the grass when Jordan and Kyle walked over to the group.

"Hey, guys," Jordan began. "Do we have everyone here?" He quickly glanced around to see if he noticed anyone missing.

Kyle held a clipboard in his hands and had been checking off names as he saw each of the boys. "It looks like everyone is here, Coach," he said, handing the clipboard over to Jordan.

"Okay, good," Jordan replied. "Guys, this is our last game of the season. It's also the last game of their high school baseball career for Alex and Brady. I know they both are going out on an incredible high. You have all had a fantastic year. Now, since Coach Kyle is largely responsible for some of our team members making it onto the field this year, I thought I would turn over the last pre-game pep talk to him."

"Thanks, Coach," Kyle said, shaking hands with Jordan. "Well, guys, it's hard to believe we have come this far. You guys have more determination than a lot of kids, and every one of you deserve to be here. I have watched you pour your heart and soul into every game, particularly in the past couple weeks. I'm proud of you guys. And on a personal note, you guys have made my first year of coaching something I'll never forget. I'm proud to be your coach, and like to think we have become friends as well.

"In a few minutes," Kyle continued. "We'll be heading onto the field for our last game. It's going to be a tough game. You don't get this far into the State playoffs without bumping up against some tough competition. But you guys have fought your way to the top. Right now, before even stepping back onto the field, you are in second place in your division. Think about that. This team has never made it to the State playoffs before, and here we are, guaranteed to take home the second-place trophy. That's quite an accomplishment. So, I want you to go out there and give it all you've got. But remember, whether we win or lose this last game, we know we are walking off with a trophy. And whether it's a first-place trophy or a second-place trophy, we'll be walking out of here with our heads held high. So, what do you say, guys? Let's go do this!"

* * *

As the day wore on, it was evident all the players were getting tired. Not just the Huskies, but all the high school boys. It had been a grueling tournament, but was winding down. The Huskies scratched their way into a guaranteed second place finish, and were fighting hard in their final game. The score had bounced back and forth, with both teams taking the lead at various points. Getting ready for their final at bat in the top of the seventh inning, the Huskies trailed by two runs.

The lead batter flew out to deep left field. Brady, one of the team's seniors, hit a sharp line drive just inside the third-base line. His hustle enabled him to turn the hit into a nice double. The next batter went down swinging when he reached for an outside pitch. A single by the fourth batter left runners on first and third, with the remaining senior on the team coming to bat. Alex took it to a full count before smashing the ball over the center field fence, allowing the Huskies to take the lead in the game once again.

The crowd was on their feet, cheering on their respective teams. The final batter for the Huskies popped the ball up right behind the shortstop, who caught it for the final out. The Huskies dugout emptied as the players raced back onto the field, hoping to maintain their one-run lead for the game's final three outs.

Excitement was high after the Panther's lead batter struck out on three pitches. A weak single to the shortstop took down their second batter. The third batter lucked out when the second baseman bobbled the ball and didn't get the throw to first in time. The Panther's next batter stepped to the plate, settled into his stance, and swung at the first pitch, sending it deep into right field. The right fielder, one of the youngest members on the team, ran toward the fence, never once taking his eyes off the ball. He made a dive for the ball as he slid across the grass, closing his glove and his eyes simultaneously. The crowd roared, and began stomping their feet on the bleachers.

The center fielder ran over to his teammate, yelling, "You did it, Derek! You did it!"

Derek opened his eyes and looked at his glove in disbelief. There was the ball representing their victory, tightly nestled into the pocket.

* * *

Two school buses, followed by a long caravan of cars, pulled into the high school parking lot just before sundown. Most of the players on the buses were fast asleep, exhausted from the grueling weekend tournament. Once the buses were stopped, the groggy players exited the buses with their duffel bags in tow. They were tired, but happy. Every boy on the team sported a huge grin as they gathered in front of one of the buses. With the two coaches flanking the team, the boys proudly hoisted their first-place trophy high into the air as cameras from the local newspaper snapped a series of pictures. One young player, not quite able to reach the trophy, had the largest grin of all as he held his glove high above his head. The winning ball still tightly nestled within the pocket of the glove.

Chapter Twelve

Now that school had released for the summer, the center was getting busier. When school was in session, afternoons, early evenings, and weekends were the busiest times at the center. JC's Hope had increased staffing for the summer, in anticipation of both larger crowds and the fact that several people would be out of town for the Cooperstown trip.

Josh chuckled as he walked through the gym and saw a group of teens huddled around the two arcade games. "Hey, guys," he greeted. "I thought you would have had enough baseball for a while after that grueling tournament."

One of the boys clutched his chest in mock horror. "Enough baseball? JC, everyone knows there's no such thing as enough baseball."

Another boy added with a laugh, "We're getting a jump on training for next season."

"By the time we get back from Cooperstown," JC said with a smile. "You'll either be on a baseball high, or will be ready to take a break from baseball."

One boy kept his focus on the arcade game as he replied, "My guess is baseball high. That trip will be awesome!"

Josh smiled as he continued working his way through the center, as he did multiple times a day, checking to see how everyone was doing. An older teen was helping two younger boys work out on the weight machines, while a couple teenaged girls worked their way up the rock-climbing wall. Looking in the window to the door of one of the classrooms, Josh saw that his dad had another good turnout for Bible studies.

It was encouraging to see how many of the local teenagers were utilizing the center, and how many had begun taking advantage of both the Bible studies and the individual counseling that was offered.

As was the case nearly every day, music drifted into the hallway from the music room. Josh opened the door, already guessing it was Brandon at the piano. Zach was in one corner of the room giving guitar lessons to a boy and girl, while another boy played his guitar at the back of the room. It pleased Josh to see how well everyone got along and tried to be considerate of each other. There had been a few issues at the beginning, but they were easily resolved. For the most part, the kids tried to respect each other and allow space to work on their own things.

Josh sat down at the keyboard next to Brandon. "It sounds like you're working on that song we were writing the other day. I like what you did with the introduction. It definitely has your signature style."

"Thanks, JC," Brandon replied with a smile. "I'm still having some trouble with the chorus, though. It doesn't seem like it flows very well."

"Play just the chorus for me and point out where you think the problem area is," Josh suggested.

Brandon began in the middle of the song, playing a portion of the chorus before stopping. He pointed to the sheet of music and said, "See, that spot right there seems almost like it doesn't fit. But I can't figure out what to do with it."

Josh turned to the keyboard, while looking over at the sheet music, and began playing. He would play a few notes, stop, go back and revise, then play a few more notes. He moved over and sat next to Brandon on the piano bench, and scribbled a few notes on the page of music.

Pointing to the music, Josh said, "Okay, why don't you start at the beginning of the chorus and play through the entire chorus. See what you think of those little changes."

Brandon played through the chorus, then went back and played through it again. Turning to Josh, he smiled and said, "That's great! It's amazing how that little change made it flow so much better. What was I doing wrong?"

"It's not that you were doing anything wrong. But that one little section felt forced. You just need to let the music flow. You're normally very good about feeling the music. My guess is you got interrupted or disturbed in the middle of working on the chorus, and you lost the flow. It happens. You're doing great, Brandon. I can check back later if you're still here. In the meantime, I have to finish checking on a few more things."

"Thanks for the help, JC," Brandon replied, turning back to the sheet of music. "Catch you later."

* * *

"Okay, guys, quiet down so we can get started," Josh addressed the excited group of boys gathered for the final meeting to discuss the Cooperstown trip.

The group of boys from the high school baseball team, along with the two coaches, Mike Slater, and several other adults from the center, were gathered in one of the classrooms, reviewing the final trip details.

Josh took the lead in the discussion. "I don't know of any last-minute changes, so we'll just give a general overview of the schedule before we leave in two days. I believe we have all the boys here from the team. As you know, both coaches are coming along on the trip. There will be several adults from the center who will be going along as well. Pastor Harmon and my mom, my cousin Aiden and uncle Todd, Matt's sister Amy, and, of course, Mike Slater.

"One of the bus drivers from school will be driving the bus over to the airport. All you guys from the team, along with Jordan and Kyle, will be riding on the bus. The rest of the adults will be driving private vehicles to the airport, but we will be going in a caravan so we're all together. We'll fly out Wednesday. The first day will be traveling and settling in at the hotel. We'll plan to spend most of the day on Thursday at the Baseball Hall of Fame."

The group of boys cheered and whooped and hollered their approval.

Josh turned to Mike and said, "I have no doubt your trip is going to be the highlight of the year, Mike."

Mike grinned and replied, "You boys worked hard and deserve the trip."

"Friday," Josh continued. "We'll do a few other small things around Cooperstown before heading home on Saturday. As we've discussed before, we're going to expect all you guys to be on your best behavior. Just like you always are here at the center. We don't want Mike to regret giving you guys this trip. So, let's make him proud of our entire group."

Josh looked at the other adults in the group and asked, "Did I forget anything?"

Travis said, "The only thing I can think of is a reminder that we're all meeting here at the center Wednesday morning at 7:00 a.m. If any of you need a ride to the center, let one of us know and we can make sure someone picks you up. But make sure you're here on time. Since we have an hour drive to the airport, and allowing time for going through security, we plan to leave the center no later than 7:30."

"Okay, I think that covers everything," Josh concluded. "Unless you happen to be at the center sometime tomorrow, we'll look forward to seeing all of you bright and early Wednesday morning."

* * *

After a long day of travel that included driving to the airport, the flight, picking up rental vans at the airport, then driving to Cooperstown, the group of tired but excited baseball fans began settling in at the hotel. The adults had agreed that everyone would meet at a nearby pizza parlor after having had a chance to rest up a bit.

Mike had called ahead and reserved an area where several tables had been pushed together to make one long table for the group. Before long, pizza, salad, garlic bread, and pitchers of soda filled the table.

Alex, one of the recently-graduated seniors from the team, spoke up. "Hey, guys, can I get your attention for a minute. We haven't even gone to the Hall of Fame yet, but already this trip has been epic! Especially for me, knowing I probably won't see you guys much after this summer, it has been great traveling together and hanging out. But, what

I really wanted to say is, on behalf of all us guys on the team, we really want to thank Mike for this trip."

A chorus of loud cheers erupted from the boys.

"Mike," Alex continued. "You certainly didn't have to pay for a trip like this, but we're sure glad you did! I can't think of a better way to finish up high school. And the support you have given to the team all season has been great. If we weren't lucky enough to have Coach Jordan and Coach Kyle on our side, along with the support from the rest of you, we never would have made it to State. And we certainly wouldn't have taken home a first-place trophy. So, I just want all of you to know how much we appreciate everything you've done for us."

The entire table erupted in another round of cheers and applause before everyone dug into the pizza and began eating. It didn't take long for the table to be filled with empty pizza pans, empty plates, and empty soda glasses.

As things were winding down, Travis spoke to the group. "Since parking anywhere near the Hall of Fame is very limited, in the morning we will take the vans to one of the trolley parking lots, then we'll take the trolley over to the Hall of Fame. From what I've been told, the easiest way to get around in the area is by riding the trolley, so that's what we'll plan to do. Both days we're here, we'll plan to drive the vans to the parking lot, then ride the trolleys or walk anywhere we need to go. At the end of the day, we'll take the trolley back to the parking lot and drive the vans back to the hotel. So, let's all get a good night's sleep so we're ready to enjoy Cooperstown tomorrow."

* * *

It was all the adults could do to restrain the boys from bursting through the doors to the Baseball Hall of Fame. Travis was not at all surprised to find his wife Meghan at the front of the group. He was quite sure she was the biggest die-hard baseball fan he had ever met, and this trip was sure to be one of the highlights of her life.

The group had opted not to join an organized tour of the Hall of

Fame. Instead, they chose to browse at their leisure, so they didn't have time constraints. They decided to start with the 'Generations of the Game' movie to get an overall feel for the history of the Baseball Hall of Fame. After the movie, the group began exploring the various museums and displays throughout the Hall. The History of Baseball exhibits were a huge hit, as well as the tour of the Babe Ruth Room. Meghan spent a fair amount of time marveling over the Women in Baseball, and the boys were fascinated to see some of their favorite major league baseball players represented in the African-American Baseball displays. Another exhibit that captured everyone's attention was Hank Aaron's 'Chasing the Dream', which detailed his life from childhood, to living his baseball dream, and continuing to his post-baseball activities.

Travis noticed that Josh stuck close to Amy throughout the entire tour. Several times he saw Josh gently place his hand on Amy's back as they entered another room. Travis tipped his head toward Meghan and whispered, "Have you noticed that Josh and Amy seem to be inseparable?"

Meghan smiled as she watched the two stroll through the Baseball Card Room while Josh pointed out some of his favorite cards. "I'm not sure Amy is as much of a baseball fan as Josh, but she certainly seems eager to learn about his passions. I think they are good for each other."

"I agree," Travis replied, taking his wife by the hand as they followed the group around the room.

"Wow!" Matt exclaimed as they entered the room housing the collection of World Series rings. "This is incredible!"

The boys all gathered around the displays, pointing out some of their favorite rings, while searching for others. "Can you imagine how much all these rings are worth?" marveled one of the boys, shaking his head in amazement. The overwhelming sense of awe seemed to be the order of the day as the boys explored the museum.

When the group entered the Hall of Fame Gallery, which had bronze plaques of all players who had been inducted into the Hall of Fame, Meghan immediately began searching for her all-time favorite player, Willie Mays. Once she located his bronze plaque, she stood next to it and begged Travis to take a picture of her next to Willie Mays.

Travis chuckled as he took several pictures of Meghan in various poses. "Who knows when you may get back here, honey, so we may as well take a lot of pictures."

Walking through the Hall of Fame Gallery was probably the quietest the group of boys had been during the entire tour. They even talked in hushed tones, almost sensing they were walking on sacred baseball ground. The adults in the group periodically scanned the room to make sure they weren't losing any stragglers. On one scan, Travis lightly bumped Meghan's shoulder and nodded across the room. Josh and Amy were walking hand in hand like it was the most natural thing in the world. Meghan smiled, secretly hoping something more than friendship was growing between the two.

One of the favorite stops of the day was a place within the Hall where the boys could create their own baseball card. They could have their picture taken, type in their name, and pick their favorite team. It would produce their very own customized baseball card.

Mike moved to the front of their group. "Okay, boys, as a memento not only of this trip, but of the great season you guys had, I want each one of you to get your own baseball card. Come on, guys, crowd on in here. I don't want anyone left out."

As the boys crowded around, they were talking excitedly about which team they were going to represent with their card. Several chose the Seattle Mariners since that was the closest major league team to where they lived. A few of the boys, even though they were Mariners fans, chose a different team as a favorite. One of the youngest boys on the team said wistfully, "Too bad we can't get two cards. Then we could have a Mariners card and another favorite."

Even though the boy had made his comment quietly, Mike picked up on it.

"I think Parker has a great idea!" Mike said happily. "Why don't all you boys get two cards. You can all get a Mariners card because, let's face it, we know you're all Mariners fans. Then you can get a second card to represent one of your other favorite teams."

Several of the boys gave high-fives as they began discussing which team they would all get for their second card.

Josh laughed as he looked at Mike and shook his head. "You know, Dad," Josh said as he moved next to Travis. "I think Mike is enjoying this every bit as much as the boys are."

"I think you're right, son," Travis agreed with a chuckle.

Mike turned to the group and said, "The boys aren't the only ones who get to have a customized baseball card. All you adults get in there and have one made too." He looked directly at Meghan and said, "And yes, that includes you ladies too."

Meghan pumped her fist in the air as she said, "Yes!"

Travis looked at his wife and laughed as he told Mike, "I was going to have her get one made anyway. I have no doubt she will have it framed when we get home!"

Mike patted Travis on the back as he said, "When it comes to baseball, my boy, we're all kids." Then Mike walked over and got in line to have his own baseball card created.

After everyone had their baseball cards made, the last stop of the day was the gift shop. It was like watching a bunch of kids in a candy store. The boys pondered all the possibilities for souvenirs. Several of them kept coming back to the commemorative Hall of Fame baseballs as they were trying to decide on which souvenir to get.

Mike walked up to the counter to get a basket for shopping, then casually walked over to the commemorative baseballs and said, "You boys all pick out something you want for a souvenir. I'm going to get one of these baseballs for each one of us, so you be sure to get something else."

The boys looked at each other and grinned as they continued their search for just the right souvenir from their trip to the Baseball Hall of Fame.

* * *

After a long day at the Baseball Hall of Fame, the group decided to have a more relaxed schedule for their last day in Cooperstown. They explored the Farmer's Museum, which gave a realistic portrayal of early rural life in America, and took in the displays at the Fenimore Art Museum.

The day's highlight was a visit to Doubleday Field, dubbed the Home of Baseball. As part of that visit, the boys were all able to take a turn in the batting cages at the Wood Bat Factory Batting Range.

By midafternoon, everyone was ready for a treat of ice cream. They hopped on the trolley and found a great ice cream parlor where they were able to relax and wind down for the day. Kyle had heard rave reviews about a burger place where they were going to have dinner before getting ready to head back to Hope the next morning.

After dinner, the entire group gathered in one of the small conference rooms at the hotel. Josh walked to the front of the room, and scanned the group as they quieted down.

"I want to personally thank Mike for making this trip possible for everyone," Josh began.

The small room erupted in cheers. Josh raised his hand to quiet the boys before continuing.

"There has been no doubt these kids turned this into the trip of a lifetime." He added, with a laugh, "Us big kids had a fantastic time too! This trip was amazing!" Josh turned to look directly at Mike. "So, Mike, since words can't come close to explaining what this trip has meant to all of us, all I can say is thank you." Then Josh walked over and gave Mike a hug.

Mike wore a huge grin as he said, "I can honestly say it has been my pleasure. I know some of you boys haven't always had things easy, but after being closely involved with most of you for the past several months, I can say without a doubt that the town of Hope can be proud of you boys. Even when things haven't been easy, you have found ways to pull yourselves up by your bootstraps and keep moving forward. What you pulled off at the State baseball finals was nothing short of miraculous. You earned this trip. You have a lot to be proud of, and I hope this little trip will be a reminder that you can do great things. We learned how some of the greatest players in baseball came from very humble beginnings and were able to do amazing things. Every one of you can do great things. Don't forget that. Don't let anyone ever tell you your dreams are too big. Prove them wrong."

Mike started to walk away, then turned with a grin and said, "Oh, by the way, when we get back home, I have dibs on the baseball game at the center." His laughter followed him out the door and down the hallway, leaving the group smiling and shaking their heads.

Chapter Thirteen

JC's Hope was filled with excitement once the group returned from Cooperstown. The boys who had gone on the trip couldn't stop talking about it. There was no doubt the trip had a huge impact on them. Several of the boys even talked about their own dreams of someday making it to the major leagues. Others admitted they weren't good enough to play big-league ball, but confessed to having other dreams. Mike had gotten them thinking about their own dreams and where life might take them after graduating from high school. It was good to see the boys have some hope. For some of them, including Matt, it was the first time Josh had heard them talk about the future in a positive way. That gave Josh even more reason to post his announcement on the bulletin board.

A few of the teens crowded around to read what Josh was tacking up on the bulletin board. One of the younger boys asked, "Hey, JC, what's a career fair?"

"I'm glad you asked, Parker," JC replied as he placed his hand on the boy's shoulder. "A career fair is when you have people from colleges and other occupations come talk to you to explain some of the options you have after graduation."

Some of the kids began talking to each other about the announcement, as other kids stopped what they were doing and wandered over to the group to see what was going on.

"A career fair?" Rick asked. "That's sounds like a great idea. What kind of people are going to be there?"

"The announcement I posted explains a lot of the details, but I can give you some of the highlights," Josh explained. "Most of you know my cousin Aiden. He served in the Army with the Corps of Engineers. He's going to be there to explain some of the possibilities and benefits of joining the military after graduation. There will be representatives from two or three colleges who will explain some of the programs offered at their schools. My uncle Todd is also planning to be there. Some of you have been working with Todd and the shop teacher in an apprenticeship program. So, Todd will talk about that and some of the job opportunities in the construction industry. And Pastor Harmon will talk about some of the options for anyone interested in entering the ministry."

"When is it going to be?" Brandon asked.

"It will be next Wednesday," Josh replied. "It's open to all teenagers in town who may want to attend. So, if you have friends who might be interested, even if they don't come to the center, be sure to tell them about it."

* * *

Word of the career fair had spread quickly, so the crowd was larger than expected. At the last minute, Josh and Aiden recruited some of the boys to move tables and chairs into the gym, since none of the classrooms were large enough to accommodate the meeting.

Josh stood at the front of the gym with his dad, discussing the large turnout. "I knew the kids who come to the center on a regular basis were excited about this, but I sure didn't expect so many people."

Travis laughed in agreement. "Yeah, I already called your mom and she's going to bring over more cookies and other refreshments. In fact, there she is now. I better go see if she needs some help bringing things in."

As more teenagers filtered in and began filling up the chairs in the middle of the gym, the various presenters were setting up their tables with brochures, pens, and other items. Travis helped Meghan add things to the refreshment tables along the wall of the gym, as Josh checked to be sure the presenters had everything they needed.

Josh stepped to the front of the gym and raised his hand. "Okay, everyone, it looks like everything is set up, so let's go ahead and get started. Let me explain how this is going to work. As you can see, there are tables set up around the walls of the gym. Each table has a representative or recruiter from a different institution or occupation. You can see where each person is from based on the large sign attached to the front of each table. For example, you all see Aiden over there at the table with a sign for the United States Army. If there is a particular area you might be interested in, simply go over to that table and you can talk to the representative. They can give you information that might help you decide on a direction to go after graduation. If you don't really know what you might want to do, you can visit several of the tables to gather information. You aren't just limited to one choice. The fair will go all afternoon, and there are tables along the wall with refreshments. If you have any questions, don't hesitate to ask."

The teenagers got up and started making their way to various tables. Some of them were hesitant and hung back until they saw what their friends were doing. Others seemed to have an idea already in mind, and headed directly to a specific table. Josh wasn't surprised to see Rick make a beeline for Aiden, seated at the Army table. He knew Rick had been talking to Aiden about possibly joining the Army after graduation. He was, however, surprised to see how quickly the Army table was surrounded by teenagers.

Matt quickly joined the group in front of Todd's table. He was one of the students who had been in the apprenticeship program at Byers Construction, and he had developed a bond with Todd. Josh was pleased to see several kids around his dad's table. He wasn't aware of any of the kids mentioning an interest in ministry, but he knew several of them were having individual Bible studies with Travis. The college recruiters attracted a lot of attention as well. Josh had been telling the kids in advance not to write off college as a possibility simply because they had no idea how to pay for it. He wanted them to be aware of what was out there, and to understand not to set limits on themselves.

Josh noticed Brandon hanging back, seemingly unsure where to start. He walked over to him and put his hand on his shoulder.

"What are you thinking, Brandon?" Josh asked.

"I'm not really sure," Brandon replied. "It would be nice to go to college, but I don't really know what to study. And there's no way I could ever pay for college."

"Remember," Josh said. "Don't write off college because you're worried about paying for it. There are scholarships, financial aid, and other programs to help. I don't want to sway you in any way, but would you like my opinion?"

Brandon's shoulders sagged with relief. "Yes, please."

"Brandon," Josh began. "You have a gift. Music is a large part of who you are. I have heard what you do with music when you put your heart and soul into it. And I have seen what a natural you are with composing music. I would be willing to bet you could get a scholarship to study music at one of the colleges."

Josh pointed over to one of the college tables along the wall. "I happen to know that college has a fantastic music program. I think it would be worth checking out."

"I don't know," Brandon said hesitantly. "What if I couldn't get a scholarship? You know my family doesn't have any money. My dad hasn't worked in more than three years. We had to sell my piano, for crying out loud. And that belonged to my grandma. If I got all excited about going to college and studying music, then didn't get a scholarship, it would be worse than not trying at all."

Josh took Brandon by the shoulders and turned him to look directly in his face. "Brandon, how many times have I told you not to set your own limitations on what you can do? There are enough people out there in the world who will put limitations on you. Don't you go limiting yourself too. I'm telling you, you have an amazing gift. It would be a shame to see that go to waste because you were afraid to try. I will never try to force you to do anything. But if you decide you want to go to college to study music, I promise, I will do everything in my power to make it happen. Do you believe that?"

Brandon looked up at Josh with a tentative smile. "Yeah, JC, I do believe that. You believed in me right from the beginning. If you think I can do it, then I'm willing to try."

Josh patted Brandon on the shoulder and said, "I'm proud of you, Brandon. You have time to work on scholarship opportunities. You're going to be a junior this fall, so you have two years to explore colleges and music scholarships. We can make it happen, Brandon. I know we can. So go over there and talk to the college reps. Talk to both of them. Keep your options open."

As the career fair began winding down by late afternoon, Josh was pleased with its success. He heard a lot of excitement from some of the teenagers he had never met, and was particularly impressed by the reaction of some of the kids from the center. He made his way over to the refreshment table and ran into Mike Slater filling a glass with punch.

"Hey, Mike," Josh said with surprise. "I didn't know you were here. If I had seen you, I would have come over to say hello earlier."

"You were busy, Josh." Mike replied with a smile. "This is a good thing you put together for the kids. Quite the turnout."

"Yeah," Josh laughed. "I had to have the guys help move things to the gym when I realized the classroom wasn't going to be anywhere near big enough. How did you find out about the career fair?"

"I was here the other day. One of the boys challenged me to a game on the baseball arcade machine. I beat him, by the way," Mike added with a chuckle. "I check out the bulletin board every time I stop by, and I saw the poster. You never know when I'll see something interesting."

Mike patted Josh on the back and said, "Well, my boy, I'm going to grab another chocolate chip cookie and get out of here. You let me know if you need anything."

The two men shook hands and Josh watched Mike walk out the door, wondering what his ulterior motive was for showing up. One thing he had learned about Mike Slater was that he always had something up his sleeve.

* * *

Amy was getting ready to head into one of the classrooms when Josh waved at her from the other end of the hall. She stopped and waited for him to catch up to her.

"Hi Josh," Amy greeted. "I haven't seen much of you the last few days. You must have been busy."

"Yeah," Josh replied. "It's been pretty crazy since we got back from Cooperstown. Now that the career fair is behind me, things should slow down to the normal dull roar soon. Are you heading in to help a student?"

Amy nodded her head. "Brittany is going to summer school to catch up on things. She's really struggling with algebra, so I told her I would meet her here to help."

"I'm heading down to work on some music while I have a little time," Josh said. "Why don't you come down to the music room when you're done here. I'd like to talk to you."

"Sure," Amy agreed. "I should only be about a half hour or so. Forty-five minutes, tops. I'll see you in a bit."

Josh watched Amy walk into the classroom, then stopped at the kitchen to grab a bottle of water before heading toward the music room. He was happy to see the room vacant so he could concentrate on his music.

He sat down at the piano, with no sheet music in front of him, and started playing the haunting melody that had been running through his head for weeks. Once he had begun composing the song a few weeks ago, he found himself absentmindedly humming it whenever Amy popped into his mind. The introduction came from a darker part of his soul that he rarely visited anymore. Once the song grew and the melody emerged, he understood why. This was Amy's song. It was her story, and it came from a place of darkness. But he had witnessed her growth, and it made him smile.

Oblivious to his surroundings, Josh completely immersed himself into the music. There were times when the music seemed frantic, like it was fighting desperately to escape. Other times, the notes were relaxed and serene, almost like the music had found its inner peace. That was the melody Josh found himself humming frequently. That inner peace was the music of victory, and it made him smile.

Sensing his composition was nearing completion, Josh went back to the beginning, to that haunting introduction, and played the song through. When the music ended, because it was certainly on a journey of its own, he removed his hands from the keyboard and sat back. He heard a movement off to the side and turned to see his parents standing there in awe. Tears were running down his mother's face.

They walked toward the piano and Meghan wrapped her arms around her son. "Josh, I haven't heard you play with that much intensity since before the accident. That was absolutely the most beautiful thing I've ever heard."

"Son," Travis added. "There aren't words to describe that. I have to assume it's one of your compositions. I know I've never heard anything quite like it before."

"It's a song I've been working on for a while," Josh said.

"I thought I heard you humming part of that a few days ago," Travis said. "Am I right?"

Josh smiled shyly before replying. "Yeah, it pops into my head sometimes and makes me happy."

"I certainly hope you're writing that music down," Meghan said. "It would be a shame to forget any of that. Do you have a title for the composition?"

Answering her first question, Josh replied. "I haven't written it down yet, but I'm going to." Moving to his mom's second question, he said, "I hadn't come up with a title for it until a few minutes ago. I'm going to call it 'Rising from the Ashes'."

Wiping a stray tear from her eye, Meghan said, "That's a perfect title, son."

Standing next to his wife, Travis smiled. "Now I have to ask you a question, son. Is that Amy's story, or your story?"

Josh looked at his dad with surprise written all over his face. "It's Amy's story. But how did you know?"

"I'm a keen observer, son," Travis replied with compassion. "But you know, 'Rising from the Ashes' could be your story as well. Your mother and I have watched your recovery and transformation since the accident. It has definitely been a rebirth."

"I guess I never thought of it that way," Josh agreed.

"You know what I think?" Meghan asked. "I think 'Rising from the Ashes' is the story of both you and Amy. Separately, and together."

About that time, the door opened, and Amy walked into the room. She saw the three of them huddled around the piano, with Meghan sitting next to Josh on the bench.

"Am I interrupting something?" she asked.

"Not at all," Travis replied, taking his wife by the hand. "We just stopped by to say hi, and now we're off. As always, Amy, it's good seeing you."

"Nice to see you two again, as well," Amy replied, before turning to Josh. "You said you wanted to talk to me. What's up? I only have a few minutes before I need to go. It took longer with Brittany than she thought it would."

Josh patted the piano bench beside him, motioning for her to sit. "This will only take a minute. I just wanted to ask you something."

Amy sat beside Josh on the bench before he continued. "This weekend there is going to be a concert in the park. There are going to be three different bands playing all kinds of music. I was wondering if you would like to go with me."

Amy smiled as she stood to go. "I would love to go with you, Josh. I can't think of a single thing I'd rather do."

"Great!" Josh replied enthusiastically. "Me too. I mean, me neither. I mean, I can't think of anything I'd rather do either. Should I pick you up around ten o'clock Saturday morning? I don't even know where you live."

Shaking her head, Amy replied. "No, how about if we just meet here at the center. It'll be fun. I can't wait."

Her smile didn't hide the faint blush creeping up her cheeks as she turned and walked out the door.

* * *

When Josh pulled his Jeep into the parking lot at the center, he smiled when he saw Amy already seated at one of the picnic tables out front.

Since it was a Saturday morning, there was already a fair amount of activity at the center, and a few cars dotted the parking lot. Josh looked around, as always, trying to see a car he didn't recognize, hoping one belonged to Amy. He silently wondered if she walked everywhere. She always turned down his offers to give her and Matt a ride home, and seemed to simply show up at the center. Maybe he would ask her sometime if she had a car.

As he walked toward the picnic table, he was pleased to see Amy smiling. "You're here bright and early," Josh said with a smile. "I figured I would beat you by getting here twenty minutes early."

"Looks like you figured wrong," Amy said with a laugh. "Are you ready to go?"

"Let me just run in and grab a couple bottles of water from the kitchen, and I'll be right back," he replied.

Returning with two bottles of water and a small sack, Josh met up with Amy as she started walking toward his Jeep.

Amy eyed the sack, then looked at Josh. He grinned and said, "Just a small snack for the ride. Chocolate chip cookies."

She reached for one of the bottles of water, shaking her head. "You do realize that the park is only four blocks away, right?"

"True," Josh agreed, grinning. "But it's a very long four blocks. We might get hungry."

"I swear," Amy said as she shook her head yet again. "Sometimes I think you're a bottomless pit. How did your parents ever keep you fed?"

"Well, it did help that my sister was nearly grown by the time I came along."

"I thought Ryleigh was younger than you," Amy said, with surprise.

"She is," Josh replied. "I meant my older sister, Kaci."

"Oh, yeah. I always forget that Kaci is your sister too. Well, hopefully, when you were growing up, you saved some of the food for Ryleigh. I don't know how your mom ever kept the kitchen stocked with enough chocolate chip cookies to feed your addiction."

Josh just laughed as he walked around and opened the door to his Jeep and helped Amy in. During the short drive to the park, he managed to polish off two chocolate chip cookies, as Amy simply grinned and shook her head. After finding a place to park, he walked around the Jeep and took Amy's hand to help her out. He kept her hand in his as they walked toward the bandstands set up in the park.

"So, what kind of music did you say they would be playing today?" Amy asked.

"I think it's going to be a little bit of everything. There's supposed to be three bands. I'm familiar with one of them, so I know they'll be playing mostly folk songs. They're really good. I think you'll like them. And I think, from what I've heard, that one of the bands plays primarily country, with some pop and other contemporary music thrown in. The last band plays mostly rock music. They're pretty good too, as long as they stay away from the heavy metal. They play good music, I'm just not a fan of the heavy metal sound."

"It sounds like it will be fun," Amy said. "You lead the way. It sounds like some of the bands are already tuning their instruments."

"Let's go over this way," Josh said, pointing. "That's the folk band."

Keeping Amy's hand tucked into his own, they walked across the park and found a place to sit on the grass near the band. They enjoyed listening to the folk band for a couple hours, until the band took a break. Josh stood, and reached for Amy's hand to help her up. She stumbled briefly and Josh pulled her close, looking down into her eyes.

Amy looked up at Josh and whispered, "My foot fell asleep from sitting too long. Sorry."

"I'm not," Josh said quietly, as he gazed into her hazel eyes, just as two young kids ran by screaming and nearly bumped into them. "I am, however, sorry those kids nearly ran us down."

"Yeah," Amy agreed. "Someone could have gotten hurt."

Josh smiled at her and said, "Yeah, and someone could have gotten a kiss."

Amy blushed lightly as she tucked her hair behind her ear.

Josh continued smiling as he took her hand and began walking across the park, humming a now-familiar tune.

Spying one of several food booths scattered around the park, Josh asked, "Are you getting hungry? It's past noon. Why don't we grab something to eat from one of the booths."

"Sure," she agreed. "What kind of things do they have?"

They continued walking as Josh surveyed the food options. "They don't have as many booths as they do when the fair is in town, but it looks like there's a place that sells burgers. And there's a pizza place. Oh, and I see the elephant ear booth is here. You have to try an elephant ear! They're great!"

Amy laughed and said, "You're a crazy man. Elephant ears? Seriously? Is that really a thing, or are you making it up?"

"No, really! They are so good! We'll get one for dessert. It's a deep-fried pastry that's sprinkled with cinnamon and sugar. A little messy, but so worth it!"

"If you say so," Amy said as she steered him toward the pizza booth. "How about pizza? That sounds better than a burger."

Josh took a theatrical bow and said, as he took her hand, "Then pizza it shall be, my dear."

After getting their pizza, they found an empty picnic table and sat to enjoy the food. They were near the rock band, and Josh was pleased they appeared to be sticking to basic rock music. Amy didn't seem to enjoy the rock music as much as she had the folk music, but she was smiling and seemed to be having a good time.

"Why don't you wait here and save our table," Josh said as he stood. "I'm going to go grab an elephant ear and I'll be right back. Luckily, the line doesn't look too long right now."

"Remember," Amy said with a grin. "Just the ear. Don't bring back the entire elephant. With your appetite, one can never be too sure!"

Josh laughed, then walked off humming once again. He returned about fifteen minutes later carrying a rather large hot pastry. He sat it down on the table, then sat beside Amy on the bench.

"I brought a lot of napkins because it can get messy. And be careful because it's hot out of the fryer."

Noticing her hesitation, Josh pulled a piece of the pastry off and tucked it into his mouth, chewing happily. "See, just pull off a piece and try it."

He tore a small piece of the pastry off and held it up to Amy's mouth.

She let him give her the bite of pastry and began chewing. "Oh, wow," she exclaimed. "You were right. This is really good!"

Josh puffed out his chest and said, "Hey, I know my food!"

After having some lunch, Josh and Amy strolled through the park, hand in hand, listening to the music. By midafternoon, they had decided to call it a day and were slowly walking toward the parking lot, with the strains of country music playing in the background. Josh could feel Amy swaying gently to the music, as she hummed along to the songs.

"So," he said softly. "You like country music. So do I."

"I have to confess," Amy said. "It's my favorite music genre."

As she continued swaying to the music, Josh stepped away from her slightly, still holding her hand, and said, "May I have this dance?"

Amy looked around shyly, as a light pink color crept into her cheeks, and asked, "Here? In the park?"

"Sure," Josh replied with a soft smile. "Why not?"

He took her in his arms, and they began swaying along with the music. He pulled her close and they continued dancing in the shade of a huge oak tree in the park. While the gentle strains of a country song faded in the distance, Josh stopped dancing and pulled away from Amy slightly. Neither spoke. Josh gazed down into her beautiful hazel eyes, then his lips met hers with their first kiss. Not wanting to overwhelm her, he pulled back slightly and peered into her face. Her eyes were still closed, but a very small smile graced her face. He took that as a sign that all was good, so he bent to place a second kiss on her lips. Amy reached her arms around Josh's neck, and pulled him gently into the second kiss, leaving no doubt in his mind that she didn't object.

Chapter Fourteen

Amy was putting supplies into the pantry, with her back to the open kitchen door. She never minded restocking the pantry shelves. It was a mindless task that allowed her time to think. She jumped when something hit the floor behind her, jerking her mind away from her troubled thoughts.

"I'm sorry, Amy," Meghan said as she entered the kitchen with her hands full. "I dropped a can of juice. I didn't mean to startle you." Meghan sat the supplies on the kitchen counter and bent to retrieve the juice can that had begun rolling across the floor.

Amy turned back to the pantry as she quietly replied, "It's okay." Then she turned to Meghan and asked, "I'm sorry. Did you need some help, or is that everything?"

"No," Meghan replied. "This is everything. As usual, I thought I could get everything in one trip, so I overloaded my arms."

Meghan began handing some of the supplies to Amy as she stacked them on the shelves in the pantry.

"Are you okay, Amy?" Meghan asked with concern.

Amy didn't turn to face Meghan. She simply replied quietly, "Yes, I'm fine. That just startled me is all."

"You've been jumpy all afternoon," Meghan persisted. "Are you sure everything's okay?"

"I said I'm fine," Amy said with irritation. After seeing the surprised look on Meghan's face, she added, "I'm sorry. I didn't mean to snap at you. I guess I'm just tired is all."

Meghan put her hand on Amy's shoulder and said, "That's okay. Just remember, if anything is bothering you, I'm a good listener."

Amy forced a smile, then returned to her task. "Thanks. I'll remember that."

Travis was passing the kitchen when he saw Meghan. He poked his head in the door and asked, "Honey, have you seen Amy?"

Meghan walked toward the door and reached up to give her husband a kiss. "She's in the pantry, putting supplies away," she said. Then she added in a whisper, "She's been jumpy all afternoon, but when I asked if she was okay, she insisted that everything's fine."

Travis shook his head sadly, then said, "I've noticed it too. Something is bothering her. Maybe I can cheer her up with some good news."

Walking into the kitchen, Travis called to Amy, hoping not to startle her again. "Hey, Amy, why don't you take a break for a few minutes. I have some news for you."

Amy came out of the pantry, closing the door behind her.

"Hi, Pastor Harmon," she greeted. "What kind of news?"

"If you're still interested, I think I've found an apartment for you," Travis said with a smile.

"Really?" Amy said excitedly.

Travis chuckled at her enthusiasm. "Yes, really. It won't be available for three weeks, though."

"Have you seen it?" Amy asked. "What can you tell me about it?"

"Yes, I've seen it. The owner is currently doing some repairs to the apartment. That's why it won't be ready until the end of the month. It's not very big, but it does have two bedrooms, so I think it would work for you and Matt. It's also only about three blocks from the center, so it would be within walking distance of the center, and the school. By the way, I've been meaning to ask you, do you have a car?"

"No, I don't have a car yet," Amy said, as some of her enthusiasm slipped away. "I've been trying to save up money to buy a cheap car. But I've also been trying to save money to get my own apartment, and that's more important. It's not a big deal for me to walk where I need to go."

Motioning toward the table in the center of the kitchen, Travis said, "Amy, why don't we sit down for a few minutes. I have some ideas that might help." Looking at his wife, he added, "Honey, why don't you join us."

Travis pulled out the chairs for the two ladies, then he took a seat.

"First things first. Let's talk about the car situation. Josh mentioned to me the other day that he didn't think you had transportation. You just confirmed that, so let's see what we can do about that."

Amy hesitated. "Like I said, the apartment is more important than a car. It doesn't bother me to walk."

Meghan reached over and put her hand on Amy's forearm. "But it bothers us. If something happened and you needed to leave in a hurry, it would be a lot easier with a car."

Amy ducked her head before saying quietly, "I do okay."

"I know you do, Amy," Meghan replied with compassion. "But we worry about you and Matt, and we want you to be safe."

"That's why the apartment is more important," Amy insisted.

Travis didn't want the discussion to get derailed, so he patted Amy on the arm and continued. "I think I have a solution to the car issue. Ryleigh just bought a new car. Well, new to her, anyway. She needed something that would work better for all her trips to and from school. She was planning to sell her old car. It's still in great shape, and would be perfect for getting around town. She just bought her new car a few days ago, so she hasn't even advertised her old one yet. I don't think she's planning to ask a lot for it. Whatever she wants for it, I'm sure we could work something out."

Meghan reached across the table and took her husband's hand in hers. "That's a great idea, honey. I can give Ryleigh a call in a few minutes and ask her about it." Turning to Amy, she added, "It really is a great car, Amy. And it would make it a lot easier for you and Matt to get around town. What do you say?"

"Well, okay," Amy replied with hesitation. "You can at least talk to her and see how much she wants for it. Then I'll decide."

"Great!" Meghan said with a smile.

"Now, about the apartment," Travis continued. "Like I said, I've seen it. It doesn't look like much right now because they are in the middle of doing some repairs, painting, and then they will be cleaning all the carpets. But it's a nice little apartment. And I think it will be very affordable for you as well. I haven't talked to the owner yet, but I've talked to the manager and put down a deposit to hold it for you. The manager needs to check with the owner since I'm not the one who would be living there. He's going to call me back later."

"Maybe you shouldn't have put down a deposit," Amy said quietly. "If I can't afford it, you might not be able to get your deposit back."

"That's not a problem," Travis insisted. "The deposit just holds it for you while the details are worked out. If you decide you don't want it, I'll get my deposit back. But let's not get ahead of ourselves. I'll wait to hear back from the manager, then we can talk more about the details. As I said, it won't be ready for about three weeks anyway."

"Okay, thanks, Pastor Harmon. Meghan, I'm finished in here, so I need to get down to the classroom to help Brittany. See you later."

Travis put his arm around his wife's waist as they watched Amy hurry out the door. "We need to get the apartment and car figured out for her. I'm worried that things are getting worse for them at home. Matt still won't talk about what happened to him. He claims he just hurt his ribs during the ballgame."

"At least he's still coming around," Meghan said with guarded optimism. "Seeing them both here at the center nearly every day makes it easier to keep an eye on them. I'm going to call Ryleigh right now and ask her about the car."

* * *

Early the next afternoon, Ryleigh and Meghan showed up at the center in two different vehicles. They went into the building in search of Amy. Spotting her in the hallway, headed toward the kitchen, Ryleigh called out to her.

"Amy! Do you have a minute? I want to show you something?"

"Hi, Ryleigh," Amy replied. "Sure. What's up?"

"Come out to the parking lot. I want to show you my car," Ryleigh said with a smile. "I don't want you to think I'm pressuring you or anything, but I really think my old car would be perfect for you. I have always loved this car, but I just needed something with better gas mileage for all my driving back and forth to school."

"I don't know, Ryleigh," Amy hesitated.

Ryleigh put her arm around Amy and started steering her toward the parking lot. "Come on," she urged. "Just look at it. Please. I really want it to go to a good home. And you would be a perfect fit for it."

As the two young ladies approached a pale blue Honda Accord, Ryleigh held the keys out to her friend. "Hop in, Amy. Let's take it for a drive to see if you even like it."

Amy smiled as she took the keys and said, "Okay, why not?" She settled in behind the steering wheel, adjusted the seat and mirrors, and they headed out of the parking lot.

After driving around town for about twenty minutes, they pulled back into the parking lot at JC's Hope.

Ryleigh turned in the passenger seat to look at Amy. "Well, what do you think?"

Amy sunk back into the seat and sighed. "You're right, Ryleigh. It's a great car. But I don't know. How much are you asking for it?"

"For my friend," Ryleigh said. "Only $1,500." Ryleigh noticed the instant hesitation on Amy's face. "But also, because you're my friend, you can make payments. No set amount. Just whatever you want when you have a little extra money. And the best part is you can take the car today. Come on, help me out here. I don't want to have to deal with trying to sell it to strangers. What do you say?"

"Are you sure you're okay with me making payments?"

"Absolutely!" Ryleigh replied.

"Okay," Amy finally agreed. "You have yourself a deal."

They climbed out of the car and Amy started to hand the keys over to Ryleigh. Ryleigh shook her head and pushed the keys back toward Amy. "Those are your keys now. You're going to love the car, Amy. I promise. And now, I need to go find my mom. She's going to give me a ride back home."

"If you want," Amy began hopefully. "I could give you a ride home. That way you won't need to bother your mom."

"Perfect!" Ryleigh said. "Let's go. It won't take long."

Josh pulled his Jeep into the parking lot just as his sister's car was pulling out. He waved, but his sister waved back from the passenger's seat. He did a doubletake when he realized Amy was behind the wheel. She returned his wave with a huge grin spread across her face.

* * *

Josh, Travis, and Todd were standing near the weight machines in the gym, discussing some equipment that was going to be added to the area. Matt and two other boys were playing on the arcade games while an older boy worked his way up the rock-climbing wall. The center was relatively quiet because it was still early in the day. The door opened and a middle-aged man walked in and looked around the room like he was looking for someone. He walked over to the boys at the arcade games and began talking to Matt.

Todd looked at Josh and Travis and asked, "Do you guys know who that is?"

"No," Travis replied. "I've never seen him here before."

"Me neither," Josh confirmed.

The conversation around the arcade games was becoming heated, as the man raised his voice to Matt. Todd started toward the games, with Travis and Josh right behind him. Just as Todd approached from behind, the man said loudly, "I said you're coming with me right now!"

The man pulled back his arm like he was going to strike Matt. Todd immediately reached over and grabbed the man's arm and spun him around.

"Don't touch that boy," Todd said firmly.

The man tried to pull free, but Todd had a firm grasp on his arm.

Todd looked over at Matt and asked, "Are you okay?"

"Yeah," Matt replied, clearly shaken.

"Let me go!" the man yelled. "You got no right to interfere!"

Todd jerked the man toward the door and said, "Let's go outside and have a little chat." Todd nodded his head, indicating he wanted Josh to stay with Matt and Travis to follow him outside.

Todd walked the man over to the picnic tables, with the man yelling obscenities the entire way. Todd pushed him down on the bench, let go of his arm, then stood right in front of him with his arms folded across his chest.

"Now," Todd began in a no-nonsense voice. "Who are you, and what are you doing here?"

The man let loose with another string of obscenities before Todd reached over and put his hand firmly on the man's shoulder. "You will talk in a civilized manner, and you will answer my questions. Now, who are you, and what are you doing here? And you had better talk nice."

The man began to mutter another obscenity when Todd bent down and stared directly into the man's face. "I said you better talk nice. I'm not going to tell you again. Now, we'll do one question at a time. Who are you?"

"I'm John Phoenix, and you got no right interfering in family business," the man finally replied.

"I'll be the judge of that," Todd said nonchalantly. "Are you related to Matt?"

"I'm the boy's father, and I came to take him home," the man answered defiantly.

"We'll see about that," Todd said. "It looked to us like you had plans to hit Matt. We're not going to let that happen."

"What I do, or don't do, with my boy is none of your business," the man said with a false sense of bravado.

"Well," Todd began. "Since I can smell alcohol on your breath, and you're on our property, that kind of makes it our business. You're not taking Matt anywhere. I strongly suggest you leave right now, and don't force me to call the police."

The man stood, careful to make a wide berth around Todd, and started toward the parking lot. He turned and pointed at Todd. "This ain't over." Then he disappeared into the parking lot.

Todd sighed as he looked at Travis. "Yeah, I have no doubt this isn't over. Let's go check on Matt."

Josh was talking with Matt just inside the main door. When Todd and Travis opened the door, Todd looked at them and said, "Josh, let's go to your office and talk. Come on, Matt."

Once inside the office, Todd indicated to Matt to have a seat at the table. The men followed and sat around the small conference table, with Todd sitting directly across from Matt.

Todd rested his arms on the table and looked Matt in the eye. "Okay, buddy, let's talk. We all know things haven't been great for you and Amy at home. We also suspected something happened to you at the end of the baseball season, and we're pretty sure it didn't happen when you made that snag during the game. Which was a great snag, by the way."

Matt didn't say anything, but gave a weak smile of thanks.

"I know both Kyle and Josh have tried to get you to talk about what happened," Todd continued. "But you have stuck to your story. We've been around enough to know when something doesn't look or sound right. And sorry, my friend, but your story just doesn't sound right. But we aren't going to dwell on that. However, when your dad comes into this building and makes a move to hit you, that changes everything.

"Matt, I like to think that you and I have gotten to be friends over the past few months. I have enjoyed having you work in the apprentice-ship program, and I don't want to see anything bad happen to you. So, I want to ask you a question and, because we're friends, I really hope you can give me an honest answer. Has your dad hit you before?"

Matt stared down at his hands and didn't say anything.

Travis reached over and put his arm around Matt's shoulder. "We want to help, Matt. And we want you and Amy to be safe. I hope you know that."

Matt looked up at Todd and said quietly. "A few times."

Travis noticed the vein on the side of Todd's neck begin to bulge. That always happened when Todd was trying to control his temper.

"That's what we thought," Todd said with sympathy. "Thanks for answering honestly, Matt. What did he want when he came in here?"

"He wanted me to go home," Matt said. "He doesn't want me hanging out here."

"Has he given you trouble before because you come to the center?" Josh asked.

Matt hesitated before replying. "Yeah. He doesn't like it that Amy and I spend so much time here."

"Any particular reason he objects to it?" Todd asked.

"I'm sure it's mostly because he wants us at home, doing chores, so he can keep an eye on us," Matt said as he shrugged.

"Matt," Travis began. "I don't know if Amy told you or not, but she has talked to me and Meghan about your situation at home. So, we know both your parents have a problem with alcohol. We smelled alcohol on your dad's breath a few minutes ago. When a person has an alcohol addiction, and has a history of physical abuse, that's a bad combination. We would all feel a lot better if you didn't go home tonight. You could come stay with one of us."

"No," Matt said adamantly. "It's better if I just go home."

Todd shook his head, not quite ready to admit defeat. "Are you sure, Matt? You could come stay with me tonight. You could sleep in Aiden's old room. It's just a guest room now."

"Thanks, Todd," Matt replied. "But I think it's better if I just go home." Matt stood and started toward the door.

Josh reached out and put his arm around Matt's shoulder. "I know Amy has a cell phone, and she has all our phone numbers. Please call one of us if you guys have a problem and don't feel safe. Okay?"

"Thanks, JC," Matt agreed. "I know Amy will call you if she thinks we aren't safe. I think I'm going to head out. Thanks."

The three men stood and watched Matt walk down the hallway, carrying the weight of the world on his shoulders, and out the front door.

Josh sighed. "I hope that's not the last time we see him here. If he stops coming, Amy will leave too. They both need this place."

"Don't worry, Josh," Todd said as he patted his nephew on the back. "We're not giving up on them. And we're all going to keep an eye on them. It certainly helps that Amy bought Ryleigh's car. At least now we know they have reliable transportation if they need to get out in a hurry."

"Thank, God," Josh said quietly. "That couldn't have come at a better time."

Chapter Fifteen

The warm summer night was perfect for sitting out on the front porch. Josh walked onto the porch carefully carrying three tall glasses of iced tea. Letting his mom take one, he then handed a glass to his dad, keeping the last glass for himself, and sat in one of the chairs along the front of the house. When Meghan designed their home, before she and Travis were married, the wrap-around porch was her favorite part of the design. She had many fond memories of sitting out on the front porch with her dad when she was younger. So, she knew she needed to incorporate a wrap-around porch in the design of her home. The entire family loved the way it wrapped all the way around to the back of the house where it became a large deck. The perfect place for summer barbecues.

"It's nice to have a relaxing evening for a change," Josh said to his parents. "It's been crazy busy at the center." Turning to his dad, he said, "I often wonder how you even have time to prepare your sermons and do all your work at the church. You spend almost as much time at the center as I do."

Travis simply shrugged. "I enjoy the work, so it doesn't seem exhausting. Most of the time," he added with a laugh.

"Well, I can't tell you how much I appreciate everything you do at the center. You both amaze me, and I'm sure I don't thank you nearly enough."

The three sat in a comfortable silence, simply enjoying the peaceful setting. The silence was broken by the sudden ringing of Josh's cell phone. A quick glance at the caller ID revealed it was Amy.

"Hey, Amy," Josh greeted as he answered the phone with a smile on his face. "Wait a minute! Hold on! Slow down!" Josh was now standing, listening frantically, trying to make sense of what Amy was saying.

"Okay, Amy. Just calm down and listen to me," Josh said, sounding much calmer than he felt. "You're in your car. Where are you?" Josh listened for a minute as she explained. "You took Ryleigh home the other day after buying her car, right? Do you remember where we live?" Another pause as he listened to her reply. "Okay, good. No, don't go to the center. Come out to our house. Do you want me to stay on the line until you get here? Okay, just drive safe, and we'll see you in a little bit. Call me back if you get lost."

After disconnecting the call, Josh turned to his parents who were both on their feet by now.

"What's going on, son?" Travis asked as he put his hand on his son's shoulder.

"Amy's dad got violent again during another one of his drinking binges," Josh said as he began relaying the phone conversation. "He started throwing chairs and stuff at both Amy and Matt. Matt tried to stop him and got hit in the back with a chair. They grabbed a few things and ran out the door. They are heading over here now."

"Thank God Amy bought Ryleigh's car," Meghan said. "Who knows what would have happened if they couldn't get out quickly."

Meghan looked at her husband, who was already on his phone.

"Todd," Travis began. "Can you and Aiden come over to the house? There's been a problem with Matt's dad. He and Amy are heading our way." Travis listened to Todd's reply before turning to his wife and son. "Thanks, Todd. See you in a few minutes."

"Todd and Aiden are on their way," Travis said. "They will probably get here before Amy does. I thought it would help to have their input. And Todd will probably want Matt to stay with them."

Josh paced back and forth on the porch, absent-mindedly rubbing the scar that ran along his jawline.

Travis walked over to his son. "She's going to be okay, son. They both will. We'll see to that."

Less than ten minutes after the call to Todd, his pickup skidded a bit as he turned quickly into their driveway. Todd and Aiden hopped out of the truck and ran straight to the porch.

Looking around for Ryleigh's old car, Todd said, "Looks like we beat them here."

"Yeah," Josh replied. "They were probably about twenty minutes away when she called. She's only been here once, so hopefully she doesn't have any trouble finding the place."

Josh and Travis had joined Todd and Aiden on the sidewalk leading to the porch. Josh relayed the phone conversation he had with Amy, so everyone was brought up to speed.

Travis could see the vein in Todd's neck begin to bulge. "Is Matt okay?" Todd asked Josh.

"Probably," Josh replied. "But we really won't know until we see them."

"Okay," Todd began. "I guess we formulate a plan once they get here, and we make sure they are both okay. As long as they are okay, then we just make sure they have a place to stay. Matt can stay with us."

"Amy can stay here in Kaci's old room," Meghan added.

Aiden looked over at Josh, who was still pacing. "You can come bunk with me at my apartment, JC."

Josh had only been half listening, and asked, "What? Why would I need to bunk at your place?"

"If Amy's going to be staying here..." Aiden began.

"Oh, yeah," Josh agreed. "It wouldn't look right. I'll just bunk with you. Thanks, Aiden."

Josh looked up when they heard a car pull into the driveway and park alongside Todd's pickup. He hurried over to Amy's car, and pulled her into a tight hug the moment she got out of the car.

Todd was the first to get to Matt as he got out of the car. He put his hand on Matt's shoulder and asked, "Are you okay, Matt?"

Matt smiled weakly and said, "Yeah, I'm tougher than any broken-down chair."

When Travis and Meghan joined the group, Travis said, "Why

don't we go around back where there are more chairs on the deck. Then we can all sit down and hash things out."

As everyone started around the house, Meghan asked, "Would anyone like something to drink? Iced tea or soda, maybe?"

Matt replied, "I could use a soda, if it's not any trouble."

"No trouble at all, Matt," Meghan assured him. "Amy, would you like something?"

"Sure, iced tea would be great," she said. "Thanks."

Aiden walked back toward Meghan and said, "I'll go help you get the drinks, Aunt Meghan."

Meghan said, "Thanks, Aiden," as they began walking toward the front door.

A few minutes later, Meghan and Aiden walked out onto the deck carrying trays with drinks and cookies. Once everyone got something to drink, they sat back down to sort through the situation.

Travis looked over at Matt and asked, "Are you sure you're okay, Matt? We should probably take a look at your back."

"No," Matt replied hesitantly. "I'm okay. I just want to forget about it."

"How about you, Amy?" Meghan asked with compassion. "Are you okay?"

"Yeah, I'm okay," she replied. "Just a bit shaken up." She snuggled in close to Josh on the love seat, as he pulled her close, keeping his arm around her shoulder.

"Amy," Travis began. "The apartment we discussed is yours as soon as it's ready. It will still be a couple weeks, though, until it's finished, and you can move in. In the meantime, you guys will be staying with us."

"But what if I can't afford the apartment?" Amy asked with concern. "I don't even know how much the rent is."

"You don't need to worry about that right now." Travis assured her. "I know for a fact it will be affordable for you. The manager didn't call me back, but the owner did. Turns out the owner of that apartment complex is Mike Slater. He assured me that he's going to give you very reduced rent for the first year, so you have a chance to get on your feet."

"Really?" Amy asked in surprise.

"Really," Travis said. "So, the apartment is not an issue. For the next couple weeks, Amy, you will be staying here with us. You can have Kaci's old room. Josh is going to stay with Aiden while you're staying here."

"Matt, you can come home with me and stay in Aiden's old room," Todd said. "Something else I've been wanting to talk to you about, Matt, so now's as good a time as any. How would you like a summer job at Byers Construction?"

"Are you kidding me?" Matt asked with excitement. "I would love it!"

Todd chuckled at his enthusiasm before replying. "You have been one of the best apprentices I've had from the school. You're a quick learner, and you have some natural ability working with wood. It's not going to be a glamorous job. You would be doing a lot of gopher work, helping load trucks and things. Maybe help out with some of the smaller jobs. Are you okay with that?"

"You bet!" Matt replied. "When would I start?"

"I'll give you a couple days to get settled in at the house, then I'll take you to the shop with me. You will be paid a fair wage, so you'll be able to help your sister out with expenses once you move into the apartment."

"That will be awesome!" Matt said. "Thanks, Todd."

"I have to tell you, Matt," Todd continued. "It does come with a stipulation. I know a lot of teenagers, once they get the taste of a steady paycheck, decide that beats staying in school and taking tests. This job offer is only valid as long as you stay in school and graduate on time. I don't want you thinking you can quit school and work for me full-time. That's not going to happen. If everything works out, and you're doing a good job, there's a good chance you will have a full-time job waiting for you after graduation. Do you think you can live with that?"

Matt jumped up, wincing a bit as he did so, and walked over to shake Todd's hand. "You won't regret it, Todd. I promise."

The discussion continued for a while longer as some of the initial panic and stress wore off. Everyone settled into a comfortable visit, and soon found themselves talking about more pleasant subjects.

"Todd," Meghan began. "Did you find out if Nicole has this coming weekend off, or is she working at the hospital? We're going to have the big family barbecue on Saturday, and it would be great if she could be here."

"She has four days off," Todd replied. "So, you can count us in."

"Great!" Meghan said. "Amy, you and Matt are invited as well. You will be staying with us anyway, so you will join the family at the barbecue. It will be a lot of fun."

"Will Ryleigh be here?" Amy asked.

"Yes, she will," replied Meghan. "It will be a nice-sized group, but not so big it's overwhelming. It will be me, Travis, Josh, and Ryleigh. Kaci and Jason will be coming with the twins. Then Todd, Nicole and Aiden will be here. And, of course, you and Matt."

"Honey," Meghan addressed Travis. "You're going to invite Mike over for the barbecue, aren't you?"

"I invited him when I talked to him on the phone about the apartment," Travis said. "He said he wouldn't miss it."

Todd stood and stretched his back as he looked over the yard at the sinking sun. "Well, it's been a long day. What do you say we head home? Come on, boys. Matt, you can grab whatever you brought with you from the car, and we'll head over to the house."

"Dad," Aiden said. "I'll ride back to my apartment with JC. That way you don't have to make an extra stop."

"Sounds good," Todd agreed.

Josh started into the house, and yelled over his shoulder to Aiden. "I'll just grab a few things, then I'll be right out."

Everyone met out in front of the house as they were getting ready to leave. Amy told Matt to be sure to listen to Todd, and Todd assured her they would get along just fine. Aiden climbed into JC's Jeep and waited for him to say goodbye to Amy.

Josh pulled Amy into a tight embrace as she rested her head against his chest. She finally looked up at him just as he lowered his head to place a tender kiss on her lips. She returned his kiss and hugged him tightly before stepping out of his arms.

"Goodnight, Josh."

"Goodnight, Amy. Everything's going to be okay. I promise."

"I know," she replied as she placed another quick kiss on his cheek. "Thanks for everything."

Then Josh climbed into his Jeep, looked at his cousin, and said, "Let's go." He was determined to do everything in his power to protect Amy. The woman he had just realized he loved and planned to marry.

* * *

Although a summer storm had originally been in the forecast, the weather turned out to be a perfect day for a barbecue. As was normally the case when the Byers/Harmon family had a barbecue, everyone decided to make a day of it. Todd, Nicole, and Matt showed up shortly after breakfast. Josh and Aiden pulled in right behind them, and Josh immediately began looking around for Amy. By the time he located her on the back deck, he heard voices around front and suspected Kaci and her family had arrived. His suspicions were confirmed when two small tornados came around the side of the house and headed straight for the Bobcat, each clutching a yellow plastic hardhat.

Ryleigh stepped out onto the deck from the house and shook her head. "Well, we won't see anything from the twins until it's time for food."

Amy and Matt watched Aaron help his sister climb up onto the Bobcat, then he climbed up and sat beside her in the seat. Amy was surprised at the nonchalant attitude the other adults had. It didn't appear that any of them were concerned about the little kids climbing around on construction equipment.

Her curiosity finally got the best of her, and she asked Ryleigh, "Isn't anyone afraid those little kids will get hurt?"

Ryleigh laughed along with the rest of the family as she replied, "No. The twins have been climbing around on that Bobcat since they were big enough to walk. It's part of the fun of being born into this crazy family. We all grew up climbing around on construction equipment. JC and I played on it all the time when we were little. Kaci did too, from what I've been told."

"She's right, Amy," Kaci confirmed with a laugh. "It's part of our DNA. Mom and Uncle Todd grew up playing on everything from Bobcats to bulldozers and road graders. Most of us learned to drive heavy equipment before we could drive a car!"

"How did that ever happen?" Amy asked, shaking her head in amazement.

Meghan explained, "Our dad started Byers Construction. It was part of our life when Todd and I were kids. When Dad passed away, we took over the business. So, all our kids grew up in the construction business too. Kaci, Josh, Ryleigh, and Aiden. They are all experts."

"Wow," Matt said in amazement. "I sure wish I had grown up like that. That would be awesome."

"Well, Matt," Todd said. "If you stick with me and show a willingness to learn, it won't be long before you'll be an expert driving heavy equipment too. But first things first. Since you haven't grown up around the construction industry, you have to learn as you go, and you have to be willing to listen to instruction."

"Then I'll be able to drive Bobcats and bulldozers?" Matt asked with excitement.

Kaci laughed as she said, "Now he sounds like my kids!"

A voice came from the side yard. "Hey, it sounds like you guys started the fun without me."

From across the yard, two small voices yelled, "Mr. Mike! Mr. Mike!"

Jason yelled for the kids as he started across the yard toward the Bobcat. "You two be careful climbing down from there. Mr. Mike isn't going anywhere."

Aaron and Sophie scampered down from the Bobcat, only a little slower than they had started after seeing Mike. They met him halfway across the yard, each kid taking one of his hands, and steered him to the back deck.

"Did you come to eat with us, Mr. Mike?" Sophie asked as she looked up at him.

"I sure did," Mike replied. "I heard it's going to be the best food ever."

Aaron laughed at what he thought was a silly statement. "Of course, it is, Mr. Mike. Papa cooks the best burgers and hotdogs."

Everyone relaxed and visited for a while before it was time to heat up the grill. The twins asked Mike about a million questions before Kaci stepped in and told them they were wearing out Mr. Mike's ears. Matt convinced Aiden to go show him the Bobcat, and he climbed up into the seat and looked right at home. Josh and Amy sat side by side on the loveseat, seeming to be very content.

Meghan stood and started into the kitchen. "Honey, why don't you go ahead and fire up the grill. I'll get the hamburger patties ready for you. The baked beans are already in the oven."

"Okay," Travis replied. "Ryleigh, why don't you go ahead and bring the plates and utensils out. It won't take long to grill the burgers and hotdogs."

"Is there anything Matt and I can help with?" Amy asked.

"Sure," Meghan replied. "Matt, why don't you check the cooler and see if we need to add more drinks to it. If so, you can grab them from the fridge. Amy, maybe in about fifteen minutes you can get the dish of cantaloupe and Kaci's macaroni salad from the fridge and bring them out."

Before long, the food filled a table along the back of the house, and people began working their way down the buffet line to fill their plates. Once everyone had dished up, Travis offered to say grace.

"Dear loving Father, thank you for this bounty and for the many hands who prepared it. We ask that it might nourish and strengthen our bodies. We thank you, God, for your loving protection over Amy and Matt these past few days, and pray you will continue guiding and directing their lives, and the lives of everyone present here this afternoon. In Jesus's precious name, we pray. Amen."

A chorus of amens followed, then the feast began, and conversation flowed effortlessly.

After a few minutes, Amy asked Meghan. "Did you say Kaci brought the macaroni salad?"

"Yes, she did," Meghan confirmed.

"Kaci," Amy asked. "Where did you get this? You didn't make it, did you?"

"Yes, I made it. Do you like it, Amy?"

"It's the best macaroni salad I've ever tasted!" Amy said.

Meghan smiled and said, "It's kind of Kaci's specialty. Whenever there's a barbecue or potluck, someone requests her macaroni salad. It's a staple in this family."

Amy turned to Josh, "You know, Josh, this barbecue has been so much fun. And the food is fantastic! You should have a barbecue like this at the center. The kids there would love it!"

Josh looked at his dad, then said, "I think that's a great idea, Amy! We barbecue all summer long. I don't know why I didn't think of that before."

Mike pushed his chair back from the table after polishing off his second plate, and said, "Josh, if you guys want to plan the barbecue, I'll supply everything necessary for the food. Kaci, you'll need to let me know what ingredients you need for your macaroni salad. I'm sure we can round up three or four grills to haul down to the center. I think it's a fantastic idea. Just make sure I'm on the guest list!"

Mike raised his arm as he walked away, "See you all later."

Everyone simply shook their heads at what they had come to learn was Mike's incredible generosity. Josh hugged Amy a bit closer and said quietly, "God is good."

From a couple seats away, Travis added, "All the time."

Chapter Sixteen

A few days after Amy and Matt left their house, Josh drove them both back home so they could pick up a few more things. Travis and Todd followed in Todd's pickup to make sure everyone stayed safe. Amy and Matt sat in Josh's Jeep, not making a move to get out.

Josh reached for Amy's hand. "Are you okay? I'll go in with you and Matt. Dad and Uncle Todd will wait out on the porch in case we need them. It will be okay. You're not alone, remember."

Amy took a deep breath, then said, "Okay, let's get this over with."

The three climbed out of the Jeep and started up the sidewalk, with Travis and Todd close behind. Amy reached into her purse and got her house key, not sure she would even need it. In their frequent condition, her parents often forgot to lock the door. As expected, the door was unlocked. Amy looked at her brother, who nodded and followed her into the house.

They looked around the living room, seeing no one. Josh followed them through the room to the kitchen, again finding no one. Matt looked out the kitchen window into the back yard.

"The car is gone, Amy," Matt said. "Maybe we lucked out and they aren't home."

Josh motioned for his dad and Todd to come into the house. "It looks like their parents aren't home."

They looked around the cluttered living room and kitchen, which obviously had not been cleaned in a while. Matt noticed them eying the surroundings and said, "It never looked this bad when we were here.

Amy and I always tried to keep their messes cleaned up. They pretty much do nothing," he said, pointing to empty pizza boxes and take-out containers.

Josh patted Matt on the back and said, "Their lifestyle is no reflection on you and Amy. Everyone makes their own choices."

"Yeah, I know," Matt agreed. "I'm going to grab some clothes and a few things from my room so we can get out of here."

Josh followed Matt down the hallway and noticed Amy standing in the doorway to her bedroom. He stepped up behind her and put his arm around her waist.

"Are you okay?" he asked softly.

"Yeah," she replied. "I was just thinking that I should have some sentimental attachment to my home. But I don't. This place means nothing to me. It has been the source of lots of heartache, and very little happiness. I'm just going to grab some clothes and I'm ready to leave. I'll get what little I have left when we are ready to move into the apartment."

It took Amy and Matt less than fifteen minutes to gather what they wanted. When they walked out the door, she left it unlocked. Just like she found it. Neither of them bothered to look back.

* * *

JC's Hope was in full swing for the summer. There was the usual group of kids who had been coming to the center ever since it opened, in addition to other teens who stopped by occasionally. A couple scout masters from one of the local Boy Scout troops had been coming by, hoping to encourage some of the kids to join the scouts. Their efforts had proven to be successful. Several of the boys had decided to join the scouts, and were quickly making a few friends outside the center.

Mike Slater had generously donated half a dozen computers to the center, and it was a common sight to see several of the older kids bent over computers as they browsed college websites. Even with an influx of new kids, Josh was pleased that there had been very few problems.

Other than the incident with Matt's dad, things had run smoothly. All the teenagers appeared to abide by the Code of Conduct, and they held each other accountable for their actions.

There were always activities scheduled, both inside and outside the building, and the grassed picnic area had proven to be a popular place to hang out in the summer weather. The picnic area and the parking lot were hubs of activity on this warm morning, because of the barbecue scheduled for midafternoon.

Once a notice had been posted on the bulletin board to let everyone know about the upcoming barbecue, several of the kids had offered to help in any way they could. Mike had recruited a handful of boys to help him load and unload barbecue grills to use for the event. As Josh walked out of the center, Mike was just backing his truck up to the picnic area to unload grills. Four boys hopped out of the truck and climbed into the back.

Josh walked up and began helping Mike unstrap the grills. "Thanks for your help rounding up the grills, Mike," Josh said as he worked. "That will make the barbecue go a lot smoother."

"Okay, boys," Mike said. "Don't forget how heavy those grills are. Just be careful and don't hurt yourselves."

"We got it, Mike," said one of the older boys. "Not a problem."

Within fifteen minutes, there were four large grills lined up alongside the grassed picnic area. Todd and Aiden brought in additional fold-up tables and chairs to add to the existing picnic tables. Travis had several boys helping him rope off a section of the parking lot near the park area where the extra tables and chairs would be set up. Josh poked his head into the main door of the center and asked for help to unload and set up the tables and chairs. Within a few minutes, more than a dozen teenagers were eagerly carrying tables and chairs from Todd's pickup, and setting them up in the roped-off area.

When Meghan and Ryleigh pulled into the parking lot, their car was surrounded by kids anxious to help carry food and supplies into the kitchen. Kaci and Amy had been doing preliminary meal prep for a couple hours, and the refrigerator was already filled with food for the barbecue.

Amy spotted Brittany carrying in a large bowl of salad. "Brittany, would you go out and tell Josh to let everyone know we have sandwiches, chips, cookies, and drinks ready for a snack. I'm sure they are ready for a little something to eat, and the barbecue won't be until later this afternoon."

"Sure, Amy," Brittany replied with a smile as she headed back outside.

Word must have spread quickly outside, because it didn't take long before hungry teenagers and adults swarmed the large kitchen. Everyone took a paper plate from the counter and filled it with a sandwich and cookies, then grabbed a small bag of chips and a drink from the table, before heading back outside to eat.

A light breeze blew through the trees, welcomed by everyone who had been busy setting things up outside. By the time people had settled in to enjoy their lunch snack, things outside were ready for the afternoon event. After having a bite to eat, most of the kids went back into the center to continue their activities, while the adults sat outside visiting at the picnic tables.

"You know, JC," Mike said, looking across the table at Josh. "You should be proud of yourself. The center has come together nicely, and it has sure been a hit with the kids in town. You've done a good thing here, son."

"Thanks, Mike," Josh said. "But it's been a team effort. None of this could have happened without you and my family. I am beyond blessed. And we have met so many great kids who have come into the center. Kids who were so shy and emotionally beaten down when they started coming around, you wouldn't even recognize them now. And kids like Brandon, who has so much musical talent but had no way to develop it. And Rick, who could have very easily fallen in with the wrong crowd and gone down a destructive path. Now he's looking at joining the Army. And Matt. I can't begin to tell you how much he has changed since I first met him. The changes in some of these kids have been phenomenal. Kids can flourish if they are given encouragement and have a safe environment."

"And you are providing both those things, Josh," his uncle Todd said in agreement. "You don't give yourself enough credit. I have seen you with some of these kids. You have been able to reach them in ways other people only dream of. You have been blessed with an incredible gift, JC."

"Any gift I have comes from God. So He gets all the credit. I'm just the messenger," Josh replied.

"Amen," Travis said as he stood. "Well, gang, should we get this barbecue started?"

Mike stood and patted his stomach as he said, "Sounds like a good idea to me. That snack has had plenty of time to settle. Let's get the show on the road!"

As the group of adults walked toward the building, Mike looked at Josh and asked, "What do you want me to do, JC? I didn't come here just to eat. I plan to help out just like everyone else."

Josh nudged his dad's shoulder as he said, "Says the man who supplied all the food." Turning to Mike, he said, "What would you like to do? I'll leave it up to you."

"I grill a pretty mean burger, if I do say so myself," Mike replied with a grin. "I could man one of the grills, if you want me to."

"That sounds like a great idea," Josh agreed. "We've got four grills. Why don't we plan to use two of them to grill the burgers, one for hotdogs, and the other one to grill corn on the cob. Uncle Todd, you grill the best corn on the cob I've ever eaten. Would you mind grilling the corn?"

"You got it, JC," Todd agreed.

"Mike will handle one of the grills for burgers," Josh said. "Who wants to man the second grill for burgers, and the grill for the hotdogs? I can do one of them, if you guys want me to."

"Josh," Travis began. "This is your event. You should probably be free to roam around and make sure everyone is getting what they need. Aiden and I can man the other two grills. Does that work for you, Aiden?"

"Sure," Aiden agreed. "And don't worry, I won't eat more than I cook!"

In no time at all, the aroma of barbecued food filled the air. Kids were drawn outside by the tantalizing smells, and were milling around the picnic area offering their assistance. A handful of teenagers were tossing around a frisbee off to the side, making sure not to interfere with the grills.

When the food was nearly done, teenagers began making trips to and from the building, carrying the remainder of the food from the kitchen. Two long tables had been set up behind the grills. They were soon loaded with baked beans, several salads and other side dishes, fresh fruit, and an assortment of desserts. An empty place was left in the middle of one of the tables to put the platters of burgers, hotdogs, and corn from the grills.

Josh stepped off to the side of the grills and raised his hand to get everyone's attention. "It looks like the food is ready to go. Why don't we have a quick blessing on the food, then you guys can dig in." Turning to Travis, Josh asked, "Dad, would you mind asking the blessing?"

"I'd love to," Travis replied. "Dear loving God, thank you for showering your blessings on JC's Hope, and for providing a haven for these young people. We ask that you bless this food, and the many hands who made this event possible. In Jesus's name, we pray. Amen."

"Okay, let's eat!" Josh said with a smile. "There's plenty of food, so don't run. Once everyone has made it through the line, you're free to return for seconds. Enjoy!"

The adults stood back and watched as the teenagers made a mad dash for the buffet tables. When all the kids had grabbed plates of food, the adults began working their way through the line, chattering nearly as much as the kids had. Josh and Amy were at the end of the line, talking to each other as they filled their plates. They each took a bottle of water from the cooler at the end of the food line, then looked around to find an empty place at one of the tables. They spotted an empty table at the edge of the grassy area and sat down beside each other. They were soon enjoying the food and quiet conversation, seemingly oblivious to all the excitement around them.

Sitting next to Travis at a table across the small park, Mike nodded in the direction of Josh and Amy. "Those two seem to be rather fond of each other."

Travis smiled as he looked at his son, who appeared to be laughing at something Amy had said. "Yeah, they've been spending a fair amount of time together. And I've noticed that Josh is very protective of her. I think they're good for each other. He has helped her relax and come out of her shell a bit. Especially after the trouble with her dad. And I don't really know how to explain it, but Amy seems to have helped Josh get back some of who he was before the accident."

"She's a remarkable young woman." Mike said with admiration. "I'm glad you guys were able to help her and her brother out."

"Me too," Meghan added. "Do you know how the apartment is coming along, Mike? Amy has been enjoying staying with us. She and Ryleigh are becoming great friends. But I also know she's anxious to get into her own apartment with Matt. I think she misses having her brother around."

"I stopped by there yesterday," Mike replied. "It looks like it should be ready by the end of the week. I'm going to move some furniture in there too, so it will be a furnished apartment. I don't imagine she has much in the way of furniture."

"You're right," Meghan said in agreement. "They don't have much more than their clothes and a few meager belongings. I'm sure she and Matt will appreciate anything they get."

"Travis," Mike began. "Why don't you and Meghan contact me in a couple days, and we'll set up a time for you to go look at the apartment. That way maybe you can tell me if there's anything else they might need to make it comfortable for them. They should be able to move in this coming weekend."

"It's a good thing I put Matt to work at the shop," Todd said. "That way I'll still be able to see him nearly every day. I'm going to miss having him at the house. He's a good kid."

* * *

Early Saturday morning, Josh pulled into the driveway at his parents' home. As much as he enjoyed the guy time with his cousin Aiden, it would be nice to have his own room back. He told Amy to be up early and ready to go this morning, because he had a surprise for her. Just as he climbed out of his Jeep, his uncle Todd pulled his pickup into the driveway behind him. Matt sat in the passenger seat, also clueless to the surprise that awaited them.

Travis and Meghan had met up with Mike yesterday and had gotten the keys to the apartment. As expected, Mike had done a fantastic job furnishing the small apartment. It looked very homey. The three of them were waiting for Josh and Todd to bring Amy and Matt over to the apartment complex. Then they would go over to their house and gather the last of their belongings and get them officially moved into their own place.

Amy walked outside and started toward Josh's Jeep. She looked at her brother in surprise. "Hi, Matt! I didn't know you were going to be here this morning."

Matt just shrugged his shoulders and said, with a sleepy expression. "I don't know what's going on. Todd just dragged me out of bed and said he had a surprise. I hope at some point the surprise includes breakfast. I'm starved!"

Todd laughed as he patted Matt on the back and said, "Don't worry, kiddo, I'll make sure you get breakfast." Turning to Josh, he asked, "Are we ready to go?"

Josh grinned as he said, "Let's go!"

Twenty minutes later, Amy looked over at Josh as she spotted Meghan's Jeep Cherokee in the parking lot of a nice apartment complex. "Isn't that your mom's car, Josh?"

Josh looked in the direction she was pointing, and replied with feigned innocence, "Boy, it sure looks like it."

Amy could no longer contain her excitement as she climbed out of the Jeep and took Josh by the hand. "Well, come on! Let's go!"

Amy released Josh's hand the moment she spotted Meghan standing in front of a ground-floor apartment nonchalantly holding up a set of keys. She rushed up to Meghan and asked, "Is this it? Is this really our apartment?"

Turning to Josh, she said, "Oh, my gosh! There's going to be so much to do! I'll have to find some used furniture, get groceries, move our things over here. It's going to be a busy day!"

Josh took the keys his mom was still dangling, and handed them to Amy. "Why don't you go inside and look around. Then we can help you decide what you may still need."

Amy took the keys from Josh, then looked around for her brother. She reached her hand out for him and said, "Here, Matt, you unlock the door. My hands are shaking."

Matt gladly took the keys, unlocked and opened the door, then motioned his sister into the apartment. He stepped in behind her and nearly bumped into her because she had come to a complete stop just inside the door. Matt walked around to stand beside her as they surveyed the scene in front of them.

Without saying a word, Amy and Matt wandered through the apartment as the others remained in the living room. A few minutes later, they returned, and were both shaking their heads.

"I don't believe it," Amy said, with tears in her eyes. "This place is already furnished. We don't need anything. It's beautiful."

Being a typical teenager, Matt said, "Well, we'll need to go to the grocery store."

Todd grinned as he put his arm around Matt's shoulder and steered him toward the kitchen. He opened the refrigerator, which was already completely stocked. Then he opened several of the cupboards, revealing a well-stocked pantry, along with the essential dishes, cookware, and utensils they would need.

Amy walked over to Josh, buried her head in his chest and began sobbing. He pulled her into an embrace and simply let her release her emotions. After a few minutes, she pulled away and turned to looked at the others.

"Who do I have to thank for all this?" she asked, her eyes still wet with gratitude.

Josh nodded in Mike's direction and said, "Mike owns the apartment building. He had the furnishings delivered and stocked the kitchen."

Amy looked at Mike and shook her head. "You didn't need to do all this," she said as she walked over and gave him a big hug.

Mike laughed as he replied, "I rarely do what I need to do. It's a lot more fun to do what I want to do. And I wanted to do this for you and Matt. Why don't we all look around and you can let me know if there is anything else you need."

Everyone let Amy lead them through a tour of the apartment. She pointed out that there was even a small desk, already set up with a laptop computer, in Matt's room. There was another small desk off to the side in the living room. Each room had the basic furnishings, along with a few little extra touches.

As they were returning to the living room, Amy asked if anyone knew where Matt was. He had not joined them on the impromptu tour.

Todd laughed as he pointed to the kitchen, where Matt was happily munching on chocolate chip cookies, washing them down with a tall glass of milk.

Matt looked at the adults and shrugged, while he wiped the milk off his mouth with the back of his hand. "What? I told you I was starving!"

Mike started herding everyone toward the door as he laughed out loud. "Let's go feed this boy! Breakfast is on me!"

Chapter Seventeen

Todd stood in the shade alongside one of the buildings at Byers Construction, his arms folded across his chest and a satisfied grin on his face. He was watching Matt maneuver the Bobcat through a course of traffic cones set up in the parking lot. True to his promise, Matt had proven to be an outstanding apprentice at the construction company, so Todd gladly held up his end of the promise. He had been teaching Matt how to drive some of the equipment. The teenager was proving to be a quick learner and an eager student.

Matt pulled the Bobcat to a stop in front of Todd and climbed out of the cab sporting a huge grin.

"How'd I do, Todd?"

Todd smiled as he patted Matt on the back.

"You never cease to amaze me, Matt," Todd replied. "You're maneuvering that Bobcat like you've been doing it for years. Do you think you're ready to learn how to operate the bucket on it? Driving it is the easy part."

"You bet!" Matt said excitedly. "When can we start?"

Todd laughed as he replied. "I remember being that excited when Dad taught me how to use the Bobcat. Then you move on to the bigger pieces of equipment and begin to think of the Bobcat as a Tinkertoy. How about we grab a bite of lunch, then jump on the bucket training right after lunch."

"Sounds great!"

After wolfing down his lunch in a hurry, Matt urged Todd back out to the parking lot for more training. Todd showed him the basics of how to operate the bucket on the front of the Bobcat, then instructed Matt to follow him around to the back of the shop. Matt pulled the Bobcat to a stop in front of a large pile of dirt.

"Do I get to move some dirt?" Matt asked hopefully.

"Yes," Todd laughed. "You get to move some dirt. I want you to start moving some of the dirt from the large pile over about ten yards or so and start a new pile. Now, Matt, it's important that you remember what you've learned. Don't get cocky. Don't lift the bucket too high. Remember, baby steps. You'll get the hang of it, but don't forget that you're still learning. Safety first. You understand?"

With determination showing on his face, Matt nodded and said, "Got it. I promise, I'll go slow and not do anything stupid."

Todd stepped back and watched Matt approach the pile of dirt cautiously. He pushed the bucket into the soft dirt, lifted it slightly, then tipped the bucket back like Todd had taught him. Raising the bucket a couple feet, he backed away from the dirt pile and drove over to where he would start his new pile. He raised the bucket a little more, tipped it forward, and dumped the contents onto the ground. Backing away from the small mound of dirt, Matt returned to the larger pile to scoop up another bucket of dirt.

Todd nodded with satisfaction as he watched Matt's small mound of dirt grow with each new bucketful.

"Hey, Dad!" Aiden yelled across the parking lot to get Todd's attention.

Aiden looked over at Matt's progress as he walked up to his dad.

"Matt seems to be catching on quick," Aiden said.

"Yeah," Todd agreed. "He's a determined kid. He wants to learn everything, and learn it now. What's up?"

"Aunt Meghan needs you in the office," Aiden explained. "There's a problem with one of the suppliers and it looks like you may have to cut them off. She wants your opinion."

"Okay," Todd replied as he headed toward the office. "You stay here and keep an eye on Matt. Give him another twenty minutes or so, then have him park the Bobcat and go help the guys in the warehouse."

"You got it, Dad. Even though, from the looks of it, I may have to drag him off the Bobcat."

"You could be right, son," Todd replied, laughing. "Just drag him off gently."

Todd looked back at Matt happily moving dirt with the Bobcat, then reluctantly walked toward the office. As much as he would rather be operating the heavy equipment, he realized the management part of the business was a necessary evil he couldn't avoid.

Aiden allowed Matt to work on the Bobcat for another half hour before waving him to a stop. Matt drove the Bobcat over to Aiden and shut down the engine.

"What's up, Aiden?" Matt asked.

"Dad had to go up to the office, but he said that's enough work with the Bobcat today. He wants you to go help out in the warehouse now."

"Okay," Matt reluctantly agreed. "Where do you want me to park the Bobcat?"

"Why don't you park it alongside the shop, and I'll meet you over there," Aiden instructed.

Aiden walked over to the shop where he watched Matt carefully park the Bobcat next to the building.

"Nice job, Matt," Aiden said, shaking Matt's hand when he climbed down from the Bobcat. "You did a great job out there today. Dad was very impressed at how quickly you caught on. You're a natural."

"Thanks, Aiden," Matt said with a huge grin. "You and JC were so lucky, getting to grow up working with all that equipment."

"Don't forget the girls," Aiden laughed. "You should see Aunt Meghan operate a bulldozer! She can work circles around most men in the construction industry. It's pretty cool."

"That's awesome," Matt replied. "Do you think Todd will teach me how to operate the bulldozer one of these days?"

"I have no doubt, Matt. You have shown a real eagerness to learn, and that's important to Dad. And you appear to have some natural ability, which helps too."

The two continued talking as they walked over to the warehouse. Once inside the large building, Aiden instructed Matt to continue working on straightening items on the shelves, and to help the other men wherever he was needed.

Before he walked off, Aiden put his arm around Matt's shoulder. "You know, Matt, Dad really likes you. He has a lot of respect for you. He doesn't always tell people how he feels, but he's going to miss having you around here when school starts back in a couple weeks."

"Wow, really?" Matt asked quietly. "I wish I had grown up with a dad like Todd. You're pretty lucky, Aiden."

"Believe me, Matt, I know how fortunate I am. And I realize not everyone was blessed with parents like mine and JC's. Just remember, it doesn't matter where you came from. What matters is where you're going. You have the opportunity to do big things with your life."

Matt looked down at the ground as he dug the toe of his boot into the dirt. "Aiden, do you think Todd would hire me to work full time for him?"

"That's kind of up to you, Matt," Aiden replied. "You know Dad's rules. You have to stay in school, get good grades, and graduate on time."

"Yeah, that's what I mean. After I graduate."

"Obviously, I can't speak for Dad," Aiden said. "But you're a good worker. You learn new things quickly, and you're willing to start at the bottom and do whatever he needs you to do. Those are important qualities to Dad. Of course, it doesn't hurt that he likes you too," Aiden added with a chuckle.

"Don't worry, Aiden," Matt said confidently. "I'm going to graduate on time, and I'll make Todd proud of me."

"He's already proud of you, Matt," Aiden replied. "Now get in there and get to work."

"I'm on it, Aiden!" Matt said as he walked away. "Talk to you later. I've got work to do!"

* * *

As she heard the doorbell ring, it made Amy smile. She had never before had a reason to smile at the sound of a simple doorbell, but life was a little different now. The doorbell meant someone had stopped by her apartment to see her. Or to see her brother Matt. Either way, she always smiled at the prospect of visitors. After peering through the peephole in the door, her grin widened when she saw Josh standing on the porch.

"Hey, Josh," she said after opening the door. "This is a pleasant surprise."

After stepping inside the apartment, Josh greeted her with a kiss.

"I stopped by to see if you had any plans today. I was hoping you might be free to go on a picnic. There's a nice lake about twenty-five miles from here, just as you start toward the mountains. It's a perfect place for a picnic. What do you say?"

"Well," Amy began. "I was going to take advantage of Matt working today and get the apartment cleaned. A picnic would be a lot more fun. Aren't you working at the center today?"

"No," Josh answered. "I gave myself the day off. There are plenty of others there to hold down the fort today."

"Okay," Amy agreed. "It sounds like fun. Let's do it! We'll have to throw together some food though. I should be able to scrounge up something."

Josh reached out to take her hand as he said, "Not to worry, my dear. I already have a cooler packed and in the Jeep."

Amy nudged him with her shoulder as she remarked, "You must have been pretty sure I would agree to go."

Josh simply shrugged and replied, "Of course. Who wouldn't want to go on a picnic with me? Besides, if you turned me down, I already had a big lunch packed."

"Let me just grab my purse," she said laughing. "A picnic beats cleaning house any day of the week!"

As the two walked toward the Jeep, Josh said, "I hope you don't mind. I put the top down on the Jeep. The weather is perfect, and I love driving with the top down."

"I don't mind at all," Amy reassured him. "Having the wind blow through my hair as we drive toward the mountains has a sense of adventure to it. I could pretend to be one of those movie stars you always see cruising down the highway, wearing sunglasses with the wind blowing her hair."

"I knew I liked you," Josh said with a smile as he helped her into the Jeep.

As soon as they were out of town and headed toward the lake, Josh cranked up the music. He already knew how much Amy loved country music, so he had one of his favorite Garth Brooks CDs playing. He glanced over to see her swaying in her seat to the music.

"Sing it, girl," Josh said with a smile. "You know you want to. Belt it out!"

By the time they arrived at the lake, Amy had convinced Josh to join her in singing along to the music. They pulled into a parking spot just as a song ended. Josh jumped out and walked around the Jeep to help Amy out. He pulled her into his arms and placed a tender kiss on her lips, before reaching into the back of the Jeep to grab the cooler.

Walking toward the lake, Josh asked, "Do you want to eat at one of the picnic tables, or would you rather sit on a blanket on the ground? I'm prepared either way."

"Oh, a blanket on the ground, absolutely," Amy replied. "That sounds like the only way to enjoy a picnic at a lake."

"I agree."

"Oh, Josh, let's go over there where we can watch the ducks."

"Lead the way," Josh replied before adding with a laugh. "As long as you don't make me pack the cooler all the way around the lake!"

Amy found the perfect grassy area for their picnic, and Josh sat the cooler down and spread out the blanket on the ground. Amy sat beside Josh on the blanket, and he pulled her close as they watched the ducks and enjoyed the beautiful weather. When they began to get hungry, Amy peeked inside the cooler and was impressed at what she found. He had packed sandwiches, a container with macaroni salad, a second container with cut-up cantaloupe and watermelon, a container with chocolate chip cookies, and cans of soda.

"Wow," Amy said. "I'm impressed. Just how many people did you think were going on this picnic?"

"Hey," Josh replied with a shrug of his shoulders. "I'm a growing boy."

Amy laughed as she began removing containers from the cooler. "I seriously doubt you're still growing, Josh. We'll just chalk it up to the fact you like to eat."

After enjoying the lunch, Josh began packing things back in the cooler. "Let me run the cooler and blanket back to the Jeep, then maybe we can walk around the lake for a bit."

"I'd like that," Amy replied. "The weather is absolutely perfect."

Josh met Amy back at the lake where she was enjoying watching the antics of the ducks. He took her by the hand, and they began slowly strolling around the lake, stopping periodically to look at things that caught their interest. On the far side of the lake, Amy spotted a large log among some cattails. She released Josh's hand and worked her way through the reeds, climbing onto the log and sitting down. She looked so incredibly happy and peaceful, staring out at the lake. It made Josh's heart melt. He pulled his cell phone from his pocket and snapped several pictures of Amy. After reviewing the pictures with satisfaction, he put the phone back in his pocket and walked over to sit beside her on the log. They sat for a long time in companionable silence, simply enjoying each other's company and the gorgeous scenery.

When they were ready to continue their trek around the lake, Josh reached out his hand to help Amy from the log. After making their way back through the cattails to the grassy area, he put his arm around her waist as they gazed out onto the lake. He turned her toward him so her back was to the lake, and pulled her into his arms. He placed a tender kiss on her lips, then backed away slightly, still holding her in his arms.

"You know, Amy," Josh said quietly. "You are the most beautiful woman I've ever known."

Amy looked down and blushed slightly before replying. "I think the scenery has clouded your vision. I'm not that beautiful."

"Oh, but you are, Amy. And you are just as beautiful on the inside as you are on the outside."

Amy smiled up at Josh and said, "Thanks, Josh. No one has ever said that to me before."

"Then everyone must be blind." Josh simply gazed at her as he continued holding her in his arms. "Amy, there's something you need to know."

She looked into his eyes, wondering what was on his mind.

"I love you, Amy. And I really hope you have feelings for me as well."

Amy reached up and wrapped her arms around his neck. She looked into his eyes and smiled as she said, "Yes, Josh, I definitely have feelings for you. I think I've known for a while. I love you too."

He pulled her close as they shared a kiss with new meaning. This was the woman he loved, and he was never going to let her get away.

Suddenly, Amy released Josh's hand and took off running toward the Jeep, laughing all the way. "Last one to the Jeep has to walk back to town!"

Josh laughed as he shook his keys in the air. "I won't be walking if I have the keys!" Then he took off at a dead run, attempting to catch her. On his way to the Jeep, he ran past another young couple sitting on a blanket on the ground. He looked at them, grinning, and yelled, "She said she loves me!"

The young man chuckled and yelled back, "Then you better hurry and don't let her get away!"

"That's the plan!" Josh yelled over his shoulder.

Chapter Eighteen

JC's Hope was a hub of activity as the center began transitioning from summer crowds back to school being in session. School would be starting in a few days, so life at the center needed to adjust to different crowds and different schedules. Many of the teenagers who were regulars at the center during the school year had only shown up sporadically during the summer months. They had quickly snatched up what few local summer jobs were available for teenagers, and treasured the opportunity to earn some money. Now that school would be back in session, the center would begin seeing some of those kids again after school let out for the day.

Matt fell into that group of teenagers. He had been fortunate to get a summer job working at Byers Construction, so he didn't spend as much time around the center. Travis saw him walk in the front door as he came out of one of the classrooms.

"Hey, Matt," Travis called to him. "It's good to see you. We've kind of missed you around here this summer."

"Hey, Pastor Harmon," Matt replied as he shook his hand. "Well, you'll be seeing more of me in a few days. I've only got a couple more days working with Todd, then it's back to school."

"How have you liked working over there?" Travis asked.

Matt's face lit up as he replied. "It's been great! I love it! Did Todd tell you he let me operate the bulldozer a little bit?"

"Yes," Travis replied with a smile. "He said you had a grin on your face for a week afterward."

Matt laughed. "Yeah, probably. It was a ton of fun! I can't wait to get more time on it, but it will probably be a while now, since school will be starting."

"Patience, my boy," Travis laughed. "Todd was also very impressed at how quickly you learned to operate the Bobcat. You may very well have found your calling in the construction industry, Matt."

"I hope so," Matt replied. "I'm hoping Todd will hire me after I graduate. He already said I have a job for next summer if I want it."

"That's great, Matt," Travis said. "Well, I was just heading out for a meeting at the church. It will be nice seeing you back here at the center. Just let me know if you need anything. Oh, JC is down in the music room. Why don't you stop by and say hi? I know he'd love to see you."

"Thanks, I'll do that. See you later."

Matt walked down the hallway toward the sound coming from the music room. He heard voices and suspected Brandon might be in the room with JC. Not wanting to interrupt, he opened the door quietly and slipped inside. Brandon was playing the keyboard, while JC was at the piano. Once the music stopped, Matt clapped his hands in appreciation. JC and Brandon smiled as they turned to greet their fan.

"That's a pretty cool song," Matt said. "I don't think I've heard it before."

"I would be surprised if you had," JC replied. "It's a song Brandon and I have been writing. Do you like it?"

"Yeah! You guys wrote that?"

Brandon smiled and said, "Yeah, JC writes a lot of good music. We've been working on some together this summer."

"Don't sell yourself short, Brandon," JC reminded the teenager. "I couldn't have written some of this stuff without you. You're very talented."

Matt looked over at Brandon, still seated at the keyboard. "I knew you played the piano, Brandon, but I didn't know you wrote music too. That's pretty cool."

"I had never written any music before," Brandon replied. "JC has written several songs, and he started working with me on some songs together. I have written one on my own now, and JC said it's pretty good."

"Correction, Brandon," JC interjected. "It's very good! In fact, Matt, Brandon and I are working on recording some of our original music on a CD."

"Really?" Matt said in surprise. "You two are going to record a CD? That's awesome! I wish I had that kind of talent, but I'm all thumbs when it comes to playing a musical instrument. I'm more comfortable with a baseball in my hand."

Brandon laughed. "And I would be lucky to catch a baseball with a bucket."

"You both have talents that are perfect for you," JC replied. "Brandon has been spending part of the summer developing his musical talents, and you Matt, have been developing skills for use in the construction industry. And I understand from Aiden that you're getting very comfortable on the Bobcat."

"Yeah, it's been fun learning how to operate some of the equipment. Todd gave me my first taste of driving the bulldozer the other day. I can't wait to learn more about that. But I also want to learn how to do the carpentry. It would be fun to be able to build houses and stuff."

"Did you know my mom designed and built our house?" JC asked.

"No! You're kidding!" Matt said in surprise.

Brandon looked at JC and asked, "Are you serious, JC?"

"Yep," JC said proudly. "My mom has a lot of hidden talents. In fact, that's how my parents met. Dad also built custom houses, and he stumbled across Mom using a bulldozer to clear the property where she eventually built the house. Of course, Dad didn't know when he stopped to watch the bulldozer that the operator was a woman. It was quite a shock to him!"

"Yeah, I bet," Matt said with a chuckle. "I didn't know Pastor Harmon built houses. I should talk to him about that sometime. That's something I could see myself doing some day."

"I'm surprised Todd didn't mention it to you," JC said. "If that's something you might want to pursue as a career, Dad and Mom would be great people to talk to. They've had decades of experience. And, of course, working with Todd will be a huge benefit. You can learn a lot from him if you pay attention."

JC stood and stretched his back. "Well, guys, I've got some work to do so I'd better get going. Good job today, Brandon."

"Thanks, JC," Brandon replied. "See you later."

Matt sat down at the piano bench vacated by JC, and the two teenagers began talking. JC watched them as he turned to close the door behind him, and marveled at how different the two boys were. Yet they seemed to be good for each other. It shouldn't, but it always amazed him how the kids at the center became support systems for each other. Those friendships were vital to the success of each kid who passed through the doors of JC's Hope.

* * *

Things were settling into the new daily routine at the center, with the mornings being a bit quieter. Travis was able to spend some time working on his sermons in the office, Josh was able to focus on his music a bit more, and Amy had taken charge of keeping the kitchen stocked and handling the bulk of the tutoring. The afternoons kept everyone hopping as teenagers once again filled the gym shortly after school let out for the day. The computers had become so popular in the classrooms that Josh had to implement sign-up sheets so everyone would have a chance to use them. A scout master from one of the local Boy Scout troops made arrangements to use one of the classrooms once a week to help some of the younger boys work on merit badge projects. All in all, Josh was pleased with how busy the center had become. If the center was busy, that meant kids were being helped.

Mike Slater walked in the front door and immediately headed over to the arcade games. He looked over the shoulder of the boy playing the baseball game and remarked, "I see no one has beat my best score yet."

Without taking his eyes off the game, the boy said, "It's only a matter of time, Mike. Kyle isn't far behind you."

Mike laughed and said, "It's bound to happen eventually. Do you know if JC is around?"

The boy nodded his head in the direction of the hallway and replied, "I think he's down in the office."

"Thanks," Mike replied. "Catch you later."

Mike tapped on the open office door before walking in. "Hey, JC, do you have a minute?"

Josh stood and shook Mike's hand. "I always have time for you, Mike. What's up?"

"I thought you and maybe one of the other boys could help me bring some things in from the truck."

As they walked back down the hallway, Josh asked, "What have you done now, Mike?"

"Nothing much," Mike replied with a wave of his hand. "Hey, Rick, can you come give us a hand for a minute?"

Rick tossed a basketball to another boy and jogged over toward the two men. "Sure, Mike. What do you need?"

Mike led them to his pickup parked just outside the door. "I picked up a couple more laptops for the classrooms. I saw the sign-up sheet the other day and figured you could maybe use a couple more."

Rick looked inside the pickup, then turned to Mike. "I always thought a couple meant two."

Josh peered over Rick's head and said, "I'm not sure Mike can count very well. There must be boxes for at least six laptops there."

Mike started handing boxes over to Josh and Rick, then said, "Oh, there's a printer in there somewhere too."

Josh shook his head and said with a smile, "What are we going to do with you, Mike?"

"Just invite me over for dinner next time Kaci fixes spaghetti, and we'll call it square."

"I think she's planning that for Saturday night," Josh replied. "I'll tell her to set an extra place at the table."

"Now see," Mike said with a chuckle. "That wasn't so hard, was it?"

The three headed back into the center, their arms loaded down with computer boxes, and Josh said, "God is good."

Without hesitation, Rick added, "All the time."

* * *

Before school started, Josh had given Brandon the task of researching what they needed to do to record their CD. Mike also put them in touch with a friend of his from the local radio station who offered his help, along with use of the studio at the radio station. It had become quite a task to coordinate everyone's schedules to make it happen, and the school year was well underway by the time they were able to do the recording.

Brandon was all smiles as they walked out of the radio station with several copies of their new CD, hot off the press. He looked at JC in awe as he ran his fingers over the CD cover.

"We did it, JC," Brandon said in amazement. "We really did it. We recorded our own music."

JC put his arm around the teen's shoulder and replied, "We sure did, Brandon. And I want to thank you for pushing me to do it. I had never considered recording any of my music until you mentioned it. Heck, I hadn't even written some of it down. I kept a lot of it in my head. I'm glad we did it."

"Thanks for helping me with my music, JC," Brandon said. "I never dreamed I would be able to write my own music. Then to hold it in my hand on a CD...I can't even describe it. When we had to sell my grandma's piano, I didn't think I would have a chance to play again. I sure didn't think I'd ever be able to compose music. I'm going to send a copy of the CD along with my college application. Maybe I can get a music scholarship to that college you were telling me about."

"That's a great idea, Brandon. As I've told you many times, you have a lot of talent. I'm confident you can get into a good music program. You have a bright future ahead of you. Just remember, don't ever sell yourself short."

"Thanks, JC," Brandon replied. "I can't believe how much my life has changed since I wandered into the music room during the center's open house."

"It's been a two-way street, Brandon. You have certainly enriched my life."

"Can I ask you something, JC?"

"Sure."

"You recorded one of your songs on a separate CD, as a single. I'm guessing it has a special meaning to you because you wrote lyrics and sang it too. You recorded your other songs as instrumentals. I had heard you play the song before, but today was the first time I heard you sing along as you played. It's a powerful song."

"Thanks, Brandon," JC said. "You're right. I usually write my music as instrumentals. I've only written lyrics to a couple of them. But this one is special."

As they drove out of the radio station's parking lot, Brandon turned to JC and said, "Someday, when you're ready, you need to tell me why it's special."

JC smiled and said, "You know, Brandon, if music doesn't work out for you, you should consider going into counseling."

* * *

Josh sat back and looked at the finished CD with satisfaction. He had printed a nice label and affixed it to the CD. He had also designed a cover using his favorite photo of Amy sitting on the log at the lake. After printing the cover on high quality paper, the finished CD looked as professional as anything you could buy in a music store. "Rising from the Ashes" by Joshua Christopher Harmon.

The next step...presenting it to Amy, along with a ring, when he asks her to be his wife.

Chapter Nineteen

Josh sat in his office at the center, watching the hands on the clock turn slowly. It was almost three o'clock, so school would be letting out in a few minutes. Matt had been coming to the center right after school every day for the past several weeks, and Josh hoped today would be no different.

Maybe I'll wander down to the gym, Josh thought to himself. *I'm going to drive myself crazy staring at the clock.*

Picking up a basketball from the cart, Josh took advantage of the empty gym and started shooting baskets. He had already made several free throws in a row and backed off to attempt a long shot. Just as he released the ball, the front door opened, and he turned to see Matt standing there.

"Nice shot, JC!" Matt said with a grin.

Josh turned back toward the basket in time to see the ball bounce off to the side of the court.

"I missed it," Josh laughed. "Did it go in?"

"Yep," Matt replied. "A three-point swisher. It's a good thing you finished with a nice basket because the court is about to be overrun. Some of the guys are right behind me, and they're already choosing sides for a game."

"Oh," Josh said with disappointment. "Were you planning to play?"

"No," Matt answered. "I was thinking I'd try to snag one of the computers and work on my history paper."

"If I guarantee you'll have a computer to work on, do you have a few minutes to talk first?"

"Sure. What's up?"

Josh put his arm around Matt's shoulder and said, "Let's go down to my office for a few minutes."

After motioning for Matt to take a seat, Josh paced back and forth in front of his desk. Matt quietly watched him pace for several minutes before speaking up.

Matt smiled as he said, "JC, you look like a caged animal. What's up?"

Josh stopped pacing suddenly, as if he had forgotten Matt was in the room.

"Oh, sorry," Josh apologized. "I guess that was rude of me."

He leaned back against his desk, facing Matt. "I wanted to talk to you about something."

"Did I do something wrong, JC?"

"No!" Josh instantly replied. "Not at all. I want to talk to you about your sister."

Matt jumped to his feet. "Did something happen to Amy?"

"No, she's fine," Josh replied as he patted Matt on the shoulder. He pointed to the chair Matt had been sitting in and said, "Sit back down, Matt."

Josh pulled up a chair and sat facing Matt. "I'm sorry, Matt. I didn't mean to worry you. I'm really messing this up. I've never done this before, and I don't have a clue what I'm doing."

"Well, you sure have me confused," Matt said with a laugh.

"I bet," Josh laughed. "Let me start over. Matt, you know I've been spending a lot of time with your sister."

Matt grinned. "Yeah, you're all she talks about."

"Really?" Josh asked, unsure of himself.

"Yes, really," Matt laughed. "JC, just say what you need to say. Unless you plan to do something that hurts my sister in some way, I've got your back."

Josh relaxed and sat back in his chair. "First of all, Matt, I would never do anything to hurt Amy. She's very important to me. I love her."

"So that explains the goofy look on your face," Matt said with a grin.

"I suppose it does," Josh agreed. "Matt, you're the most important person in Amy's life. You mean everything to her. Until your dad decides to quit drinking and be a father to you and Amy, you're the man of the family. As the man of the family, I want to ask if you have any objections to me asking Amy to marry me."

Matt didn't answer. He simply sat in his chair and let the grin on his face grow. He suddenly jumped up, grabbed Josh by the hand, and pulled him into a bear hug.

"JC, I think that's fantastic! I've always wanted a brother. You would be great for Amy. It will be nice for her to have someone besides me who would always watch out for her. Man, this is going to be so cool!"

"So," Josh began. "Does that mean you approve? Can I ask her to be my wife?"

"Yeah! When are you going to ask her?"

"I thought I would ask her to go on another picnic up at the lake before it gets too cold. Maybe tomorrow. Do you happen to know if she has any plans tomorrow afternoon?"

"I don't think so," Matt replied. "Do you want me to find out?"

"No," Josh said. "That's okay. She should be coming in before long to do some tutoring. I'll ask her then."

"Okay. Well, that history paper isn't going to write itself, so I better get to work on it."

"Let me know if there isn't a computer available for you," Josh said as a reminder.

Josh watched Matt walk down the hallway to one of the classrooms. Just before entering the classroom, he jumped in the air and pumped his fist, then casually walked through the door.

* * *

The fall weather was almost too cold for a picnic, but Amy had quickly agreed to go back to the lake. Dressed in jeans, boots, and hooded sweatshirts to ward off the cool breeze coming from the lake, Josh and Amy walked toward one of the picnic tables. Josh sat the small picnic basket on the bench before helping Amy spread a blanket over the table. Since neither had eaten lunch, and it was now mid-afternoon, they decided to go ahead and eat before taking a walk. Amy had packed the basket with a small, heated dish of lasagna, along with garlic bread and a thermos of hot cocoa.

"I'm glad you decided to make lasagna for our picnic," Josh said, as he helped take things from the cooler. "It's colder than I thought it would be today."

"But it's a perfect day for a picnic, Josh. The fall colors around the lake are beautiful." Then Amy added with a smile, "Besides, if it gets too cold, that just means you'll have to snuggle a little closer."

"That's a sacrifice I'm happy to make," Josh said as he leaned over and gave Amy a tender kiss.

The two ate in silence, as they watched ducks waddling in the grass along the lake. After finishing their meal, they packed things back into the picnic basket, keeping the thermos of hot cocoa out on the table. Amy folded the blanket and laid it on top of the basket.

"I'll run the picnic basket and blanket back to the Jeep," Josh said. "Then we can take the thermos with us and go for a walk around the lake. I'll be right back."

Amy picked up the thermos and began slowly walking toward the lake, giving Josh a chance to catch up to her. When he appeared at her side, she reached out for his hand, and they began walking in silence. This was only their second time to the lake together, but Amy already thought of it as their special place. This was where they both said 'I love you' for the first time.

They slowly made their way around the lake, stopping occasionally to watch the ducks. When they reached the big log on the opposite side of the lake, Josh took Amy by the hand and helped her up on the log. She started to turn so she was facing the lake, but Josh took her hand and turned her to face him.

"Amy," Josh began, still holding her hand. "Sit down for a minute."

Amy sat on the log, facing Josh, wondering why he didn't want her looking out on the lake.

Josh reached into the front pocket of his Levis and pulled out a small box, then knelt on the ground in front of the log.

Amy sucked in a breath of air, then covered her mouth with her hands.

"Amy," Josh began, as he opened the box to reveal a beautiful, yet simple ring. "I can't believe how lucky I am that God brought you into my life. There was a point after my car accident when I thought I would never feel whole again. But the day I spotted you sitting alone on the bleacher next to the baseball field, I knew you were going to change my life. Amy, I love you. Will you make me the happiest man alive and agree to be my wife?"

Amy practically launched herself off the log and into Josh's arms. She wrapped her arms around his neck and buried her head in his chest, tears streaming down her face.

Josh pulled her away from him slightly and looked into her eyes. "Uh," he began with a smile. "Does that mean yes? I'm going to need an actual answer."

"Yes, yes, yes!" Amy replied. "Yes, Josh, I will marry you!"

"Well, okay then," Josh said as he removed the ring from the box. "Let's make it official." And he slipped the perfectly-sized ring onto her finger, wrapped her in a tight embrace, and tenderly kissed his new fiancé.

Josh looked lovingly at Amy as she admired the ring on her finger. "When we get back to the Jeep, I have another little present for you."

"You mean there's more?" Amy asked, looking into his eyes.

"My dear," Josh replied. "There will always be more."

Amy reached over and took Josh by the hand and said with a grin, "I think it's time to head back to the Jeep."

The walk was brisk, partly in anticipation, and partly because the sun was dropping in the sky, and it was turning cold. Josh helped Amy into the Jeep, then got in on the driver's side, turned the key, and cranked up the heater.

As the Jeep warmed up, Josh reached into the pocket of his hooded sweatshirt and took out a CD, handing it to Amy. She stared at the picture of her sitting on the log next to the lake.

"I didn't know you took a picture of me that day," she said in amazement. "What is this? 'Rising from the Ashes' by Joshua Christopher Harmon. Is this a song you wrote?"

"Yes, it is," Josh replied. "I wrote this song for you. For us. It's our song, Amy."

She ran her fingers over the picture on the CD cover and asked, "Can we listen to it?"

"I would love for you to listen to it with me," Josh replied.

He popped the CD in, fastened his seatbelt, put the Jeep in gear, and drove away from the lake. Their lake. Listening to their song.

"God is good," Josh whispered.

"All the time," Amy added in a quiet voice.

* * *

Travis started a small fire in the fireplace at home while Meghan and Kaci put the finishing touches on dinner. Since Josh had called a family meeting on short notice, the girls opted for their old standby, spaghetti, tossed salad, and garlic bread. Jason was keeping the kids entertained in the family room until the doorbell rang and Mike Slater walked in.

"Mr. Mike! Mr. Mike!" Aaron and Sophie yelled in unison. "We didn't know you were coming over for dinner."

Mike let the kids take his hands and lead him to the sofa to sit. "I didn't know either until about an hour ago. But when your Uncle Josh told me your mama and grandma were making spaghetti, and I was supposed to come for dinner, I wasn't about to argue with him."

"Do you have any idea what this is all about, Travis?" Mike asked curiously.

Travis chuckled as he replied. "Not a clue, Mike. Josh just told me he had something important to discuss, and he wanted the whole family here. He made a point to say you needed to be here too."

Meghan walked in from the kitchen and greeted Mike with a hug. "Josh just texted me and said they would be here in a few minutes. So, I guess we'll find out soon enough." She looked across the room at her brother and sister-in-law and added, "I'm glad you happened to be off work tonight, Nicole."

"Me too," Nicole replied. "I have no idea what's going on, but if he wanted the whole family here, that's what he's going to get."

Travis heard Josh's Jeep pull up out front and said, "Well, it looks like we're about to find out what the big mystery is."

Josh and Amy walked in the door and were greeted by Josh's entire family. They looked around the room and smiled. "Good," Josh said happily. "It looks like everyone was able to make it. Matt, I'm glad you were able to come too. Thanks."

Meghan held her cell phone up for Josh to see. "I called Ryleigh, so she's on the phone and can hear what's going on too."

"Thanks, Mom," Josh said. Then added a little louder, "Glad you could phone in, Ry. I wanted you here too."

Ryleigh said through the phone, "I wouldn't miss whatever is going on that would cause you to call a family meeting. You hate family meetings."

Unable to contain their excitement any longer, Aaron and Sophie ran over to give their uncle a big hug. "Hi, Uncle Josh!" Sophie said.

"We came for spaghetti, Uncle Josh!" Aaron added.

Josh bent down to give the twins each a hug and said, "I'm glad you came for dinner, munchkins."

"We also came to find out what the big secret is," Aaron said.

"Well," Josh explained. "It's not so much a secret as it's something that people just don't know yet."

"If it's something people don't know," Sophie asked. "Doesn't that make it a secret?"

Travis laughed as Sophie climbed into his lap. "She's got you there, son."

Josh took Amy by the hand and faced everyone in the room. "We might as well clear up the secret," Josh said as he winked at his little niece.

"I have asked Amy to marry me," Josh said happily.

The clamor of voices filled the room as everyone began talking simultaneously. Josh and Amy were swallowed in a sea of hugs and hand-shakes as everyone offered their congratulations.

"Hey, wait a minute!" Travis said from the corner of the room. "These congratulations are all well and good, but I haven't heard if Amy has agreed to this plan."

Josh's dad quickly worked his way across the room and stood in front of Amy. "So, my dear, what was your answer?"

"Yes!" Amy stated emphatically. "My answer was yes!"

"Well," Travis said, as if that settled everything. "In that case, let me be the first to welcome you to the family!"

Everyone began working their way to the dining room as soon as Kaci announced dinner was ready. As was customary whenever Mike was over for dinner, Sophie and Aaron sat on either side of him. Once everyone had found a seat, Travis offered the prayer.

"Dear Loving Father, thank you for bringing our family together for this wonderful announcement. I have no doubt you were responsible for bringing Josh and Amy together, and we humbly thank you. When you protected Josh during his accident and returned him to our family, we knew it was because you have great plans for him. We're thrilled to know Amy is part of those plans, and we lovingly welcome her to our family. Now, Father, we ask you to bless this gathering, and bless this food. In Jesus's name we humbly pray. Amen."

A chorus of heartfelt amens followed, then conversation flowed easily around the dinner table.

Matt leaned over to Todd, who was seated next to him. "JC told me about this yesterday."

Todd raised his eyebrows in curiosity. "He did?"

"Yeah," Matt confirmed. "He said since I was the man of our family, at least until Dad gets his act together, he asked me if I had any problem with him asking Amy to marry him."

Todd nodded his head in admiration. "Good for him. That was a classy thing to do."

"He also showed me the ring," Matt said proudly. "He asked me if I thought Amy would like it. I told him it was perfect for her."

"You know, Matt," Todd said. "That's going to make JC your brother-in-law."

"Yeah," Matt grinned. "That's just like a brother. I've always wanted a brother. Hey, that means you will be kind of like my uncle too."

"Yes, it does," Todd agreed. "And I would be proud to be your uncle, Matt."

"Wow," Matt said in amazement. "We're going to be like one great big family. How cool is that?"

"That's very cool, Matt," Todd said in agreement. "Very cool, indeed."

Chapter Twenty

Word of Josh's and Amy's engagement spread quickly. All the teenagers who were regulars at the center had become good friends with not only JC, but Amy as well. Excitement was high, and everyone wanted to know when the wedding would be. A few brave souls even asked what all the kids wanted to know. Would they be able to attend the wedding? Josh chuckled as he explained to a group of kids that it was still early in the planning process, so none of the details had been worked out yet. But he assured them, he would let them know as soon as decisions had been made.

Josh was doing some work at the center before the afternoon crowds hit. He had just finished tidying things up in the gym and had started down the hallway toward the office when the front door opened, and a middle-aged man walked in. The man was dressed in dirty jeans, and a filthy shirt that had seen better days.

"Dad," Josh said quietly. "You're going to want to come out here."

Travis stepped into the hallway, and Josh pointed toward the man looking around the gym and arcade area.

"Isn't that Matt and Amy's dad?" Travis asked.

"I think so," Josh agreed. "I've only seen him the one time when he showed up here."

"Let's go see what he wants before a bunch of the kids start showing up," Travis said, as he started in that direction.

"Hi," Josh greeted the man. "Can we help you with something?"

"Uh, yeah," the man replied with uncertainty. "You probably don't remember me, but I'm John Phoenix. Last time we met, it wasn't under very good circumstances."

"I thought I recognized you," Josh confirmed.

"Can you tell me if Pastor Harmon is here?" John asked.

Travis reached out his hand in greeting, and said, "I'm Pastor Harmon. What can I do for you?"

John shook Travis's hand, but didn't reply immediately. He was looking down at the floor, shuffling his feet back and forth nervously.

"Uh," he began. "Is there someplace we can talk?"

Travis looked around at the empty gym, but knew kids, likely Matt as well, would be showing up in the next half hour. He hoped to get some idea of what John wanted before taking him down to the office to talk.

"Why don't you tell me what's on your mind," Travis suggested. "Then maybe we could go down to the office."

"You know my kids moved out," John began, still looking at the floor. "I haven't seen or heard from them in months. Not that that should surprise me. I've never been much of a father to them." He finally raised his head and looked Travis directly in the eyes. "My wife and I, we know we really messed up. We want to see if you could help us get clean."

Sensing what he hoped was sincerity in the father's request, Travis put his hand on the man's shoulder and said, "Let's go down to the office and talk."

Travis then leaned toward Josh and whispered, "Watch for Matt and Amy. If either of them show up, let them know he's here so they aren't blindsided if they happen to see him."

Josh nodded, then decided he would keep himself busy in the gym area so he could watch the front door.

Travis led John down the hallway, and pointed to the office. "Let's go in here where we can talk. Have a seat."

John sat in a chair opposite the desk, and looked around the room nervously.

Travis pulled up a chair and took a seat in front of the other man.

"So, Mr. Phoenix," Travis began.

"Just call me John."

"Okay, John," Travis agreed. "I'm sure you have probably guessed your kids have told us about their home life, and the problems you and your wife have had staying clean and sober."

"Yeah," John replied, looking down at the floor. "I figured you probably knew about all that."

"I want you to know, John, that we are also responsible for helping them find an apartment so they could move out. Their safety has always been our primary concern. We're not going to let them get hurt in any way if we can prevent it. So, I just want to make sure you understand our position."

"I do," John replied. "I stopped by a few days ago. I was going to try to talk to you then. I heard some of the boys talking about my Amy being engaged to your son. It cut me like a knife, finding out that way. Knowing my little girl is getting married and she didn't even tell us about it. I think that's when I hit rock bottom. I went home, without even looking for you. When I told my wife about it, she just sat there staring at the floor for the longest time. Didn't say a word. Then she got up, walked over to the sink, and poured her drink down the drain. She said, 'I don't know about you, but I'm done.' I'm done too, Pastor."

John folded his hands in his lap and simply stared at the floor.

"So," Travis began. "You think you are both ready to get the help you need?"

"We don't really have a choice," John replied sadly. "We missed their entire childhood, such as it was. I'm sure they don't think they had much of a childhood. They won't even talk to us. Now my little girl is getting married, and we will probably miss that too. I don't even know what my boy is doing."

"Matt's doing fine," Travis interjected. "We're all very proud of him."

"He probably hates me for everything I've done to him," John said, still staring at the floor.

"I doubt he hates you, John," Travis said. "I don't think Matt could ever hate anyone. But that doesn't mean he's going to welcome you back into his life. Or Amy either, for that matter. You and your wife have caused a lot of hurt and a lot of trauma for your kids. They have both been working very hard to deal with that trauma and hopefully have a normal life. You must understand something. Even if you both go into rehab and are successful at staying clean and sober, your kids still may not want to reestablish a relationship with you. So, you need to understand, if you want to change your life, you need to do it for you. Not for them. I pray they will both want to invite you back into their lives. But that's a choice they will have to make. You can't force them. You've done enough of that already."

John's shoulders sagged in defeat. That wasn't what he wanted to hear, and this was going to be much more difficult than he ever imagined. He suddenly sat up straight in the chair, and squared his shoulders in determination.

"I guess we need to take this one step at a time, then," John said. "We need to find out what we need to do to get clean. We need to get our acts together. Then all we can hope is the kids will want us back in their lives. What's the first step, Pastor Harmon? What do we need to do?"

"I'm going to be brutally honest with you, John. There is a very good possibility that you won't be able to see your daughter get married. You and your wife will likely need three months, minimum, of inpatient rehab. Then, when you get out, you will need to be able to stay clean and sober. That's a tall order, and I doubt Amy will delay her wedding for that. Both you and your wife will need to understand that and come to terms with it."

"I know," John replied. "I don't like it, but I understand it. At this point, the best we can probably hope for is they will let us back in their lives eventually, so we won't miss out on grandkids and stuff."

"Okay, as long as you have realistic expectations," Travis said as he handed John a business card. "I want you to call this man. He's a counselor and rehab specialist at the best rehab facility in the area. It's about fifty miles from here, but it's your best bet. After you talk to him, if you are both committed to making this change, and you need transportation to get there, let me know. I will make sure you get there."

Handing John another business card, Travis said, "And here's my card. Call me if you need something. Make the call to the rehab center today, John. Don't wait. Do it today, okay?"

John stood and shook Travis's hand. "I will. Thanks for your help."

"Good luck, John."

Josh walked up to his dad as John walked out the front door. "Do you think he's going to get help, Dad?"

"I think so, son," Travis replied. "I really do. I gave him the information he needs. Now all we can do is pray he does his part."

At that moment, the front door opened, and Brandon burst in waving an envelope over his head. Behind him, the afternoon crowd of teenagers filtered into the center and began scattering to different areas.

Brandon ran up to Josh, still waving the envelope. "I did it, JC! I did it! I got in!"

Josh and Travis looked at Brandon in confusion. "Slow down, Brandon," Josh laughed. "What did you do?"

Brandon was still breathless with excitement. "I was accepted to Northwest University! They accepted me into their music program. I got a scholarship, JC. A music scholarship." Brandon was so overcome with emotion that tears began pooling in his eyes.

Josh grabbed the boy and wrapped him in a hug. "That's sensational, Brandon! I knew you could do it!"

"It was the CD," Brandon explained. "They loved the CD, and said I was a perfect fit for their music program. Can you believe it, JC? Can you believe it?"

Josh chuckled at the boy's excitement. He patted him on the shoulder and said, "I told you you had talent. Congratulations, Brandon. I'm really proud of you."

Travis patted Brandon on the shoulder and said, "That's great, Brandon! You're going to love it there. I can't wait to see where your music takes you."

Brandon shook his head as he clutched the prized letter in his hand. "JC, I never could have done it without you. You have encouraged me and my music since the first day I came to the center. You pointed out the college opportunities when you had the career fair here. And you helped me learn how to compose music. Thanks, JC. For everything."

"You're welcome, Brandon," Josh replied humbly. "But you did it. I just helped guide you. You're the one who put in the time and work. You should be proud of yourself."

Brandon turned and started down the hallway. "I'm going to go work on my music. It's got to be university level now!"

Travis put his arm around Josh's shoulder as they started back toward the office. "Son, look what your little brainchild has turned into. This youth center started as just a little dream you had. Look at it now. Look at all the kids you're helping, the hope you're giving them. You're helping them believe in themselves, Josh. You're helping them believe in their dreams while you're living out your own dream. It's a good thing you're doing, Josh."

"We're all in this together, Dad," Josh replied. "Me and these kids. Me, my family, and everyone who has helped the center become a reality. And God. With God, all things are possible."

* * *

For the next several weeks, life got incredibly busy for Josh and Amy, as well as for his family. The center continued growing and was busier than ever. Josh had hired one more full-time employee, and two of the local Scout Masters volunteered at the center on a regular basis. Travis was now teaching Bible study classes three days a week, as well as offering one-on-one counseling, along with Josh. There was a steady stream of teenagers going through the doors and making good use of everything JC's Hope offered. Mike Slater stopped by several times a week to make sure the center wasn't lacking anything that would make the kids' lives easier.

Josh and Amy had begun planning for an early spring wedding, so wedding plans filled all their free time. Amy and Matt were cautiously optimistic about their parents' rehab, but had decided they weren't going to put their lives on hold for them. Their parents delayed entering rehab when they fell into a bout of self-pity, but had finally been admitted. Neither Amy nor Matt were in any big hurry to talk to them, so any information they learned came through Travis's limited contact.

Josh and Amy had joined Travis and Meghan in the office at the center for an impromptu planning session. Seated around the table, they had just begun their discussion when they heard a knock on the open door.

"Am I interrupting?" Mike Slater asked as he poked his head in the door.

"You are always welcome, Mike," Josh replied with a smile. "I saw you out there earlier, honing your skills on the baseball arcade game. Do you still have the high score?"

Mike laughed. "So far. But that Kyle keeps sneaking up on me. That's why I have to keep practicing."

Travis stood and pointed to a nearby chair. "Pull up a chair, Mike. We were just talking about some wedding plans."

"Then it sounds like I got here just in time," Mike laughed as he patted Josh on the shoulder and gave Amy a fatherly peck on the cheek. "Don't mind me. I'm just going to sit here quietly and see what these kids are planning."

Amy opened a notebook where they had been writing down things that needed to be done. "Well," she began. "We have some of the basic things nailed down. A lot of the kids here have been asking Josh if they would be invited to the wedding. We thought the best way to handle that would be to simply hold the wedding here. Besides, Josh and I met because of the center, so it seems like the logical place."

"We thought we could have the actual wedding in the gym," Josh added. "It's big enough to handle all the guests, and we think the kids would feel more comfortable here anyway. Since we have a kitchen and plenty of room, it would be easy to handle the food right here."

Josh looked over at Travis and said, "Dad, Amy and I obviously want you to perform the ceremony."

"I'd be honored to, son," Travis replied.

"Mom," Josh continued. "We were wondering if you would help Amy shop for a wedding dress."

Meghan reached over and placed her hand on Amy's hand. "Amy, I would love to do that. We can schedule a time this next week if you'd like. We want to make sure there is time to do alterations, if necessary."

"Thank you, Meghan," Amy replied with a smile.

"Can I interrupt here for just a minute?" Mike asked. "You all know I don't have any kids of my own. And, well, I've gotten to be rather fond of JC and Amy. Kind of look at them as my kids too."

Mike turned and looked at Amy. "Amy, dear, I would be honored if you would let me pay for your wedding dress. And your ring and anything else you might need."

Amy stood and walked around the table to Mike. With tears in her eyes, she gave him a big hug. "Mike, you have been so generous to Josh, the center, and all the kids here. You have the biggest heart of anyone I know. I can't even begin to thank you. So, all I can say is, yes, I would love to have you buy my wedding dress. That would make it very special. Thank you."

Josh reached across the table to shake Mike's hand. "Thanks, Mike. That's very generous of you. We appreciate it more than you know."

"It's my pleasure, son," Mike replied with a smile.

Amy turned back to the notebook to look at the list. "Josh and I have discussed it and neither of us want a big elaborate wedding. That's just not our style. And we don't want the kids here to feel out of place. So, we won't have a lot of attendants like most people do. I want to ask Ryleigh to be my maid of honor. That's one reason for the timing. If we have the wedding during spring break, she will be able to be here. Josh wants Aiden to be his best man, and I'm going to ask Matt to walk me down the aisle."

Travis nodded his head in approval. "I like that, Amy. Matt will be thrilled to do that for you."

Josh turned to Meghan. "Mom, do you think the twins would like to be part of the fun? If so, we'd like Sophie to be the flower girl and Aaron to be the ring bearer."

"Definitely talk to Kaci about it," Meghan suggested. "But I think they would love to do it."

"That nails down most of the major things," Josh said. "There's one other thing Amy and I were discussing, and we'd like some feedback from you guys. That includes you too, Mike."

Josh took Amy's hand in his before continuing. "It's obvious Amy's parents won't be able to attend the wedding. That's entirely their own fault. It's certainly not Amy's fault in any way. But they are still her parents, so she does feel bad about it, to a certain extent. What they are doing in rehab is more important in the long run than being able to attend the wedding. Do you think there would be a way we could maybe livestream the service so they could watch it from rehab? And do you even think that's a good idea?"

Travis and Meghan looked at each other before Meghan replied. "I think that would be a great idea, kids. From a parent's standpoint, particularly since they are working on making some significant changes, I think it would mean a lot to them to be able to watch the ceremony."

"I agree with your mom, Josh," Travis said. "We just need to see what we need to do to make that happen."

"I'm pretty sure my buddy at the radio station could help us out," Mike offered.

"Oh, that's right!" Josh agreed excitedly. "I had forgotten about that. He would have all the necessary equipment, and the know-how to be able to do that."

"I'll give him a call," Mike said as he put a reminder in his phone. "I'm sure he would be happy to help."

"That would be perfect, Mike," Amy added. "Thanks for doing that."

"Can any of you think of anything else we need to get settled right away?" Josh asked.

"There's still plenty of time to decide on the food and program, I think," Travis said. "Amy, do you have any other family or friends from out of town you might want to invite? It's probably not too early to start working on a guest list so we can get a rough head count."

"No," Amy replied matter-of-factly. "If we have any other family, Matt and I have never known them. Ryleigh has become my best friend, and all my other friends are right here at the center."

"As you know," Josh added. "All my friends and family are right here in town. Grandma and Granddad are the only ones living out of town. If their health allows it, I would love for them to be here. If not, maybe we could set it up so they could watch via livestream too."

"I'll give them a call," Travis said, making a note on his phone. "Dad has been doing much better, so maybe they could come if I go get them."

"Sounds good. I think that's everything we needed to get settled for now," Josh said. "We can work out more of the details as things get closer. Thanks for your help, everyone."

"Amy, we'll go dress shopping soon," Meghan said happily. "The wedding will be here before we know it!"

Chapter Twenty-One

The cold winter was slowly beginning to slip into spring as wedding plans were kicked into high gear. Amy and Meghan took an entire day to drive to the nearest larger city to shop for a wedding dress. Since neither Amy nor Josh wanted a fancy wedding, Josh had opted to wear a nice suit instead of renting a tuxedo. Aiden and Matt would do the same. Ryleigh already owned a suitable dress to wear as maid of honor, one she had recently worn as a bridesmaid for a friend's wedding. Amy's wedding dress was the last major clothing hurdle.

Meghan parked her Jeep Cherokee in the lot next to the bridal shop.

"Well, Amy," she began. "Are you ready to go find a wedding dress?"

Amy smiled with excitement. "Let's do this! And thanks again, Meghan, for being willing to help me with this. I wouldn't know where to begin."

Meghan linked her arm in Amy's, and they walked down the sidewalk, stopping to look at dresses in the windows. Pointing to a dress in the window nearest the door, Meghan asked, "Do you have some idea of what you may be looking for, Amy? Any particular style?"

"No, I really don't," Amy replied. "I wasn't one of those little girls who dreamed of a fancy wedding. So maybe this is one of those times when my blank mind might come in handy."

Meghan chuckled as they entered the store. "I'm sure we'll be able to find the perfect dress for you. Let's look around, and you can tell me if something reaches out to you. We might also keep an eye out for flower girl dresses and ring bearer suits. Kaci doesn't think they really need anything new, but I know Sophie would love to have a new dress for the wedding. Aaron probably couldn't care less, but we might look anyway."

"Oh, Meghan," Amy said with excitement. "Isn't this the cutest little flower girl dress?"

Meghan took the dress off the rack and begin looking at it. "You're right, this is adorable. And Sophie would look beautiful in this shade of green. Since Kaci left it up to me, I think we should get this. Let's see if we can find it in Sophie's size."

After flipping through a few dresses, Meghan found the green dress in Sophie's size. There was a rack of small suits next to the flower girl dresses, so they beginning browsing for a suit for Aaron. Being a typical grandma, Meghan always knew current clothing sizes for her grandkids, so it was an easy chore to find a dark charcoal suit in Aaron's size.

"Well, the kids were easy," Meghan chuckled. "Now why don't we see if we can find a dress for the bride."

"Okay," Amy agreed, walking toward a rack of dresses. "I don't want something real fancy and elaborate. That's just not me. Maybe something relatively simple, yet nice. I want Josh to like it."

"Trust me, Amy," Meghan said with a smile. "Josh will like any dress you choose. When you're walking down the aisle, you will be the most beautiful woman in the world to him. It wouldn't matter if you were wearing bib overalls and a flannel shirt." Then Meghan laughed at a memory as she said, "I wore my cowboy boots under my wedding dress!"

"You didn't!" Amy said in surprise.

"I sure did!"

Amy smiled at that image, not at all surprised once she thought about it, then walked over to a rack of dresses without as many frills. She pulled a dress off the rack and held it out in front of her. "What do you think of this one, Meghan?"

"Let's walk over to the mirror and I'll hold it up to you so you can see what you think," Meghan suggested.

"I really like it, Amy," Meghan said with a smile. "It's simple, yet elegant. Do you like it?"

Amy nodded her head, "Yes, I do."

Meghan raised her hand to signal for an attendant. "Let's have you try it on and see what you think."

The attendant opened a fitting room, and the ladies went in so Amy could try on the dress. Once Amy had the dress on, they went out to look in the full-length, three-way mirrors.

"Amy," Meghan began. "Turn around and look at it from all angles. What is your initial reaction? Do you like it? Do you like certain things about it, but not others?"

Amy looked a bit overwhelmed, but she beamed as she turned to look at herself in the wedding gown. "I really like it, Meghan. I really do. If I had ever had an idea in my head of what kind of wedding dress I would like, I think this would be it. What do you think?"

"I love it, Amy!" Meghan said honestly. "I loved it the minute you put it on, but didn't want to influence your decision. And I think the ivory color is perfect with your red hair."

After a consultation with the attendant, everyone agreed it was a perfect fit and didn't need any alterations at all. The gown was put into a long dress bag, and the clothes for the kids were boxed up.

"Well, Amy," Meghan began. "That takes care of all the clothes. I think the last thing on the list is the ring for Josh."

"Mike wants to take me to look for Josh's ring on Friday," Amy said. "It will be nice to get a man's opinion."

"Agreed," Meghan said. "I think Mike loves being involved in the wedding plans. He thinks an awful lot of you and Josh."

"I know he does," Amy agreed. "He has become like a father to me. Between Mike and your husband, I finally feel like I have a father in my life. I feel like God has blessed me by bringing me into your family. Now I have two wonderful father figures. And before long, I'll have the most amazing husband."

Amy suddenly stopped in her tracks. "Meghan, I can't believe it. I'm getting married soon."

Meghan took Amy by the arm as they continued down the sidewalk. "Yes, Amy, you most certainly are. And we couldn't be happier to add you and Matt to our family."

* * *

Mike pulled his pickup to a stop in front of the jewelry store, then hopped out to go around and help Amy down from the truck. As he tucked Amy's arm in his, ensuring he was on the outside closest to the street, he radiated fatherly protection and pride. No one would have guessed they weren't father and daughter as they walked into the jewelry store.

Stepping up to the counter, Mike addressed the salesclerk. "My little girl here is shopping for a wedding band for her fiancé."

Moving to the display of men's wedding bands, the clerk asked Amy, "Did you have something special in mind?"

Amy looked at Mike with uncertainty. "I'm not really sure. I've never shopped for a man's wedding band before." She chuckled nervously. "What do you think Josh would like? You've actually known him longer than I have."

"Don't sell yourself short, Amy," Mike said as he patted her on the arm. "You have very good instincts. But if it helps at all, I don't think Josh would want something flashy. He's more down to earth. The perfect fit for you."

"You're right," Amy said as she began looking at some of the simpler bands. "I know I don't want it to be just a plain band. I want it to have some character, but not overdone."

She pointed to a band with some light engraving and a small diamond in the center. "What do you think of something like that? Although I'm not sure he would want a diamond."

Mike looked at the ring when the clerk pulled it out of the case. "I think I agree with you, Amy. I think he would rather have something without a diamond. Do you think he would want gold, or silver to match your ring?"

Amy laughed, "I hadn't even thought about that. But I think silver to match mine."

Mike pointed at another ring in the case and asked the clerk to pull it out so they could look at it. "What about something like this, Amy? It has a matt finish with some subtle engraving."

"I like this one," Amy agreed. "It's simple, yet elegant. I think Josh would love it. You said Josh came down last week to get sized for the ring, right?"

"Yes, he did," Mike replied. Turning to the clerk, he asked, "Do you have the ring size for Josh Harmon? He stopped by a few days ago."

The clerk pulled some records up on the computer and replied, "Yes, we do. Josh will need a size twelve. Let me see if we have that ring in a twelve."

Returning with a smile on his face and a velvet ring box in his hand, the clerk opened the box and sat it on top of the jewelry case. "Here you go, size twelve."

"Well, my dear," Mike addressed Amy. "What do you think? Is this the one?"

Amy picked up the box, removed the ring and turned it over in her hand, admiring it. "It's perfect. I think Josh will love it."

Turning back to the clerk, Mike said, "We'll take it."

After helping Amy up into the truck, Mike said, "I'm famished. Let's go grab some lunch before we head back. There's a nice little café a few blocks from here. They have some tasty salads, and the best hot beef sandwich I've ever eaten. But the best thing is their homemade peach pie!"

"Peach pie is my favorite!" Amy agreed happily.

"Then peach pie it is, my dear," Mike replied. Then he put the truck in gear and drove down the road whistling along with the country music playing on the radio.

Chapter Twenty-Two

Before Mike was able to put his pickup in park in front of JC's Hope, he was surrounded by teenage boys, anxious to unload the tables and chairs. Mike chuckled as he climbed out of the truck, then went to open the main door to the center. He poked his head inside and was amazed at the transformation. Josh's entire family, along with Amy, Matt, and the kids from the center, had been busy all morning getting the center ready for tomorrow's big wedding. Against feeble protests, Mike had insisted on having the food catered for the event. He wanted everyone to be able to relax and enjoy the wedding without having to worry about the food.

Mike walked up to Travis, who was giving the boys guidance on placement for the chairs. "Busy place in here this morning," he said with a smile.

Travis shook Mike's hand before he replied with a chuckle. "It sure is! Thanks for hauling the tables and chairs over. Setting up for this wedding has certainly been a team effort."

Spotting Todd across the gym, Travis called to him. "Hey, Todd, can you and Aiden help Brandon move the piano down from the music room? Josh can show you where he wants it placed."

"We're on it," Todd replied, looking around for Aiden.

Matt appeared next to Todd. "I'll help you and Brandon with the piano. Aiden is working on setting up the sound system."

Todd and Matt walked toward the music room where Brandon was getting the piano ready to move down the hall. One of the younger boys grabbed the piano bench and started toward the gym. Back in the gym, teenagers were carrying in flower stands and other items to be used for decorations. Josh was coordinating the placement of everything, while Amy and Meghan talked to the florist about the arrival of the flower arrangements. In a few short hours, the building had been transformed from a youth center to a wedding venue.

Travis and Mike joined Josh, Todd, and Aiden in the middle of the gym.

"I think Matt just brought in the last of it," Todd said, as they looked around the room. "It doesn't even look like a gym anymore."

Josh shook his head as he took in the scene around him. "I can't begin to thank you guys. Everyone has been amazing. The place looks great!"

"Well, JC," Mike said, patting him on the back. "It looks like you're all ready to go for tomorrow. And Charlie said he has the livestream all set up. He provided the link to the counselor at the rehab center, so Amy's parents should be able to watch the ceremony."

"Thanks, Mike," Josh replied. "I know Amy really appreciates that."

Mike turned to Matt, who had just joined the group. "I would be willing to bet you have a loud whistle so you can get everyone's attention."

Matt grinned and said, "You bet, I do!" He put his fingers to his mouth and let out a shrill whistle. As expected, all the noise and commotion came to a halt.

"That's what I thought," Mike said with a chuckle as he patted Matt on the shoulder.

"Can I have everyone's attention for just a minute," Mike requested. "I promise, I'm not going to make a big speech or anything."

After the chuckles died down, Mike continued. "I can honestly say, this warehouse has never looked so good! I know you all have been working hard to get things set up for the wedding tomorrow. So, I have arranged to have a bunch of pizza delivered from Luigi's. They should be showing up in the next few minutes. When they get here, just help yourselves. There will be pizza, salad, garlic bread, and drinks. Just don't make a mess on all your hard work!"

The room erupted in excited cheers as everyone began thanking Mike. He simply dismissed the attention with a wave of his hand and headed toward the kitchen to dig out some paper plates. Keeping all the volunteers fed was important. Tomorrow was going to be a very big day at JC's Hope.

* * *

Meghan and Ryleigh were in the office at the center, which was being used as the bride's dressing room, helping Amy with the finishing touches on her dress and hair. Ryleigh pinned a small rosebud in Amy's hair, just above her ear, then placed the bridal bouquet in her hands.

Turning Amy toward the full-length mirror, Meghan said, "You look beautiful, Amy."

"Mom's right, sis," Ryleigh added. "Josh won't know what hit him when he sees you walking down the aisle."

"Thank you both so much," Amy said, with tears pooling in her eyes. "I can't believe how lucky I am to be a part of your family. I never could have done this without you." She then reached out and gave them both a big hug.

Ryleigh reached up and dabbed Amy's tears with a handkerchief, then said with a smile, "Hey, now, don't go smudging your makeup. We worked hard on that."

Amy smiled before giving Ryleigh another quick hug. "I'm sure my face will be a mess by the end of the day."

"You're going to do just fine, Amy," Meghan said after a brief hug. "Ryleigh, we better get in there before the boys send out a search party."

"See you inside, Amy," Ryleigh said. "Matt is already out here waiting for you."

Amy stepped into the hallway and was greeted by her brother. "You look very handsome, Matt. Thanks for doing this for me."

Matt simply stared at his sister adoringly for a moment before saying, "Wow, Amy, you're beautiful. Well, are you ready? Kaci already has the kids out front, waiting to go inside. We'll go out the kitchen door and meet them around front."

Matt took his sister by the arm and led her outside and around to the front of the building where they met Kaci and the twins. Through the closed doors, they could hear Brandon on the piano, playing the music Josh and Amy had selected. Matt and Amy stepped off to the side so Kaci could open the door and guide the kids inside.

Sophie held the flower basket tightly in her hand, while Aaron guarded the pillow and rings with his life. They had both been practicing their roles for days, wanting to get it just right. At a signal from Travis, the kids started up the aisle. Sophie carefully dropped flower petals along the way, at first placing them neatly on the floor. About a third of the way up the aisle, she began tossing them from the basket with a theatrical flair that caused Aaron to giggle.

When they reached the end of the aisle, and her flower basket was empty, Sophie stopped to ask Mike, "Did we do okay, Mr. Mike?"

Mike smiled, patted Sophie on the back, and said, "No one could have done it any better, honey."

Sophie beamed as she stood next to her brother, who was guarding the rings with all the seriousness of a guard at Buckingham Palace.

Standing outside the closed doors, Matt and Amy heard Brandon play the opening strains of the wedding march. Just before the doors were opened, Matt looked at his sister and said, "You know, sis, JC is a very lucky guy. I think it's great that he's going to be my brother, but he's getting the best end of this deal. You're amazing, Amy. I really mean that. And I'm honored to be walking you down the aisle."

With those words, he took his sister's hand, stepped back, and gave her a bow fit for a queen. Then he looked at her with his boyish grin and said, "Let's do this!"

The doors opened and Amy gazed at the packed crowd, overcome with the knowledge this was now her family. She raised her head and looked toward the front of the room where her future husband stood, waiting for her. For her. Because she was worthy of his love.

As the wedding march continued, Matt placed his sister's hand in the crook of his arm, gave her a little wink, and they started down the aisle. Amy looked straight ahead, her eyes glued on Josh, still not believing this was all real. At the end of the aisle, Matt gave Amy a peck on the cheek, then handed her over to Josh.

"Friends and family," Travis began. "We're gathered here today to share in this happy occasion as Josh and Amy pledge their love to each other. They have chosen to hold their wedding here at JC's Hope for two reasons. First, they met because of the center. Second, everyone connected with the center, and all the teenagers who come to the center, are part of their family. And they wanted you all to be able to share in their special day.

"A few months ago," Travis continued. "Josh wrote a very special song for Amy and recorded it on a CD. He was originally going to have the CD played today because he wasn't sure he would be able to sing such an emotional song. However, he has decided to give it his best shot and pray God will grant him strength to make it through the song."

Handing Josh the microphone, Travis said, "Brandon will accompany Josh on the piano. So, here is the first public performance of 'Rising from the Ashes'."

Brandon began playing the introduction, then Josh added his rich baritone voice, completely captivating the audience. When the song ended, a hush fell over the crowd before a few 'wows' escaped the lips of some of the teenagers.

Travis again addressed the audience. "Amy and Josh have written their own vows which, honestly, are better than anything I could have come up with. Amy, why don't you go first?"

Amy took the microphone from Travis and turned to look at Josh. "Josh, nothing I could put into words would adequately express how I feel about you. You befriended both me and my brother and treated us like family right from the beginning. You made me feel like I belonged whenever I came here to the center. You have always treated me with kindness and compassion. When I realized I had fallen in love with you, I didn't dare hope you might love me too. But when you told me you loved me, I honestly felt like I had won the lottery. I don't know how I could have been so lucky. I wouldn't have believed this a few years ago, but I now know that we are together because God planned it that way. I love you, Josh, and can't wait to see where God takes us."

Travis took the microphone from Amy and handed it to his son.

"Sweet Amy," Josh began as he looked deep into her eyes. "You are my heart and my soul. When I first saw you sitting alone on the bleachers at the ball field, I knew you were special. I never dreamed I would learn just how special you are. You are an amazing woman, Amy. Your devotion and commitment to your brother Matt showed me how important family is to you. Now you're going to be part of a large family, and we couldn't be happier. You have become one of my biggest supporters. Whenever I wasn't sure I could do something, you convinced me I could. Whenever I had doubts about anything, you found a way to remove those doubts. I love you, Amy. And I'm going to spend the rest of my life making sure you know how much you are loved."

"Now, Ryleigh and Aiden," Travis began. "If you'll retrieve the rings from that handsome little ring bearer, we'll move on to the ring exchange."

As they retrieved the rings from the ring pillow, Aaron leaned forward and whispered, "Did I do okay, Papa?"

Travis smiled and whispered his reply. "You did great, Aaron."

Travis looked at his son and smiled before proceeding.

"Joshua Christopher Harmon," Travis began. "Do you take this woman to be your lawfully wedded wife?"

"I do," Josh replied as he looked into Amy's eyes.

Turning to Amy, Travis asked, "Amelia Lane Phoenix, do you take this man to be your lawfully wedded husband?"

"Yes, I do!" Amy replied.

Travis chuckled at her enthusiastic reply. He nodded to Aiden, who handed Josh Amy's ring.

"Josh," Travis said. "Place the ring on Amy's finger and repeat after me. With this ring, I thee wed."

Josh slipped the ring onto Amy's finger, squeezed her hand, and said, "With this ring, I thee wed."

Ryleigh then handed Josh's ring to Amy, and Travis said, "Amy, place the ring on Josh's finger and repeat after me. With this ring, I thee wed."

As Amy slid the ring onto Josh's finger, she repeated, "With this ring, I thee wed."

Travis smiled as he looked at the newlyweds and said, "I now pronounce you husband and wife. Josh, you may kiss your bride."

Josh took Amy into his arms and kissed her tenderly. Travis had them turn to face the audience.

"I present to you," Travis said with pride. "Mr. and Mrs. Joshua Harmon!"

Josh looked at his new bride, took her hand and raised it high in the air. "God is good!"

Amy looked at her husband and said, "All the time!"

* * *

After the wedding ceremony, people began milling around and visiting with each other while professional photos were being taken. Mike had hired a photographer for the wedding, and she had been taking photos and video during the ceremony, and was now gathering people for the family photos. A nice assortment of photos were being taken, making sure to include all the attending family members. Once most of the photos were finished, Amy pulled the photographer off to the side and whispered something to her. The photographer walked over to Mike, took him by the arm, and escorted him back to the group.

Amy took Mike by the hand and said, "Mike, you have become like a father to me. We would be honored to include you in some of these photos."

Mike began to protest, but soon learned it would do him no good.

Josh smiled as he instructed Mike where to stand. "Mike, we want a photo of me, Amy, and you. We also want you included in a photo of us with Mom and Dad. Then, of course, you have to be in one of the photos with the entire family. Like it or not, Mike, you're part of our family now."

Mike chuckled as he said, "Well, son, I can't think of a better family to be part of. I've grown rather fond of you all."

The last pictures took a fair amount of coordinating. Josh and Amy wanted a picture that included all the kids from the center. Once everyone was gathered, the photographer climbed up on a ladder to be able to get a good shot of the entire group. At Mike's urging, the photographer took a nice group picture, then a more relaxed and fun picture of the kids with Josh and Amy.

When all the group photos were finished, Travis directed everyone to the side of the room where a table was set up with a multi-tiered cupcake tower, with trays of matching cupcakes, chocolate chip cookies, and Oreos alongside for the guests. People gathered around while the new bride and groom shared a cupcake, after which, Travis addressed the group.

"Josh and Amy wanted everything to be informal, so the luncheon reception is set up in the kitchen area. It is buffet style, so you can form lines on both sides of the tables and work your way through the buffet. You can bring your plate back out here, and there are tables and chairs set up around the room where you can eat comfortably. After you make your way through the buffet line, don't forget there are cupcakes and cookies over here, so help yourselves."

As the crowd of people moved toward the kitchen, Matt elbowed Aiden, and said with a grin. "I'm going to snag one of those cupcakes and a couple Oreos on my way to the kitchen, so I don't miss out on them."

Aiden chuckled as he replied. "I like the way you think, Matt. Grab one for me too and I'll save your place in line."

The afternoon was a relaxed time of visiting and fellowship. It wasn't long before Brandon found his way to the piano and began playing. Josh slipped in occasionally and joined him, filling the room with a mix of country and worship songs. The end of the afternoon found Josh and Amy, who had long since changed into more comfortable clothes, seated at a table with Mike and their family.

"You know," Mike began, as he settled back in his chair. "When Jason first introduced me to your family, I had no idea how much you would change my life. You have taught me what family is all about, and it's been incredible seeing how you all support each other. Your family and the kids here have blessed me beyond words."

"You have been the true blessing, Mike," Josh added sincerely. "After the accident, I felt like I was floundering and wasn't sure what to do. I knew I still wanted to work with kids, but I thought the idea of opening a youth center for troubled teens was just a dream. You were a big part in making that dream a reality. I can never adequately thank you for everything you have done, not only for me and Amy, but for the center."

"One thing I know for sure, JC," Mike continued. "You certainly came up with the perfect name for the center. Every single day you are living your dream and extending JC's hope to every kid who walks through those doors."

Josh simply smiled and said, "God is good."

Matt patted his new brother on the back and replied, "All the time!"

Epilogue

The gymnasium at Hope High School was filled nearly to capacity for this year's graduation. Josh's family, along with Mike Slater, filled an entire row in the audience for this special occasion. Several of the graduating seniors had been regulars at JC's Hope. Many of them never would have made it to graduation if it weren't for the existence of the center. Sitting with Josh's family were two adults who likely would not have been here if this graduation had been a year ago.

John and Vicki Phoenix sat nervously beside their daughter Amy as they watched graduating seniors walk across the stage to collect their diplomas. They fully admitted they were never the parents Amy and her younger brother needed, and deserved, but they had made significant strides in the past year toward a better life. After spending more than three long months in a drug and alcohol rehabilitation center, they had both been sober for over six months. A feat they never would have believed possible a few years ago. They were now taking small steps toward rebuilding the relationship with their two kids, who had finally agreed to allow them back into their lives.

"Matthew John Phoenix," the high school principal announced into the microphone.

Matt stood tall and proud as he stepped onto the stage and approached the principal. With one hand, he shook the principal's outstretched hand. With his other hand, he gladly accepted his high school diploma, which had a special medallion affixed to it designating him as an honor student.

As he continued across the stage, he proudly flipped the tassel on his graduation cap to the other side, indicating he had successfully completed his high school career. He walked down the first step to join his classmates and, with a huge grin on his face, raised both arms in victory.

Mike had insisted on throwing a graduation party for the seniors from the center. JC's Hope was decorated with the red and white colors of Hope High School. Tables and chairs were set up in the gym, and tables loaded with food lined one wall.

Most of the adults were at the center, awaiting the arrival of the graduating seniors. Travis and Meghan were trying to make Matt's parents feel more at ease, so they made sure they weren't left alone for long.

The front door opened, and a group of teenagers burst through the door, led by the six newly-graduated seniors. Matt ran up to Josh and wrapped him in a hug.

"I made it, JC!" Matt said happily.

"I'm proud of you, Matt," Josh replied with a smile. "You worked hard for that diploma."

Todd, Travis, and Aiden crowded in to offer Matt their congratulations as well. Mike stepped up beside Matt and wrapped his arm around Matt's shoulder. "Congratulations, son. You have a lot to be proud about." Then Mike nodded his head toward the middle of the gym. "There's someone over there I think you need to go talk to."

Matt looked in the direction of his parents, who looked completely out of place standing beside Amy, then walked toward the middle of the gym.

"Dad, Mom," Matt began. "Thanks for coming."

Tears were reluctantly forming in John's eyes when he reached out to shake his son's hand.

"No, Dad," Matt said. "I just graduated from high school. I think that's a hugging occasion, not a handshake." Then Matt, with all the maturity an eighteen-year-old boy could muster, wrapped his dad in a long-overdue hug.

* * *

Mike Slater stood outside the Major League Baseball Hall of Fame in Cooperstown, New York with a small group of people. It didn't take a lot of arm twisting to convince Josh and his family to make a second trip to Cooperstown. This trip was not for the high school baseball team. This was a family trip. Aaron and Sophie had insisted if Mr. Mike was taking their family to the Baseball Hall of Fame, they were going too. Mike wouldn't have it any other way.

As the group stood on the steps before entering the building, Sophie was holding one of Mike's hands, and Aaron had the other. Never having been to the Hall before, the two kids had no idea what to expect. They only knew that Mike had been keeping a secret.

"I know I've been pretty vague about the reason for this trip," Mike said.

"You've been keeping a secret," Sophie said knowingly.

Mike chuckled as he agreed. "Yes, Sophie, I've been keeping a secret. Why don't we go inside, and I'll show you what the secret is."

Mike led the family into the building and down several hallways before stopping in the middle of a wide hallway. He stepped over to a covered bench and instructed, "Why don't you all move in a bit closer, so we don't block people's path. Josh, why don't you come up here and stand beside me."

Josh had the same confused look on his face as the rest of the family, but he did as Mike asked.

"Josh," Mike began. "When you first told me about your dream for the youth center, I asked if you had a name for it. You told me it would be called JC's Hope, meaning it was your hope for a better life for the kids in our town. I took that name at face value, until I began spending more time at the center. With your insistence that it be a place where the kids knew it was important to have God in their lives, it began to change my perspective. As I watched that godly influence change the lives of those kids, it suddenly dawned on me that JC's Hope could just as easily stand for Jesus Christ's Hope. It's a good thing you've done,

Josh, and I wanted to do something to acknowledge everything the center stands for. So, I have purchased a commemorative bench right here at the Baseball Hall of Fame."

Mike pulled the cover off the solid oak bench to reveal an engraved plaque on the front of the bench.

JC's Hope
A place where God and baseball
make a difference in the lives of kids

CPSIA information can be obtained
at www.ICGtesting.com
Printed in the USA
LVHW100042280323
742726LV00005B/198